Lock Down Publications and Ca$h

Presents

I0664113

BLOODLINE
of a SAVAGE

(A Bill Hilliard Trilogy)

By
Gritty and Raw Crime Novelist
Prince A. Tauhid

Lock Down Publications
P.O. Box 944
Stockbridge, GA 30281
www.lockdownpublications.com

Like our page on Facebook: Lock Down Publications
www.facebook.com/lockdownpublications.ldp

Stay Connected with Us!

Text **LOCKDOWN** to 22828 to stay up-to-date with new releases, sneak peaks, contests and more…

Like our page on Facebook:
Lock Down Publications

Join Lock Down Publications/The New Era Reading Group

Visit our website:
www.lockdownpublications.com

Follow us on Instagram:
Lock Down Publications

Email Us: We want to hear from you!

Prologue

2014...

The robber was given inside knowledge of an elderly lady who was perceived suffering from a case of dementia. She was identified as being the one holding money and kilos of heroin for her grandson. Mrs. Edna Dietrich was a biracial 73 year-old woman of African-American and German lineage. Her Mother was German top and bottom, and her father was a black man born and raised in Philadelphia, Pennsylvania. North Philly specifically.

Mrs. Dietrich was admitted into a hospice-type nursing facility in Northeast Philadelphia. She'd been diagnosed with memory and concentration issues at the onset. Then later, it was determined that the early phases of Alzheimer's disease had developed. She'd been living in Pleasant Grace for the past three years, and received the best of treatment and care the entire time she'd inhabited the studio-styled apartment lodge. Family and staff adored Mrs. Dietrich, but held grave concerns for her at any time the condition showed a heightened intensity. But whether known or not, Mrs. Dietrich had a propensity to manipulate certain situations, especially so if her one and only grandson stood to benefit from her perpetuated acts.

The grandson, Trevon Rommell Dietrich-Savage, was the son of Lilly Dietrich, Mrs Edna's daughter, and a man by the name Cornelius Savage II aka "Little Hound." Lilly's Father was African-American top and bottom. Cornelius' parents both was African-American.

Trevon, known on the streets as "King Von," "SK Von," "Killer Von," or simply "Vonnie," depending, was a 22 year-old dynamic and vicious goon, who'd gained notoriety on the streets of Philly through his Father's family namesake, then with his own breakout moment to make a name for himself, and commanding a crew. They maintained a stronghold over certain drug territories through the city and elsewhere.

Von stood at six foot three, weighed two hundred and ten pounds, and possessed an athletic build. He had a walnut complexioned hue of skin, kept a low temp fade Caesar haircut, and a one-inch full beard that had a razor sharp line-up to it. Von was well-groomed, well-dressed and well-paid. His grandmother oversaw large amounts of his money and a lethal cache of the product he pumped through the veins of the underworld.

Some of the contraband was stashed in her residence. This arrangement had been in play for the past year leading up to the day. And then, a motherfucking thief had the balls to carry out a caper, and went to work once put up on game of the potential lick. The sly crook was eager to see what the old lady had tucked away in her domain and what all she knew.

There was a female cousin of the thief who worked at the facility. The two held a conversation. A plot was hatched.

"Carl, how about, I recently found out that the boy Von, got a grandma who live at the nursing home I now work," Beade said to her cousin, Carlton Parker, aka "CP."

"Von!" he retorted "Shit! Which one?" CP now wanted to know.

"Von, nigga! *King Von!* Ain't but one I know! Not nary one of them broke Von niggaz who go by *that* name! I'm talking about the one who got Darien street on lock. Them niggaz on Erie Ave work for him too. The blocks around E.A. as well.

"SK Von! Killer Von! The rich nigga in the streets with the deep pockets and the black on black seven sixty with a chrome plate on the front that got a scary clown face on it! *That* Von!" CP sought clarity.

"Yeah cuz. *That* Von! The rich nigga in the streets, with deep pockets, and the work laid out in the *Badlands*," Beade replied. "*His* grandma. He comes to see her every week like clockwork. Some days he brings large bags, and some days he doesn't. But I don't understand, what the hell does an old lady need with Louie and Gucci bags? Designer suitcases and shit? I've seen designer shoe boxes and all, cuz," the girl informed.

"Oh yeah!" CP salivated at the thought.

"Hell yeah!"

"And how long have you had that job now?"

"About a month. But from what I've been told, he has been consistent with his visits every Thursday at four o'clock for the past year. I saw a few people meet him there too. A Spanish *jawn* and a white boy. It's probably more going on than meets the eye," Beade declared.

"You think so?"

"I *know* so."

"But why you think he'd risk it like that, to handle his business at that type of place? As slick as that nigga thinks he is! I don't know too much about the nigga. But I do know that much. The cops can't even pinpoint dude or catch him up on anything. And the blood-thirsty hyenas who want him, not able to run down on the nigga to rob him for what he got. Dude a moving target. But why you passing on what you know to me?"

"Cuzzo, you don't think I know what you're into? You do more than sell coke, nigga. But I'm telling you because, I want in. I'm curious to know what that long money nigga got going on there myself," the girl uttered. "And his grand mom, she's got a bad case of Alzheimer's. What the fuck type of conversation they able to have!"

"His grandma got old-timers bad! What the fuck! She probably don't even know who the fuck he is!"

"*Alzheimer's* cuz. Not *old-timers*. And no. She may not have any idea who he is," Beade corrected.

"Do he know you?"

"I doubt it. I'm just like everybody else who knows of him, and he doesn't know of them. Not at all."

"Have y'all ever said anything to one another when he was there at the nursing home?"

"Nope. I've only looked at him with lust in my eyes and fantasized how lovely it must be for all the side pieces he got lined up. He made my pussy get wet with the swag he got though. Dude is like that," she complimented.

"So, why the hell you want me to rob the nigga, when you can get something out of him by fucking him!"

"Because, I don't know if he'll go for me like that. And, even if he does, I know I won't get the type of money out of him with love, like we could by doing it your way. And I know that nigga holding onto a grip too."

"Before we can do anything, you gotta do your homework. Von ain't no ordinary duck, you know. You ever been inside his grandma's place?"

"Yeah. We have to change out her linen, clean up the place, and check her vitals. We issue pills to her too."

"Well, good. You scope out the place. When you go back in there, snoop around a little bit and see what you may come up with. Then, let me know. That way, we can go from there."

"Cuz, even if I do stumble up on something, I can't leave work with anything in my possession. Too many of them dirty bitches done stole from the patients already. And my boss and them have gotten strict about that," Beade made her cousin aware.

"I see. Well, just snoop around and let me know from there."

"I can do that. Miss Dietrich doesn't talk at all now. And probably don't know night from day. Let alone, she doesn't know how to feed herself anymore. Staff has to. But I'll get back to you next week. Next Thursday after he leaves. As I said, Von normally stays an hour or so each visit."

"No doubt cuz. Do that. I'm out," CP ended the call.

Beade put her mind to work on how she could ease into Mrs. Dietrich's suite and rummage around to see what she may come up with.

***

Tyese Smith aka "Beade," applied for a job at the hospice center and got hired. Her experience as a certified nursing assistant helped her land a position in the facility where Mrs. Edna Dietrich resided, While doing her work inside Mr. Dietrich's suite, she merely greeted the old lady and attempted to make small talk only a time or two. But when met with muteness and a blank stare, Beade never wasted time looking to converse anymore. She only did her work and exited,

The following day after speaking to her cousin CP about the potential of doing a stick-up or a theft, Beade took the initiative herself to see what Von was hiding in his grandmother's domain. A hood-nigga visiting a nursing home with designer bags and products, was so out the ordinary, but not far-fetched. Either way, she felt certain that he had something going on. The only thing to do from there was to find out what.

Beade entered Mrs. Dietrich's suite and found her seated in front of the TV on the couch watching *The Price Is Right.* The time was 11:10 a.m. the usual scheduled routine when the aides would show up to perform duties.

"Good morning Miss Dietrich! How are you today?" Beade greeted.

She was alone this day. Her help was told that the work could be done by one person. It was a Monday.

Mrs. Dietrich didn't so much as offer a glance in Beade's direction nor utter a word in reply. Her eyes were facing directly at the TV and her body produced no motion. She sat with her hands palm down on her thighs, feet flat to the floor, and back ramrod in a vertical position.

Beade paused in front of Mrs. Dietrich momentarily with her palms planted on her hips and stared at the dementia patient.

"This bitch ain't got the slightest idea of who I am, what's going on, where she's at, or the day of the week it is," Beade worded in a low tone.

She took up no more time from there. Her footsteps into the bedroom were swift and sudden as lightening striking.

Beade darted straight to the closet. She opened the door and noticed it was filled with clothes from front to back. Top label designer clothes. Some for women. Most for men. She then spread the ones hanging to create an opening to the back. Shoe boxes upon shoe boxes lined to the wall from right to left and top to bottom. Beade held first-hand knowledge that dope dealers—no matter the age or experience in the game—have an obsession with using shoe boxes in a closet at home to stash bread, as if it was some type of safe or security lock box to keep money, jewelry and other valuables. Die-hard hustlers trust these over banks, for some strange reason. And Von, although only 21 in age, was a die hard tight-fist negro with money.

This nigga gotta have something in here! All this shit ain't for nothing!

Beade went for the boxes, rapidly lifting tops and knocking them over, Then, lo and behold, a sneaker box for females loaded with rolls of $20 bills tumbled to the floor.

I motherfucking knew it! Beade exclaimed in thought.

She grabbed two of the rolls and stuffed them in her overcoat pocket. She needed to search for more. She'd discover all there was to know.

Beade then re-situated everything that was messed up, stood to her feet, closed the door back, then proceeded to perform her duties as an aide to Mrs. Dietrich.

While in the kitchenette, Beade unlocked the window and eased it up and down to be sure it opened properly. She then rolled up a large sheet-sized portion of saran wrap, raced to the bathroom, closed the door, situated the two rolls of money with the wrap, lathered them with Vaseline, lowered her pants and panties, then slid the rolls inside of herself. She got back together at that point, exited the bathroom, and stood in front of Mrs. Dietrich once more to say goodbye for the day.

"You have a nice day now, Miss Dietrich! Okay," she said.

To her surprise, Mrs. Dietrich's eyes roved from the TV screen towards her direction. The old lady looked on at Beade's shirt and then into her eyes. The colorful attraction of her scrubs must have appealed to her. She returned her focus back to the TV screen.

Beade left the suite, then went to the bathroom. Shortly after, she reported to her supervisor that she wasn't feeling too well and needed to go home early for the day. She did so. While en route, she called CP to relate what she now knew.

"What's up, Beade! I hope you got some good shit to tell me," CP answered upon noticing her number.

"I knew Von had something going on, cuzzo. I checked it out myself. Dude got boxes of money up in that bitch!. That's where he keeps his paper!"

"Word!"

"Word cuz! I took some of it myself."

"*Some of it!*" CP retorted. "Why the fuck you didn't take it all!"

"Because, I couldn't. I already told you, we can't leave work with anything. But I was able to sneak two rolls out. I stuck them up in me," Beade said.

"Bitch, you wild! But you did what you had to do. So what the fuck am I supposed to do?" CP now wanted to know.

"I left the kitchen window unlocked. You got to go tonight. It has to be tonight, cuz. Meet me at my house in an hour. I'mma show you how to get to where I work. You can figure out the rest from that point."

"I goddamn sure can! I'll be there."

Beade made it home. Withdrew the money, and unwrapped it. She unrolled the cash and began counting. Each roll was fifty $20 bills. She had $2,000 total.

CP arrived. The two then got into Beade's car and she drove to where her workplace was located. She pulled around towards the back of the facility to point out the window to Mrs. Dietrich's suite.

"The window there with the purple-looking curtains, cuzzo. That's where Von's Nanna lives."

"And she's gonna be the only one there, right?"

"You think I'm gonna lead you into a trap or something, nigga? That old dementia having bitch is there all day every day by herself, except for Thursdays, and on occasion, Sundays. And like I said, you gotta go tonight. Von will be by Thursday."

"I got that part. No need to say anymore."

At 1 a.m. that night, CP took to the task at hand. He made his way to the facility. He had two black backpacks with him.

All the lights except for the night light in the kitchenette were out. He took a look through the window. No movement. He then tried the window to be sure it was unlocked. It was. He eased it up and slithered inside. Moving and tip-toeing like a cat burglar, he made his way to the living room, checked the front door, then headed to the bedroom. A dim light effect from the lamp on at the stand illuminated. Mrs. Dietrich lay on the bed sleeping peacefully.

CP leaped atop and began to bind her hands and feet with a roll of duct tape he had. He gagged her with a sock and wrapped her mouth tightly with the tough material. Beade already gave him the info on where to locate the boxes. He went straight to the closet where awaited the grand prize. He snatched down clothes and knocked over all the shoe boxes.. He found what he was looking for, plus more.

CP began stuffing the rolls of loot into the backpacks. Along with the money, there were 10 kilos of heroin, 2 kilos of fentanyl, and 3 forty-five caliber automatic pistols. All two backpacks were now loaded with contraband. He then got the hell out of there, the same way he'd gotten in. CP didn't even bother to cut Mrs. Dietrich free from the tape. He left her ass wrapped tight laying across the bed for staff to find her the next few hours to come.

He then went to his daughter's mother's house where he'd been staying. The both of them counted the money together. It totaled $500K in all. The kilos of heroin sold wholesale at $50K each at the time, and the fentanyl, he had no knowledge of the base price for a brick of that, nor how much it was in demand. He would have to look into that so as to not cheat himself. He had it in mind to give Beade $60K. CP felt that that was enough for her services. Dude was happy to have a cousin like her to have that type of job. But above all, he was glad to know Beade had the ability to peep game and comprehend what was going on around her. The eyes doesn't lie. Never have, and never will. The ears may be deceived. But not the eyes. Trust no man who may say anything different.

***

Forty Days Later . . .

A little known fact about people who suffer from Alzheimer's disease is that, the mental faculties of the patients have the ability to heighten and fade at sporadic points throughout the process. Luckily for Von, his grandmother experienced a moment or so through her day when the robbery plot was carried out.

The name *Tyese Smith* was scribbled on one of the pages of the coloring books Mrs. Dietrich had. The grandson, Vonnie, bought those for her. Mrs. Dietrich possessed a fond love for the craft as she loved crayons, different types of flowers, and floral art. She often referred to the female doctors and nurses as "flower girls," due to the many different colorful scrub suits the aides wore, especially the CNA's. The writing was barely readable and appeared as if "chicken scratch" on the page. But nonetheless, Von knew how to decipher any formality of letters his Nanna wrote out or had trouble wording.

"Flower girl, Vonnie! Flower girl!" granny conveyed. She then went mute once more, and he knew it may be days or weeks before he could get more out of her regarding the perpetrators of the robbery.

At the time the staff discovered Mrs. Dietrich taped and gagged on the bed in her suite hours after the robbery, they'd never suspected anyone to have entered and stolen anything from the place. They thought maybe a cruel prank was played on her, as the staff there had a history of neglect and mistreatment. And not once was it contemplated that the family was using Mrs. Dietrich's place to stash money, drugs, and guns. Nothing was ever reported to the police, and there weren't any signs to indicate anything was missing. But Von knew that there was, and merely kept it to himself, until the proper time. He took the report as a slap in the face, the one made by the shift supervisor to the facility, that *"his grandma had acted out and ransacked her own closet."* And to get even by way of a prank, an unknown staff member, bound her with tape to subdued her. He knew personally, that that couldn't have been any farther from the truth than it was. Von took action into his own hands.

He made it his business to go to a shop that sold spyware. He bought several mini cameras, batteries and other materials to help catch a thief. He didn't change up the routine he'd established. He'd still shown up on Thursdays at his regularly scheduled time.

After nearly a month of him collecting footage, he then retrieved the data recording devices from his grandma's suite and went to his house to review. The cameras were left in place with Mrs. Dietrich.

Von took notice of the many "flower girls" and a "ferry" who'd moved in, about, and out, of his grandma's space. He observed name tags and all. But one in particular stood out.

"Tyese Smith! That's the bitch right there who Nana was talking about! A flower girl!" he worded aloud to himself upon observation.

Mrs. Dietrich's mind was working fairly good the day when she rotated her eyes from Beades' shirt, towards her eyes, then back to the shirt. It was the name tag she'd committed to memory.

***

Since the day CP paid Beade those $60K, she'd upgraded herself in a decent way. She'd gotten a brand new car, kept her hair and nails superbly up to par, and looked like she'd come into some money. It was the month of August. Therefore, all the funds from her income tax returns was long gone, and the three kids she had, exhausted any additional money for the need of school clothes that had to be bought. Not that he knew she had kids. However, Von knew enough about women with children to know that August is a month when women were at their most broke point. Much like October and January.

Von and his right-hand man, Eunice Coleman, aka "Cold Heart," set out to get Beade on this particular day, the flower girl had to be dealt with.

The two sat low key in a discrete car in the parking lot of Pleasant Grace to await Beade to exit the building to go home. Her shift ended at 8 p.m.

Finally, Beade came walking out the front door into the parking lot. Von and Cold Heart decided that the best way to deal with her was to kidnap the bitch, torture her to near death to get her to tell who else had anything to do with the robbery, then, as a finality, execute Beade in horrendous fashion.

The henchmen studied her movement so as to know which vehicle she drove. Beade navigated cleanly through the other automobiles that dotted the pavement en route to a Nissan S.U.V. It sat off to itself at the farthest end of the lot, making it an easier task now for the two to snatch her up and make a clean getaway.

Beade was about thirty feet from her vehicle when Von pulled up in the Dodge Charger he drove. Cold Heart, a somewhat muscular and athletic guy at 6'1" and 220lbs, hopped out the passenger seat and rushed the girl with a tackle. She attempted to scream. Cold Heart punched her out then and there. He'd broken her nose with the blow. Von reached over and opened the door on the right side in the back. Cold Heart quickly lifted and tossed her into the backseat, lowering his full weight atop of her. Von pulled off with Cold Heart closing the door at the same time and tying Beade with the shoelaces he had to serve the purpose.

Nightfall was now set in. Von drove to the house he owned on Darien Street. He pulled up through the alley behind the place and into the garage. Cold Heart had Beade bound tight and mouth gagged. They yanked her from the car down to the gritty concrete floor. Cold Heart was instructed to drag her by the ankles to the basement from the carport. Beade banged her head each step along the way.

The basement was an area where Von fought his game-bread pit bulls and sometimes kept them chained. He had a spring leash hanging from a cross-beam above. Cold Heart tied Beade's wrists with the thick nylon dog collars and connected her to the chain that dangled.

Whop!

Von backhanded her in the mouth. Beade's lip puff instantly.

"So you wanna steal from me, bitch!" Von spat.

Whop!

He fired her up once more.

Whop!

Then again.

Cold Heart handed Von her purse. He went inside and discovered she had money there. It Was $5,000 in $100 bills and $500 in $20.

Von took a hard look at the bills. The $100's most of all. He knew then without a doubt that the money Beade had belonged to him.

"Bitch, this is my motherfuckin money!" he vented.

Von made it his business at the time, to place distinguish dotted markings on all his large bills he kept with his grandma. His favorite color was Royal Blue. He'd used a fine point ink pen to put snake-eyed dots in this color on the forehead between the eyes of Benjamin Franklin, and one dot on the earlobe of Andrew Jackson, as if he had an earring in his ear. Von was very meticulous in this way and made the time always to mark everything he owned. He even made his girlfriends and side pieces all get a tattoo that says "SK Von" (hence: "Street King Von"). Dude had terrible control issues.

"You wanna steal from me! Huh bitch! Take that tape off this bitch mouth, bro," Von said.

Cold Heart yanked the tape free.

"How the fuck you get my paper, bitch!"

Whop!

"Huh!"

Whop!

"Speak up!"

Whop!

"Who helped you! Who else involved! You better talk! And now!"

Beade broke. She told him everything. The relentless series of backhands caused her to cave.

"Cold Heart! Murk this bitch!" Von dictated.

The right hand man began to maliciously beat Beade in the head with a hammer. He bashed her skull in so bad to the point her brain sloshed like wet noodles in warm tomato sauce.

The two unchained her arms and allowed the body to plop onto the thick plastic beneath. They rolled her into the black plastic spread and loaded her in the trunk of the car.

Von and Cold Heart drove the body to the outskirts of the city, to the Pennsylvania countryside. They dumped Beade alongside the road just within a wooded line of trees there, hopped back into the car, and got back on Interstate 676 headed east to the city. The *"Flower Girl"* who loved to wear the periwinkle colored scrubs, was no more. She'd paid the ultimate penalty for her plotting and thievery. In the end, the risk of such magnitude wasn't worth the short-lived reward that was gained. Had she only taken heed.

***

Ten Days Later . . .

The two hitter friends was at it once more. Von and Cold Heart set out to track down the elusive possum named Carlton Parker aka "CP." He'd managed to burrow himself deeply in the various ghetto havens of Philly after the robbery. The chase became a scenario similar to *Coyote after Road Runner.* CP was difficult to locate and get a hand on. And Von found himself bloodthirsty behind the loss of his money and Kilos of narcotics. In a sense, he was Wile E. Coyote himself. A predatory killer on the loose.

The streets put it out that a known dude for pulling capers, had batches of heroin he was busy trying to get rid of. For a low price at that. Word also had it that this same cat had some type of other powerful drug that wasn't too common in the hood. Beade already provided a name before her inevitable end, and Von had knowledge of who it was he was now looking for. He went to a hired hand to assist with locating the perk. A cop his cousin had on the team.

Von held a business acquaintance with this Philadelphia City policeman he paid well monthly. Pervis sherron Dillion was the uncle of one of Von's girlfriends. Von and the female had a daughter together. Her name was Brianna Dillion. Her Father was the brother of Pervis. Von let Pervis know who he was looking for and how badly he wanted him.

"I'll be sure to track down this chump for you, Von," advised the 41 year-old Pervis. "It shouldn't take too long. Maybe a few days."

"Please do. He and I need to have a little meeting, so I can know what the fuck he was thinking when he decided to take what belonged to me. I need to know!"

Von seethed with anger in his heart and held vengeance on his mind.

The two met at the Riverside location of Penns Landing, a tourist spot where they chose to discuss the matter. At no time would they talk over the phone. They'd only send coded text messages to set up a meeting. Or Von would have Brianna relate his words to her uncle. Von and her had been acquainted for the past few years. She was 24. Their daughter was 3.

Pervis retrieved the arrest record of CP. It was discovered that the guy not long before the day, been arrested for a domestic dispute with the Mother of his son. He'd beat on her and she called the cops. He posted bail to the same address that was on file to a home in Southwest Philadelphia. It was the residence of his grandmother. Pervis made a call there posing as CP's friend to confirm whether or not this was the correct location. It was. Von and Cold Heart again went to work.

CP made his way to his grandmother's home at 11:30 p.m. on a Sunday. He entered where the elderly lady lived alone, for the most part, expecting to find her in the bedroom sleeping like always when he came home late. But what he found instead, was something far more horrible altogether, and paralyzed him with fear.

CP eased open the door to his grandmother's room and immediately took notice of Von standing over her with a large automatic pistol. It was firmly planted against the back of her head. She was tied tightly and stretched out across the bed.

"What the fuck! No! Please no!" CP pleaded for mercy. He pissed on himself from fear.

Cold Heart then came up from behind and wrapped his left arm around CP's neck, pinning a pistol to the right temple of the dude and whispered in his ear.

"Thought you got away, didn't you!" Cold Heart hissed through clenched teeth. He pushed CP to the floor face first and proceeded to tie him up.

Now secured and no longer a threat, Von began to speak, "Don't even think about telling me a lie, nigga! Your cousin Tyese, already told me everything before we knocked her off. And now to you. Where the fuck is my money and my dope!" Von demanded to know.

CP didn't hesitate to speak up.

"I got the money and what's left of the work down in the basement. Just please, leave Nanna out of it. A'ight. Don't hurt her. Your beef is with me. No one else."

Von and Cold Heart then dragged them both to the basement. CP told them where they could find what they came looking for. They'd gotten it. From there, it was to the part Von couldn't wait to get to.

He had Cold Heart pass him the claw hammer which was in his waistband. Von palmed the weapon tightly. At that point, he came down hard on CP's head with a devastating blow. Then again. And again. And again. And again. The old lady began to cry at the sight of the ski-masked assassin viciously bludgeoning her grandson to death. She couldn't scream. Her mouth was gagged. All she could do was cry. And that, she did a lot of. The fear was, she'd be done the same way as her grandson. But fortunately for the old lady, Von had mercy and compassion in his heart. The thought of his own grandmother compelled him to refrain from doing her dirty in this way. He did, however, stomp on her hand and made a statement before the two were to flee the scene.

"I'm sure you spent some of my money your punk-ass grandson stole from me! But I'mma give your ass a pass this time. *Grandma!* Consider yourself lucky. And continue to thank God," Von spat.

He then brought down the hammer hard, smashing the concrete directly in front of her face. Pieces of rock particles popped in both her eyes. Opposite of that, she would however, live to see another day.

"Thank you Lord, that those demons didn't kill me!" The old lady said aloud to herself.

***

The cops were called by neighbors. Suspicious activity was reported. They were now there at Cp's grandmother's house with the crime scene investigative unit. The old lady was removed and taken to the hospital to be treated for a minor eye injury. A particle from the smashing of the concrete caused her issues. She would need counseling afterwards.

The lead homicide detective, William Edward Hilliard, better known as "Bill Hilliard," a 44- year-old African-American male, was present to begin the investigation. Bill stood at five foot eleven, rather chubby at 240 lbs, had a slightly deep variation in voice, and wore a crew-cut hairstyle. His nose was broad—shaped like an Ace of Spades—and his lips thick and wide. The detective was clean-shaven, and religiously put a razor blade on his face each morning before work. His military routine carried over from service to the police force. Bill loved his job and was good at what he took an oath to do.

"So we got a maniac robber slash killer on the loose, I see," Bill remarked to his detective partner of many years, a Hispanic named Valente Canelo. "The worst part about it is that, he doesn't discriminate. Now, all that's to be done is make the connection between this murdered victim here, and the others that's occurred. If there's any. Most recently, the incident which one of the females killed is the same fashion, was discovered by the D-O-T (Department of Transportation) and reported. While trimming bushes and trees along the roadside out in the county, they stumbled upon her.

"There is a pattern to it, huh," said Canelo. "I'm only wondering, what's the motive inside the mind of this killer, to make him bash his victims repeatedly with a hammer!"

The Puerto Rican veteran on the force was just as serious about his work as was Bill, if not more.

Bill paced around in the basement, scanning the area more for any potentially overlooked evidence. He spoke more.

"The grandmother stated that a few days ago, her grandson here (he pointed down at the victim sprawled out on the floor) had given her a lot of money to pay bills and finish off the mortgage. His rap sheet reveals he's a robber and a drug dealer. She also mentioned that the person who did this, brought it to her attention that her grandson supposedly stole something from the guy. Money. The only likely conclusion I see is that, this was an act of retaliation. Karma coming back to claim the perpetrator of the bad deeds he'd done," Bill said, and jotted notes onto the yellow paper pad he had.

"It seems to be the obvious to me as well. Nothing appears fishy. And the body of the female you mentioned, a Tyese Smith, confirmed to be one of the females who was abducted in the parking lot of her job at a nursing center. Her vehicle had been abandoned. This is what raised suspicion. She was added onto the missing persons' list, until of late. We need to run a check to see if any connections exist between her and him. Rather by relationships, family, or otherwise," Canelo declared.

"I'm more than sure that something should connect the two. Phone records, family members, an ex-girlfriend, or something. You watch. We just need to get busy trying to capture this guy, before his hammer comes down on yet another victim. Or on us by the Mayor or Captain, since we're in mid-term, and the crime rate needs to be reduced before the election in November. And I don't like this bad boy by any means. The style of his slayings is too brutal. For some strange reason, I have an eerie gut feeling this may be someone we've encountered before. Or perhaps, these may be people whose crossed our path," remarked Bill. "But nonetheless, this bastard belongs to us! And we won't stop or rest until we nail this motherfucker, Valco! You with me on this partner?" asked Bill.

"I am! To the death of me, Bill!" Canelo responded.

The two then bumped fists and stared at one another in serious solidarity.

"To the death of me as well! We can't stop until this killer gets the death penalty. Understood?"

"Understood."

"Hup!"

"Hup!"

PART ONE

One

Trevon Rommell Dietrich-Savage, was born November 21,1991. His family on the father's side maintains a legacy of infamy that stretched from the late 1940s to the present. The Savages had a gritty and raw reputation of street and ghetto lore, from Georgia, to Pennsylvania, to Florida. Von's grandfather, Cornelius Aaron Savage, aka "Big Hound Savage," was one of the original founders of the notorious yet business savvy "Black Mafia Incorporated," and played an instrumental role in empowering the many underworld narcotics suppliers who made millions of dollars illegally, prior to going legit in their efforts to buy back the hood and rebuild it properly.

Von's Father would go on to carry the tradition of BMI by him and his cousins and brothers, establishing Junior Black Mafia (JBM), dominating the 1980's and 1990's underworld of Philadelphia city.

Cornelius II aka "Little Hound," fathered three kids. However, Von was the one and only by his mother. Little Hound and Lilly separated on good terms, and vowed to maintain a decent friendship. The relationship they had, suffered a blow when Von's father was sent away to serve a prison sentence. The mother made him aware that she was lonely and requested permission to see other people. Little Hound understood his predicament better than most, and knew it was impossible to hold onto a woman from a prison cell. For him, the best thing to do at the time was to simply let her go. That, he did. He'd never been the type of dude to get into his feelings about a female. *"There's too many fish in the sea to be down and out about one,"* he thought. *"So long our friendship remains, and she don't ever put my business out there to some other guy, it's all good with me."*

The fact of the matter was that, Lilly knew too much of Little Hound's business. He had to move on and allow her to as well. No love lost. No harm done. No foul on the play.

Growing up as a kid, Von spent a lot of time with his paternal family members. He was very close to his grandfather, Big Hound. Out of twenty-one heads of grand kids, he found a way to become the favorite of them all. The grandfather never told Von per se that he was the "favorite." But to the grandson, it was evident. It showed in more than one way. And at the age of thirteen, Big Hound confirmed this to Vonnie by showing the kid the exact writing in his will; and what all he was to leave behind for him upon his death. The grandfather didn't give a damn about anything little Von would have going on in the street at his age or what he did. All he asked of him was for Von to graduate high school (Simon Gratz High), and go on to get a degree in College as a business major at Drexel University. Von had to carry out the wishes of his grand pop in order to inherit the benefits left to him.

Big Hound and his main two cousins were really close (Mickey Savage and Johnny Mack Savage). He wanted their grand kids in particular, to have fun, live life to the fullest, and gain a deep level of respect for money and business, especially *their* money and *their business.* Blood was shed, lives were taken and lost, love compromised, and souls were sold to the devil, to acquire the riches that they had, and they didn't want it all to go in vain.

Von had been around drugs the majority of his life. He knew what it all looked like, and had long benefited from the proceeds of narcotic deals without having ever touched so much as a baggie or a crumb. At the age of sixteen, all that changed. The teenager always wanted to live the same type of lifestyle his father and grandfather lived, if not more to a deeper degree, but never expressed this burning desire.

Fast, wild, and on the edge with excitement, proved to be the life that worked best for Von. And having long money and a fleet of women at his disposal, the same way he'd seen other kingpins maintain, motivated him to get on the ball and get to it hustling as never before. He wanted to establish and build upon his own legacy, outside the realm of what his Savage family had established already. The young buck was ambitious to make his own money, not being dependent on his mother's, father's, or grandfather's finances, and do everything his way, how he saw fit; only being sure to keep true to the promise to grand pop intact while doing so. And that appeared to be an easy thing for the athletic and academically bright kid. Von was a mastermind in his own right, and set out to prove it. Again, in his own way.

TWO

Von began his hustling career in narcotics by selling dime bags of high-grade weed and ecstasy pills. He and his closest homie, a guy street named Cold Heart (then only known as Eunice) would get money in and around the neighborhood where Von's mom owned their home, on Darien Street, and sometimes, out of the home itself. Those two would attend parties and teenage haunts to sell their product. Most notably, the place called "Dances" or "Bobby Dances," located just off Girard Avenue and Broad Street in North Philly.

Von and Eunice quickly built a client base. In the beginning, they'd started out with a half pound of bud and 200 pills. Within 90-days, between school and the streets, they'd reached fifteen pounds and 1000 beans. Once they'd come to the conclusion that customers prefer to spend $10 and get two bags of weed and $20 for three pills, they switched up the hustle to accommodate them. It was on and popping from there. Von and Eunice experienced a stark elevation in sales and recognition. Additional trap spots and a couple of trustworthy female friends had to be included in the fray for distribution in retail. There was now a team, and Von referred to himself and the crew as the "Darien Street Squad." With that, Von was sure to hold the thought that there would eventually become a point in time when enforcers and defenders of themselves, the money, and the product would be necessary. They were now seven deep, and the ranks could potentially grow.

***

Von met a female at school. A Puerto Rican chick he was somewhat familiar with. He was in the eleventh grade and she was a senior. Her name was Chloe Dominguez. She became the apple of his eye and the main attraction whom had his attention. The Spanish sensation had no boyfriend at the time and he was without a girlfriend. Von was still a virgin. But he was ready for things to change. This was a surprising thing far a teenager in North Philly. But Von however, did have an episode or two with a female for oral sex. Of course, that doesn't count as intercourse. The young lady wanted to smoke on the weed he had, and pop a few pills, but had no money, and her period was on. Nonetheless, she was in luck, because she had two things going well for her to give an advantage. Her mouth worked and her hands. She put them both to use at the party in the bathroom and got what she wanted. An even swap with no swindle. The second time for Von was by a hooker on the stroll whom he paid to please him. He wasn't willing to risk putting her tender manhood into her. Not even with a condom on. A dick-sucking worked out just fine.

Chloe was five-six in height, weighted 132 lbs, and had a fit figure. Her flowing long black hair, honey-complexioned smooth and radiant skin, pink medium-sized lips, and bumblebee-like waistline were the top features that really had Von in hot pursuit after her. Those pretty white well structured teeth of Chloe's and her seductive accent (she spoke more Spanish at home than English at school or elsewhere) turned him on in the same way. Von couldn't help himself. He had to have her. Chloe's heart was won. But at what cost.

Although a little too fast for Von's comfort and more experienced in relationship, he presented something new and refreshing for Chloe. Besides, she needed it, after ending what she had with a guy five years her senior, a dude named

Raul. He was too compulsive and controlling. Their relationship only lasted seven months. One month before Von came into her life, she and Raul ended what they had. Chloe turned over a new leaf and Von entered a new world. One in where he was now having sex and getting help from his girl in having a new supplier. The two were on the path to succeed as a couple.

The first time Von and Chloe had sex, turned out to be a magical moment they would cherish for the remainder of their days. It was on a Saturday night and the day the high school prom took place. Chloe was to graduate that year and Von was in her life to celebrate both events with her. Not only that, just past noon this same day, he'd reached a milestone in his hustling life. Von made his first $10,000 in drug sales. That was the most money he'd ever had at one time. He had it counted out in ten stacks at a "G" pile each and had $8,000 worth of product in the streets divided between the six other people on the team, four dudes and two females.

Once the prom was over and all the dancing completed, the real party began between the two lovers who'd elevated to that from being friends. Von felt the need to splurge. He wanted to really show Chloe a good time. The two checked into one of the ritziest hotels in downtown Center City Philly. They were at the Marriot, on the Seventh floor, Room 711. He didn't smoke weed, pop pills or do anything like that. Only puffed on a Black & Mild every now and again, and sip on a wine cooler. However, Chloe smoked, and liked Xanax pills, but did so with control.

"Chloe, I'm proud of you baby girl. You know that," Von said to her, then took a sip of his drink. He had on nothing but his boxer shorts and a wife-beater as they sat atop the king-sized bed in the suite.

"I know you are, Papi. I'm glad to have you in my life to enjoy these types of moments with me. I like you, Von. A lot. You mean well. You make me feel good inside. And you make me smile. Not to mention how good of a dancer you are. You got moves," Chloe said with a smile and a peck on the lips before she hit her blunt and took a sip of the drink they shared. She was down to her panties and bra.

"I do a little something-something, you know. Tonight is all about you though. Now that you're gonna graduate next month. What are your plans?"

"I don't know. I can't really say. You already know, I don't like to plan in advance of things. I'm more spontaneous than I am anything. I like for things to play out the way that they are supposed to. Because nothing ever goes as planned. I had to learn that the hard way one too many times."

"You don't say, I think the same way you do, Chloe. My mom says me and my pops think alike. That we are two of a kind."

"I wouldn't mind meeting your mom one day. When do you plan to introduce me to her?" Chloe asked.

"Soon. Very soon. That's a big step. And I just want to ensure you are the one. I would hate to have to explain what went wrong if we fail to make it right. And that's all I want to do, get it right the first time around, you know. So it's important that we continue to go easy and not rush a thing. I wanna take my poor precious time getting to know you, the same as I want you to do as it applies to me. You feeling that," Von responded.

"Don't rush at anything, huh? Well, what about this?" she said, then gently strode her left hand over his right thigh, finding her way to his manhood. Von's dick jumped to life instantaneously.

"Now that . . . we can go ahead and rush into," he let out with excitement and a smile.

Chloe returned a smile of her own, then eased her hand into the waistband of his underwear to grip his manhood. It was average in size, but thick and hard to the touch. She liked it and was eager to lay eyes on it and have him inside of her. She withdrew the dick from its hiding space and began to do the expected thing any older more experienced girlfriend would do to their younger boyfriend. The Puerto Rican heartthrob bobbed up and down on him with a dick sucking he would crave for come the next time around. This was the first the two had took their intimacy to this level in the two months they'd been together, and the first she'd even seen his dick. Von had something to work with, and now had a pretty and sexy Latina to exploit him in that way for his first sexual experience in intercourse.

Once Chloe primed him to a peak erection, they both got naked and began to do what sexually active teenagers do; fuck like there was no tomorrow, and as if they would never have the opportunity again.

They stayed at the hotel for two days, that Saturday and Sunday, going home that night at 10 p.m. by Cab. Von didn't have a car yet, and neither did Chloe. They were working on making that happen at some point.

***

One Month Later . . .

The relationship between Von and Chloe got deeper and far more intimate from the day they first had sex. They were now close to each other on a daily basis and appeared to be inseparable. Within the 30-days leading from prom night to the week of graduation, the two had had sex at least ten or more times. They were fucking like jackrabbits and became obsessed with the feeling and thrill. Von now spent more time around Chloe than he did on the block getting money. Although his homie Eunice, was capable of holding down the team, they all had their own money to make and agendas to work at carrying out. Von only had the connect for the product they sold.

Although Von had his nose hung far up in Chloe's ass, he still managed to go to school and maintained staying aloof from trouble.

Chloe was finally granted the opportunity to have one of the requests fulfilled. Von welcomed her over to meet his mother. The two ladies had a thing or two in common in terms of beauty, naturally long flowing hair, fair complexion in skin tone, and extraordinary levels of sex appeals. Lilly began to take a liking to Chloe before she had a chance to hear her speak. Her presentation spoke volumes, and the elegant smell Chloe had, gave her a stamp of being approved. The eye test and her energy wooed Lilly.

"Mom, meet Chloe, my girlfriend," Von introduced. "And Chloe, met my dear mother. Her name is Lillian. But please, simply call her Lilly."

"Hello, Miss Lilly. It's a pleasure to meet you," Chloe greeted.

"Chloe, huh? Nice name. You're a pretty girl, Chloe," Lilly let out in response with a smile. "It's a pleasure to meet you as well. So you're the lucky one my son has been spending all his time with, I see. How lovely life must be," Lilly remarked.

Chloe giggled shyly at Lilly's remark, then produced a welcoming smile, one showing more of those exquisite teeth. They were one of her best assets.

"She just graduated high school too, mom. She's a smart girl."

"Oh, really! That's good. Congratulations darling. Me and Vonnie gonna be sure to do something special for you, okay? You've earned it. Graduating from school is a big step. What's your plans from here? What type of career are you looking to establish?" Lilly asked.

"I don't know yet. I'm undecided right now."

"Well, I highly encourage you to take your time. You don't want to have any regrets later in life. And the way things are going with this country and economy, you just never know. You just never know."

"I appreciate your encouragement too, Miss Lilly. I needed that. And Vonnie and I have decided to wait until he graduates before we pursue a career. I don't want to leave him behind, you know. We're making plans as we get to know each other better," Chloe expressed.

"That's a good thing too, you both are taking your time."

"Yeah mom, Chloe gonna get a job and work until I'm out of school. Then we might get a house together. We are just in our beginning stages and got a ways to go," Von let out.

They all took a seat in the living room and were content on having their meaningful conversation. A lot was related about themselves. Lilly was making herself acquainted with Chloe in a way that an older woman would with a young female she was looking to have a friendship with. Chloe was just the type of female and personality Lilly needed to forage a relationship with. Not to mention that Chloe was the girlfriend of her son and potential future daughter-in-law. Lilly desired personal time together with the girl, to go shopping, to the beauty parlor, and enjoy friendship. They were off to a good start.

THREE

Von and Eunice made progress on the streets. It was basically Eunice, Kareem, and Lonnie, who moved all the work and made the money while Von would be in school or spending time with Chloe. Von's homies had long dropped out of school and fully embraced the streets. They were hoodlums to the ultimate degree, and were on pace to be a group of malicious street thugs who just sold drugs to support their livelihood and held no goals for what they wanted their lives to be. Bad influence on Von, as the peer pressure from them mounted.

Then there was Ronald Waldon, Shayla Allen, and Tangela Norwood, who all did their own thing when it came to selling the weed and the pills. Von knew them from the neighborhood. They grew up together. Actually, he and Ron had been friends since childhood. He knew Ron before Eunice. But through it all, everyone made progress and the crew was evolving. They now needed a location to sell their product. And Von had to find a new supplier. The guy he was currently buying from wasn't able to supply him the large amounts he was now getting each re-up. The guy had suffered a robbery and now down bad in product. Von knew that Chloe had family members who sold the same material he was looking for. He went to her to connect him to someone.

Chloe lived in *"Puerto Rican land."* This was a section in North Philly. She lived in the not-so-rough area though. Things was smooth.

"Chloe, I need a favor, sweetie."

"A favor on what, Von?" She responded.

"I need you to connect me with one of your people, so I can buy my supply from them. I'm really low on product, and I need to continue to make money."

"Von, how do you figure I have a family member who got what you're looking for? And why do you seem to be more focused on dealing drugs than you are on your school work?" Chloe asked, now clearly concerned.

"Chloe. For one, I'm very focused on my class work and graduating from school. Don't get that twisted. I'm definitely gonna do that, sweetie. And another, I've got to make money. I've gotta take care of you and myself. And I wanted to by my own car and not continue on with my mom's ride anymore. Besides that, school is out for the summer. And we need our own place to live now. I'm sure you're ready to be in your own space too," Von said to his girl.

It didn't take her long to respond. Her mind was already in this direction.

"The only reason I'm gonna say something to my cousin for you, Vonnie, is because yes, I am ready to have my own place to live like you mentioned, and I need a car to get around in. I find myself having to call my cousin Rosa to take me where I need to go all the time. And I don't like to be dependent on anybody for anything. So, I'mma hit my people up for you. He got some killer weed too," Chloe stated.

"Okay. Go ahead. Call him for me. Tell him to come by." They were seated in Chloe's bedroom. She took her cell phone off the charger and then called her cousin, Tito. He was one of the top suppliers in Philly on weed and pills. Tito owned a few businesses too, in the Puerto Rican community. The main place he liked to hangout was at his custom car detail shop. Rims were sold there as well as accessories like music systems. He was there at the shop this day, like most often.

"Yeah! What's up Chloe," he said in Spanish. He took notice of her number on the screen.

"Hey Tito! How are you?" Chloe responded in their cultural tongue. "I need to speak with you. I have a boyfriend I want you to meet. He wants to talk."

"You have a boyfriend I need to meet! He wants to talk?"

"Yes, can we meet you at the shop?" Tito was asked by Chloe.

"Yeah. Come on by. I'm here."

"Okay. We're on our way now as we speak. We'll be there shortly. We're at my mom's house.

The call ended.

"What did he say? You know I don't understand that Spanish *ish* y'all speak," Von said with a smile.

Chloe began to prepare herself to leave. She put on her sneakers and grabbed her purse. Von got the idea at that point.

"Let's go. He wants to meet us at his shop," she informed.

"At his shop!" Von retorted.

"Yeah, at his shop. He has a car detail garage."

"Oh, he do."

"Yes sir, he does. A nice spot too."

"Oh yeah. Well, let's go. I'm ready to meet mister Tito. Hopefully, we can work a deal," Von said, obviously happy at the prospect of meeting a more high-profile supplier.

Tito's shop wasn't too far from where Chloe lived. Maybe five minutes away. It was located on Allegheny and Glenwood Aves. Once they arrived, they went into the office where Tito sat. Chloe played her part and walked closely to Von to show her cousin she liked her boyfriend and stood with him in all he had in mind to do.

"Hey Tito," she said in English so as not to offend Von. She then gave her cousin a hug. "This is my boyfriend here. His name is Von."

Tito turned his eyes towards Von and looked him up and down. Von had the appearance and physique of a grown man. He didn't look like a 16-year-old by far. His full beard was coming in maturely, and he had the persona of a veteran street dude who'd been in the game for a long time now. Last Tito knew, Chloe was into older dudes. This is why he perceived Von as a grown man.

"What's good, Tito? Nice to meet you," Von said, then extended his hand to shake Tito's.

"Von it is, right? What's good homie? What do you want to talk to me about? Tito asked.

Chloe took a seat and allowed the two guys room to talk while they stand.

Von dug into his pocket and pulled out a roll of money. "I got a couple of dollars I'm trying to spend, Tito. Chloe told me you could help us," Von said, then began to count out his money while he awaited Tito to reply.

Tito nodded his head in approval at the action and mind-set Von put on display. "I might be able to help you. Depends on how much you trying to spend. I don't do deals for less than ten thousand," Tito declared.

Damn! That's all the money I got put up. Von thought.

"But since you're my little cousin's boyfriend, and this is our first time doing business, I'll make an exception for you, because I'm sure you're gonna do right by her. Right?"

"No doubt, Tito. Chloe is my lady and my responsibility. I've got to take care of me and her. And I got four grand I want to start out with. I've got a little crew. We get to the money together. It won't take too long to get rid of what I get from you and be back for more. Much more," Von declared.

"That's what's up. Come on with that cash there, homie, and let's get things going," Tito stated and agitated four fingers in his left hand to indicate to Von to pass over the money. He did so.

Tito then counted it all himself. There was $4,000 like Von said it was.

"And what exactly type of product are you trying to get?"

"A combination of weed and pills, homie. That's what I want," Von responded.

"You know what. I'mma do you as solid. Because you and my little cousin are together. I got a deal for you. A'ight. I'mma give you two hundred E-pills and four bags of weed. And when you come back, be sure to have ten thousand for me to send. Can you handle that?' Tito asked.

"No doubt, I could. I got you bro."

Tito made a phone call to one of his workers for them to deliver Von's order. They sat and talked over a few relevant topics related to the streets. Tito knew of a lot of people who Von mentioned he knew in and around the hood. But Von wasn't too familiar with the cats who Tito brought up. They were mostly Spanish dudes. Von did bring up his dad's name to Tito.

"Damn little homie! That's your pop? Dude had it going on during his time out here on the streets. Lil Hound! Fuck yeah! I remember holmes. Them JBM niggaz didn't play!" Tito remarked. He was 35-years old and more closely related to Von's dad generation to recollect upon their reign in Philly.

"Yeah bro. That's my pop."

"I gotta ask you bro. All that money I'm sure your dad left behind, and the type of power and influence I know for a fact he had, why you not trying to capitalize on the clout he established?" Tito wanted to know.

"Because bro, you just said it. That was *his* money and something *he* established. I'm trying to make my own dough and create my own legacy. You feel me. I don't want anything to happen for me easily or without me working for it. That's my take on it. I got a plan that's not one-dimensional. It's gonna be a diversified vibe me and my people will hustle, rock, and elevate on. I think different Tito. That's all," Von said.

"I hear you. And I see. Sound like you got your shit together, little homie."

"I do. Just sit back and watch me work. My money gonna be spent with you until it can't be no more," Von stated.

Tito smiled at his quick witty reply. He was impressed with the youngster.

Twenty minutes passed. Tito's courier finally arrived with the work. Von took possession of his purchase, situated it in the truck of the car, then drove to his grandmother's house up in Germantown. Mrs. Edna Dietrich had a nice home in this section of the city. She lived there alone mostly, until Von moved in, and only went to the house on Darien Street to sell his product in the area on a freelance basis. His grandmother's home was his main place of residence. No one other than Mrs. Edna Dietrich, his mother, and now, Chloe, know of this.

He and Chloe exited the car. He grabbed hold of the bags that had his narcotics, and they made their way to the front door.

"Von, whose house is this?" Chloe asked.

The home was average in size but looked really nice. The lawn was green and well manicured as could be, with outstanding landscaping art in its design.

Von took a look at her and smiled, then turned the key to open the lock before and after he were to answer her question. "This my grandmother's house. My mother's mother," he said.

"Oh. It's definitely nice," Chloe remarked.

The sun was now setting and the sky had an illustrious crimson glow to it. The brick home had the appearance of an efficient castle in contemporary times; like a miniature version of Buckingham Palace where Queen Elizabeth II resided, only having the royal figurehead to reside at the home in Germantown North Philly, Queen *Edna Dietrich.*

The two made their way to Von's room. He led them through the house. He entered and closed the door behind him.

"So you live with your mom and your grandma, huh?"

"Yep," Von responded. "Been here since my grandfather passed away two years ago."

"What type of work did they do for a living?"

"My grandfather retired front the military after almost forty years in service. And my grandmother retired from *Nabisco*.

"You talking about the one located on Roosevelt Boulevard?" Chloe asked.

"That be the one. Now, let's get down to business, and separate this work I got here, so to make us some money and put us in a good place to live, shall we?" Von remarked with a smile on his face and a tone of excitement. He was eager as ever to distribute the product he and his girl hustled. Von had a ton of ambition and drive.

It took them about an hour to get the material separated and packaged the way he wanted. They then capped off the evening together with a superior moment of intimacy. Chloe sucked him up really well before allowing him the pleasure they both desired; to fuck her good from the back. Von blew his load deep inside of his Latina sweetheart. He'd become infatuated with having sex with Chloe. Her love juices permeated a musk-type intoxicating fragrance he couldn't get enough of. They had interesting chemistry.

FOUR

Eunice managed to make a great deal of movement for the crew. He utilized the territory in the vicinity of Erie Avenue to sell the product he had. His mother's house was there in the area, and that served him well to keep his money and product safe. If a threat was to present itself, Eunice bought a few guns and rifles to arm himself and the crew. Among them all, he was the second oldest at eighteen; but the most fierce; and the biggest and most athletic.

Eunice bought ten handguns; two AR-15's; and two shotguns for protection. He had a cousin by the name Herb, who was heavily into arms dealing. Herb was tied in with the Russian Mafia of Philly. The majority of the $6,000 Eunice paid for the weapons, came out of his own pocket. Unlike the others of the crew he was a part of, he knew how gritty and ugly the niggaz in the hood could get, and how vicious the streets were as a whole. Therefore, all precautionary measures had to be put in place, being that they were on the rise along the food chain in the underworld. Philly was as cutthroat and as gangsta as they come, even when it came to a few ambitious teenagers selling their little weed and pills, and trying to get by. No doubt, they were food too. No one was off limits.

To properly put it in perspective, Eunice was the leader of the squad. But didn't have the backing of a reputed die-hard family on the streets as Von and his family—the Savages. Von had the connection, and Von had people he could go to for money. He and Eunice got closer and hinted that they were like- minded business partners.

Eunice hit Von up and told him to come by the house. That he had something to give him. Von did so. Eunice showed him specifically what the meeting was for.

"Check it, Von. This here for you bro," Eunice said, then presented his homie with a brand new Glock-19 pistol and a pair of black leather gloves. "I'm sure you're gonna need this. So that's why I went ahead and bought us a few hammers, a few ratchets, and a few sticks, little homie. The streets of Philly ain't nice to nobody! And we ain't gonna be sweet out here either!

"Damn, Eunice! This jawn her nice, my nigga!" Von let out, taking hold of the firearm with caution.

"It ain't loaded, nigga," Eunice said with a chuckle. "You don't have to be scared to handle this."

Von definitely had familiarity with guns. He'd been around them and had shot more than enough to know what needed to be known about them.

"I know how to work these things, homie. Trust and believe that. I'm a Savage. Remember," Von responded with a smile. "So, how many did you buy?" he then asked.

Eunice lifted the mattress to the bed in his room. It didn't have any sheets or blankets on it. Just a raw mattress. "I brought all this for us," he related, then picked up the M-16 closest to him and aimlessly waved it in a sweeping motion.

"What the fuck! Nigga we're strapped for real now, ain't we! I wish a mothafucka' would!" Von expressed.

"I know that's right! If niggaz want some smoke, we go hard with fire!" Eunice responded. "We gotta go by everybody else spot and give them theirs. You already know we gonna have to show Shay and Tangee how to use these things. I got these here for them. Or either these." He pointed a finger at the two .38 snub noses and the two small nine-millimeters.

"I'm about to text them now and let them know we on the way to see 'em," Von stated.

"For sho. But on the flip side of this, we should be ready to re-up, right? I am. I done got rid of all I had. That weed was smoking too. You're dealing with the same dude again, right?" Eunice asked.

"Nah. I ran into a new plug. A Puerto Rican cat. One of my girl's people."

"Oh, you fuck with a Rican chick now?"

"Hell yeah. I met her at school. She graduated this year. And now, she's gotta get her ass a job and go to work. But if she wanna go off to college, that shit gonna have to wait until next year when I walk the line. If I ain't gotten her pregnant by then. Shorty all that."

"You pussy whipped already, nigga! Ha ha ha," Eunice made fun of Von.

"You gotta get you a girl now, *Clubber Lang,*" Von retorted with humor, referring to Eunice's boxing ability.

"Got one, little bro. I'm just more concerned with the hustle and getting money than I am with pussy and a female. I know they're gonna be there. Once we run it up, we can have all the bitches we want. One just won't do for me," Eunice remarked.

"You probably got a point there. But I gotta live a little first, then move on to bigger and better things. Anyway, I'll make it my business to re-up Saturday, once we get rid of what's left. I gotta check with the crew and see what they got," Von stated.

He then tucked his new pistol inside his waistband and put the box of bullets in a show box Eunice passed to him.

"Let's roll bro. We gotta check in with the others. Crew love to the death of us," Eunice said then put his gun inside his waistline. He had a .45. All metal and black in color.

They got into Von's mom's car he drove. It was an Acura TL. He liked the car and had plans to buy a similar version once he got his dollars up.

They made it a priority to stop by to see Shayla and Tangee first. The two girls were best friends actually. Like sisters in many ways. They were close to each other and hung out nearly every day. The hangout spot for them was Shayla's sister's house. She lived a block away from 17th Street and Jefferson Ave, an area where there was heavy traffic for weed, pills, and syrup. Shayla and her sister did hair and nails for a living. The weed they sold along with the pills, added to their income.

Von and Eunice arrived. As expected, Tangee was there with Shayla and her elder sister, Cori. The boys entered the house.

"What's good Von . . . Eunice," Shayla greeted. Those big black lips of hers were cute. She was seated on the couch puffing on a Black & Mild. She'd not long gotten her hair re-done. Shayla had box braids.

"What's good, Shay . . . Tangee . . . Cori," Von responded.

"Yeah, what's up girls," Eunice spoke.

"Hey, you two," Tangee then greeted with a smile.

"Yeah. Hey y'all," said Cori. Her lustful eyes locked in on Von. "You know I'm ready to suck that young dick of yours,Von. When you ready for me too?" she included with a smile and a set of wet lips. "You a Savage, nigga! Your bloodline runs deep. I'll suck your dick and put this pussy on you on the GP. Your people them dudes," she added, referring to his family no doubt.

Eunice laughed like hell at the sexually aggressive energy Cori put on display.

"I may entertain that thought one day, Cori. Just be patient."

"Okay baby. Just don't have me waiting too long. I still want to be attractive for you when you finally decide to let me taste your sugar," Cori responded, then took a toke of the weed the girls smoked, and sip on her beer.

"I won't. But look, Shayla and Tangee, me and Eunice need to holla at you two," Von stated.

The girls then got up and they all stepped to the backroom—Shayla's room—and began to talk. They'd met there a few times in the past. The routine was normal.

Eunice closed the door. He then pulled two pistols out of the backpack he had. He spoke up at that point. "A'ight, look you two. We moving on up in the world nowadays. And you got haters out there everywhere. You also got robbers who think they can take shit from motherfuckas' when they feel like it. But we got something to keep them niggaz at bay. Y'all know how to use these, right?"

"No doubt, nigga. We know how to aim and shoot," Shayla responded.

"Yeah, I know how to use one," Tangee chimed in. "I want this one," she opted for the small automatic. A nine-millimeter.

"And I want this one," Shayla pointed at the .38.

Eunice handed them the gun of their choice.

"Okay, now look," Von then spoke up. "How much money y'all done made so far?" he asked.

"We got about twenty-five hunnid together so far," Shayla said.

"Where is it? We need it to re-up with. We're going big this time," Von said.

"Go get that, Tangee," Shayla told her friend,

The brown-skinned butter pecan complexioned sweetheart, sauntered towards the door of the room. Her plump round ass shifted enticingly from side to side. Tangee had on a pair of those thin material boy-shorts, the kind that made for her ass cheeks to hang out from below. It was the summer and hot out. Von had to regain his focus. His eyes momentarily looked in on the bulls eye's designed pattern on the back of her shorts. He knew he could have some of her if he wanted. But the business he maintained in mind, negated any sexual thoughts. Although young and at the age of where a teenage boy would want to stick his dick in every piece of pussy available, he had a level of discipline to him from his father and grandfather's wisdom imparted to prevent reckless sexual behavior. *"Don't put your dick and your money in the same place,"* the grandfather, Hound Savage, would say.

Tangee returned with the purse she and Shayla used as a money stash. She handed the cash to Shayla. It was counted by her for the final time and passed to Von. He put it away then made the girls aware of what to expect soon.

"A'ight look, between the both of you, y'all normally get a pound and a half, and a hundred pills to move, right? But this weekend, y'all gonna be upgraded in a major way. That's the reason for those hammers there," he pointed towards two pistols the girls had put away now in the same purse the cash was in. "To protect yourselves with."

"And y'all two bitches better bust your guns off the rip, if any motherfuckas' try to rob or take advantage of you!" Eunice spat with a bit of aggression to his tone to indicate he meant what he'd said.

"We got you, bro," Shayla professed. "Us two bitches here . . . gonna bust our guns, for sho'!"

"Damn sure is!" Tangee chimed in to cosign.

Von and Eunice then dapped up both girls with a hand slap and fist bump. They left the house and made their way to the three other dudes who were down with them, Ron, Kareem, and Lonnie. They too were to be given two handguns each.

Von then dropped Eunice back off at home. He made his way to the house of someone he had a lot of love and respect for. A man who he looked up to as "God" himself, and the woman that the man had as a wife as a "Goddess." It was his grandfather, Cornelius Savage, aka "Big Hound."

Hound Savage and his wife Henrietta, had a nice home on the far end of Philadelphia, in the Southwest section of the city, the neighborhood was posh, in a gated community. It was a location where well-to-do tax-paying affluent citizens lived. Hound was sure to prepare for a peaceful retirement in his life after many years in the underworld. He'd secured plenty of money through the decades he'd spent dealing heroin. He and his cousins Mickey and Johnny Mack. And held plans to live out the remainder of his days just as he was. Lavishly.

Von was granted access into the community. He'd pulled up into the driveway of his grand pop's home, got out of the car, and made his way to the front door. The grandparents were already expecting him from a phone call the front gate made to them.

Mrs. Henrietta opened the door to let him in.

"Hey grandma!" Von greeted. He spread his arms to give a hug.

"Hey baby. How you been?" she asked.

"I've been good, Nana. Where granddaddy at?"

"He in there," she responded and pointed to the den area of the house.

Von took a look at his watch. The time was just past 7 p.m. He knew then and there what his grand pop was busy doing on a Thursday evening.

Von entered the area of the house where Hound was situated. "What up, grand pop!" he said. "How you doing today? I had to make it my duty to come see you." Hound was seated on the thick leather couch before the 80-inch flat screen TV. Von walked up to give him a hug.

"I'm good, son. What about you?" Hound responded. He'd not long before the hour had his personal barber (one of his cousin Mickey's grandsons) give him a straight-razor head shave and beard line-up. The old man still had a level of handsomeness to his appearance, even in his late seventies. He was serious about being groomed and well dressed.

"I've been well, granddaddy. Being sure to keep to the dream and plan you have in place for me," Von responded.

"That's right. You gotta be sure to do that, son. If nothing else, you gotta keep to your word, to your promise to me," Hound reminded.

"For sure," Von confirmed. "What you got going on?"

"Just here enjoying my favorite pass time, watching the baseball game. My Atlanta Braves playing my second favorite team, the Philadelphia Phillies. This a good game too. From how the first two innings played out."

"That's right, I forgot you love them sorry behind Atlanta Braves," Von let out with a chuckle. "You originally from Georgia. I almost forgot."

"That's right, son. Baseball is my favorite sport. My daddy—your great granddaddy—played in the Negro League, for the *Atlanta Black Crackers!* I'm sure you won't know anything about them," Hound stated, reminded of how young his favorite grandson was.

"Nah, grandpa. I can't say that I do. But look. I came to see you today, because I need you."

"Oh, you do! Don't we all!" Hound responded with a bit of humor to his remark. "What you need granddaddy for?" he asked.

"You know I'm about to go into my last year of high school, right. And I need to go shopping for some school clothes before we go back, you feel me," Von related and brought his grandfather up to par with the modern lingo of his generation.

"That's right–that's right. You are on your way, ain't you? I'm proud of you too, son. I really am. How much you need to get your clothes?"

"Well . . . you know I don't like none of that cheap *ish!*" Von let out before he began to make his request.

Hound then once himself over with an open hand, implying that the grandson should look at how expensive and nice the clothes were he had on. Although the time was well ahead into the day, Hound still had on top-dollar attire, even with no place in particular to go. Especially not at that hour.

"I see you grandpa. You look nice too," Von let out with a smile, causing Hound to return the same.

"Again, how much do you need?" Hound asked once more. He didn't like anyone to beat around the bush in dealing with him. The legendary gangster loved people to be straight about everything.

"I need ten thousand dollars, granddaddy!" Von stated.

"Ten thousand dollars!" Hound retorted. "Damn! You do got expensive taste, don't you boy!"

"I'm a Savage, granddaddy. What more would you expect? I've got the same blood pumping through my veins as you do yours. That rich Hound Savage blood, that is," Von responded with a flare of flattery. He knew how to appease his grandfather with compliments.

"Well, since you said it that way, I ain't got no choice but to give you what you ask for. I'm the one who made you this way, me and your daddy."

Von nodded in agreement, added by a smile. "You got that right. You definitely got that right," he flattered him more.

Little to Von's knowledge, not only did his grandfather have his own money tucked away in the bank, in investments, and so much cash on hand at home. He held the money that belonged to his eldest son as well, that of Cornelius Savage II aka "Little Hound," Von's father. And Big Hound, had it in mind to give the grand boy $5,000 of his own money, and $5,000 from Von's daddy's pot. An even amount of gifts for the young Savage who was coming of age. And doing so faster than the grandfather originally thought he would.

Hound called out for his wife. She was in the kitchen making them a snack.

Henrietta came to the den where her husband and grandson were situated. "Yes honey?" she responded.

"Yeah baby, I didn't mean to slow you down, all right. But, I need you to get ten thousand dollars from my cash pot in the room, please," Hound asked of his wife.

"No problem, sweetheart," she replied, then made her way to their bedroom, an area of the home no one other than those two had ever stepped foot inside.

While awaiting his wife to return, Hound entertained the small talk his teenage grandson made. He thought to himself how much time had changed in terms of language, vocabulary, lingo, and values.

Henrietta made it back with the money. She politely handed it to Hound then made her way back to the kitchen to finish preparing snacks for them.

"Here you go son," Hound said and passed the two rolls of cash to Von. "I trust you're gonna do the right thing with my money, right? You just be sure not to disappoint me and my expectations of you. Deal?"

"That's a deal, granddaddy. I promise not to let you down," Von replied.

Hound asked of the last time Von had visited his father, prior to hugging the boy and planting a kiss on his forehead.

Von responded by telling him he and his mother visited three months before the day. He then let his grandfather know he'd be back to see them soon. Von left and went home.

Once there, he took a shower, put on his sleeping clothes, turned on his TV to watch a movie, then called his girlfriend, Chloe, from his cell phone. They talked for about an hour. Von then went to sleep. He had his re-up on his mind before doing so.

That nigga Tito said not to come back unless I got ten thousand or better, huh! I'mma go this time with fifteen. He's gonna love that! Von thought to himself.

FIVE

Von went to see his girlfriend once more. The purpose was different this time. The two hadn't laid eyes on each other in a day and a half and were eager to hug and kiss. Although talking over the phone is a strong form of communication (this was a time before camera phones and video-chatting existed heavily), it's nothing like the physical presence of a person there in front of you to touch and experience the intimate level of their energy. Chloe was home looking after her 11-year-old sister and 9-year-old brother. The trio was in the living room of the house.

"Hey, Von!" The two siblings of Chloe spoke seemingly at the same time. They were familiar with him from past visits.

"Hey you two!" he responded, then dug into his pockets and withdrew a small roll of $20s. He gave them one each."Here y'all go. Chloe gonna take you to the store later today so y'all can buy candy, cookies, and other snacks y'all like, okay," he said to them. He then leaned over to give both a hug.

"Thanks Von. You're the man, homie," the brother said.

"Yeah, thank you Von," said the little girl while maintaining a loving smile.

Von and Chloe then hug and kiss. The youngsters looked at them in admiration. They smiled at the show of affection placed on display.

"I need to talk to you," Von whispered into her ear. That was the cue for them to go into the bedroom for privacy.

They entered.

"What's that in your pockets, boo?" Chloe asked.

Von didn't bother to answer verbally. He simply pulled out the huge knots of money.

"You need me to call Tito again, don't you?" Chloe asked at the sight of the money.

"Yeah, baby. I do," Von responded, then peeled off fifteen $100 bills and gave them to her.

"What's this for?"

"For you to get busy trying to find us a place to live. You're gonna put everything in your name; the lease, lights, water, and gas . . . everything sweetie," Von stated.

Chloe accepted the money and put it into the pocket of one of her coats in the room closet. She then grabbed her phone and dialed Tito's number.

"What's up, Chloe? How's it going?" Tito answered.

"I'm good. My boyfriend needs to see you again," she made him aware.

"Oh, he does!"

"Yep. What do I need to tell him?"

"Tell him to come by the shop. I'm here in my office."

"Okay. I'll do that. Talk to you later. Take care."

"You do the same."

The call ended.

"He wants you to come by the shop again," Chloe mentioned.

"A'ight. You going with me, or do I go alone?" he asked.

"Well, you can't go with me. You gotta look after those two," he said while pointing towards the room door indicating her siblings in the living room.

"I'm sure he won't have any problem with you showing up without me now. Not with that type of money you trying to spend with him. How much is that anyway?"

Von cracked a smile behind the question asked. He then proceeded to offer an answer for her. "I've got fifteen Gee's I'm looking to spend with Tito. I'm moving on up. But look,

I'm about to go see him and handle this business, okay?" he let her know and they kissed. "I'mma call you later."

"You gonna call me!" Chloe retorted in a shocked way. "Von! I haven't seen you in almost two days, you know. And, we ain't spend no time together since I don't know when!" she brought to his attention.

"And guess what? It may be a little longer than that before we do," he let out with a smile, teeth showing in the process.

"Von!" Chloe protested.

"What sweetie." He smiled at her body language and reaction. "A'ight, look. Me, you, and your sister and brother, are all gonna spend the day together; tomorrow. So, you be sure to be ready. And have them ready too. Early. We going to *Six Flags Great Adventures* over in Jersey. Okay."

A loving smile now appeared on her face.

"Now that, I can go for. We haven't been there in awhile. I know they're gonna love it. I am too," Chloe responded.

The two kissed and Von exited the room, on his way to the front door.

"And don't let them know what the surprise is either, Chloe," Von said over his shoulder.

She simply smiled as a response.

Von got in the car and then made his way to go see Tito. They now had bigger business with each other.

***

Von reached Tito's shop and entered. The host was already awaiting. He smiled at Von's presence.

"Homie, Von. What's good? I'm glad to see you again," Tito charmed in greeting.

"I know you are. I'm glad to see you too. Homie!" Von replied.

"If you are here again and we're face to face, that can only mean one thing. You brought ten thousand or more with you?"

"No doubt. I wouldn't waste your time or insult you like that if I didn't," Von stated.

"So let's talk."

Von was eager to get down to business.

"Let's talk. How *much* are we talking?" Tito said.

"I've got fifteen stacks to work with."

"Ooh! You came back all the way correct, didn't you? I can respect that."

"I'm spending ten on weed, and the other five on pills," Von declared.

"Gotcha," Tito responded, then picked up his phone and dialed a number. He spoke in Spanish to the person on the opposite end of the line.

Von took a seat upon putting his order in. Tito had a big-screen TV in the office. Music videos played. And the four workers at the shop were able to tune into the upbeat and energizing sounds of their favorite artist through the large speakers Tito had situated all about the place.

"Your material will be here shortly," Tito said to Von upon disconnecting the call.

The two talked as they waited.

Thirty minutes later, the transporter arrived with a large duffle bag loaded with the goodies Von's customers craved.

"Same quality material as before, right?" Von asked.

"True indeed."

Von passed Tito the cash, and Tito in return, passed him the bag.

"I spotted you extra bags of weed and pills too, homie. You owe me five thousand now. I know you can be trusted. My little cousin knows all I need to have her know about you for me to front you work. And here's my number too. Now you can call me direct yourself. Text first though. So I'll know who you are. Have my money on hand with your re-up money when you come back. Good luck! And be easy homie. You on your way to going somewhere in the game. I can see that shit in you already," Tito stated to encourage the young hustler to keep up the good work.

Von accepted the compliment and gesture. He grabbed the bag by the handles, slapped fives with Tito and bumped shoulders altogether, then exited the shop. He wasn't too far from Eunice's house. He wanted to make a pit stop there before heading home. Von called him on the phone to let him know he was on the way towards his location. He pulled off in the Acura TL, en route to his homie's pad to break down the vacuum-sealed bags of weed pounds and bundle up the pills twenty-five to a pack.

While on the way over to his partner's crib, Von tuned in to the radio station *Power_99 FM,* One of his favorite jams pumped through the sound system. It was the song, *Position of Power,* by *50 Cent,* from the album *The Massacre.* Von loved that song. It did something to his spirit, especially so now that he was on his way to the top in the game, and had twenty pounds of high-grade weed and nearly a thousand potent ecstasy pills. He rapped along to the lyrics of 50.

Eunice was already at home awaiting. Von pulled up, retrieved the duffle bag from the backseat, and got out of the car, making steps to the door of the row house.

"What up bro!" Eunice greeted.

"What it do, my nigga! I got that work, homie." Von responded as he and Eunice dapped hands and embraced.

"I see-I see! I'm damn sure ready to get to it."

"We're about to do just that right now."

The two went inside and headed to Eunice's room in the home.

"You went harder with the re-up, didn't you?" Eunice asked.

"Had to. Plus, the connect spotted me extra on everything."

"That's what's up there. I'mma sell only quarters and better now. We can continue to let Shay and Tangee hustle nicks like they been doing," Eunice revealed his intentions.

"And, we can have those two recruit others, maybe three additional females, to help them move their portion of the product. The faster we get rid of everything, the quicker we work our way up, the more material we cop from the connect, the more money we stack. And before long, we're gonna be rich and having our way out here in these streets, bro," Von stated enthusiastically.

"Motherfuckin' right, my nigga! We gonna take over the weed and pill game in the city, Eunice responded.

"Facts!"

Von then gave Eunice five pounds of weed and 250 pills and told him a number to have come re-up time. He then left, making his way to the house of everybody else in the crew. Most of all, Ron, being that the two were closer to each other than anyone else who was in the clique.

Ron lived out in West Philly. His family moved there from North roughly six months before the day. The neighborhood was an area that wasn't too rough nor too easy. Strangely enough, it had a balance to the activities of the underworld, considering the fact that at the time, this location of the city, was notorious for all things criminal. But Ron was a rugged, go-hard, and ultra-tough type of 19-year-old, who had more gangster and fierceness in him than Von may have ever known. He didn't tolerate any form of disrespect, and his quiet easy-going demeanor was known to show flashes of rage and violence at certain times.

Von made it to the home of his closet homie. The two had known each other and had been cool since first grade.

Von got out of the car with the duffle bag clutched tightly in his fist. Ron was already put on point on what the play was, and had the front door open and standing in position so Von could make his way into the house quickly without no one noticing his movement. Ron closed the door behind his homie with Von sitting the bag to the floor and them dapping each other and embracing strongly.

"What's poppin' Von! What it do, my nigga!" the dark-complexioned slim framed friend greeted. Ron was an inch taller than Von.

"I'm cooling, bro. Just made this move on the re-up. I got something else for you too. Some shit Eunice equipped us with to keep safe." Von responded

"Hammers?" Ron asked.

"Word! He got family who's heavy into that particular world." Von then pulled two Glock .40s from the bag and handed them to Ron. He then dipped his hand back inside to retrieve the two red boxes of hollow point bullets.

"These motherfuckas' nice here!" Ron expressed.
"I've got to give these two pretty bitches a name."

Von put up a finger in gesture and slightly raised his head as if a light bulb lit up in his mind with a thought. "How about, '*Mona*' and '*Lisa?*" he suggested.

"*Mona*' and *Lisa?*" Ron retorted. "You mean like the painting '*Mona Lisa?*' But instead of it being one person's full name, make it two?"

"Exactly nigga! You already know I'm weird like that in my own way. And I'm crazy about Leonardo de Vinci. That mothafucka' was a pure unadulterated genius, bro. With everything he's done, especially with his paintings."

"Well, we gonna do some *painting* alright!" Ron quickly responded, then took aim at the poster board he had on the wall in his room with the pistols. "We're gonna paint walls all over the city, with the blood and brains of any niggaz . . . any bitches . . . or even the *police,* if they get in the way and fuck with our come-up! I put my life on that, my nigga! We 'bout to get to it!" Ron let out with passion and intensity while grimacing and clenching his teeth. He was now a monster in the making. An absolute demon in disguise.

If only it could accurately and truly be expressed in words, the type of tremendous power that a person is equipped with upon coming into possession of a gun—let alone two or more—and knowing that they could take life or spare others from death. The type of fear that goes along with the knowledge of how dangerous an average person becomes with a gun—especially a hoodlum or street thug—it's unmatched by any other factors that may exist. That's why the *"hood"* and black-on-black violence, is such a serious matter. Although legendary and sometimes a necessary evil to rid of greater evil, the point is that, guns in the wrong hands is a bad thing no matter how it is looked at. And in this case with Von, Ron, and the crew, it could go either way.

"Motherfuckin' right, nigga!" Von co-signed and gave Ron more dap. "That's what the fuck I'm talking about! Pipe up then, Ron! We out there now! The new generations of JBM! We gonna carry on tradition! For my pop and for your people, you feel me, homie!" Von let out with energy and enthusiasm. He was the motivator. He felt he needed to rally the troops.

"Word!" Ron replied.

Von then went into the bag once more and brought out five pounds one by one, then the pills. Ron received the same amount of work as did Eunice.

"Shit is getting real with the product, huh," Ron responded at the increase in material.

"No doubt, homie. Got a new plug now. A Rican dude. He's my girl's people."

"That's what's up" Ron stated, then changed the subject. "You still in school nigga?"

"Hell yeah. Last year too. This why I'm laying everything on y'all to get rid of. Because I ain't got the time."

"We got you, my nigga. And I've got to get on the ball building up my clientele over here in the West like I had it in North. That way, I won't have to go all the way over to the North to hustle every day.

"Do what you gotta do, bro. Even if you got to put those two crazy hustling cousins of yours down with you—Khaddafi and Khalil. Do what you gotta do."

"That's exactly who I had in mind. Those two niggaz right there."

The two friends continued to make small talk and make strategic plans over how the organization of the future would be constructed at that particular point, then were to operate once a certain level was reached in the game. The ideal goal was 100 pounds of weed, and 10,000 pills. The possibility existed to reach that in short order, and then more.

SIX

Three months later . . .

School resumed and Von was set to complete his senior year then move on about life how he saw fit, fulfilling the promise to his father and grandfather at the same time.

He and Chloe now had their own place to live. It was a rowhouse in Northeast Philly. There was a garage to it. The location was on Cottage Street and Frankfurt, Ave. Von no longer had a space at his mother's house. She'd replaced him with the boyfriend she had in her life, a dude by the name Bernard. He'd been with Lilly for two years, and they'd now decided to move in together.

Bernard was a North Philly native. He knew the hood fairly well and many people who dwell there. He and his male family members worked in construction and carpentry. They had a daily functioning business. Bernard and Von were familiar with each other. Although Von didn't like him personally, he respected him on the strength that his mother was in love with the guy. Lilly was crazy about Bernard. She took care of him in a way like no other. She barely wanted the man to leave the house and go off to work. Von and Bernard did get along, but barely. That lack of bonding had its roots in the relations Bernard and Lilly had. Dude had a habit of beating Lilly on occasion—something she was okay with for the most part, because she caused it. But Bernard never hit her in the face. Only about the body. Von resented him from the first time he'd witnessed Bernard chastise his mother. Those two guys never got along from that day.

Bernard encouraged Lilly to make Von get his own house away from her place before he was to move in. She did what the man told her to do. Lilly even took it a step farther and sold Von her Acura TL for little to nothing, only $5,000 in five installments of $1,000 each. Lilly placed a demand on Von to *"Man up"* as he was no longer a little boy. Although his mother restricted his access to her house, he still had full access to his grandmother's home, the place where he sometimes kept his weed and pill supply, along with money,

Von's school days were short. Only three times per week now, and classes lasted until 12 p.m., sometimes. All the seniors who maintained a high-grade level earned the incentive and leeway to enjoy half days throughout the weeks. Von was amongst them.

***

On the street side of things, the crew had made it to the 100-pound and 10,000-pill milestone. They were at 150 pounds to be exact, and had 15,000 pills of all kinds. In addition, they had three locations in the city where they got rid of the product. Shayla and Tangee had a house together now. Shayla' sister—Cori—was able to move into a bigger space, directly on 17th Street and Jefferson, and they all utilized her house to sell their product. This was a prime location.

Von was the link between Eunice and Ron. The three of them now hung tightly and had a trap spot located at 7th and Montgomery. They were booming too. Really getting money and pushing the weight.

Kareem and Lonnie were brought together by the grace of Von. Those two had very similar personalities and habits. They had a trap spot in South Philly. Everything flowed smoothly.

Mind you that this was a group of teenagers with the oldest (Eunice) being only 19-years of age, a few months ahead of another. Von was the youngest at 16 nearing 17 in two months. They still conducted and carried themselves in a way, like teenagers. They loved to hang out, do reckless things, and had that *"Fuck the world"* type of mentality; the same as all typical youngsters possessed. Of all seven, Von was the only one to stand out. He was the exception to not drop out of high school, and wAS on the verge to graduate. The others had long become street poisoned and gave up hope in the pursuit of education. Not so with Von. He was determined to make his parents and grandparents proud. All that they'd wanted from him was for the boy to graduate and at least go on to complete some level of college. Von's hope was to please them. And then, things became complicated. A *very strange* turn of events was about to happen for them all in individual ways, leaving nothing to remain the same. Problems would ensue from all ends and confrontation would begin to pop up from multiple angles. With money and narcotics, comes envy and hate. Von and the crew had the product and paper to cause others to act in this type of way.

The area of the game where Von and them now had reached, was the particular level he tried to do all possible to keep safe from and avoid, and the potential conflict that was to go along with it. However, Eunice and Ron were ready to embrace any and all opportunities and deal with the challenges attached to them. May God save the king! Because the street king that possibly there were, began to come of form in such instance. The hood and the City of Philly couldn't go without one.

SEVEN

Shayla now had a boyfriend in her life. He was a dude by the name, Stephon Richardson, aka "Feezy." He was an average dope boy, pushing coke for a living, and mostly got high and fucked off with the money he made. Shayla was getting more cash than him, and he took offense to that in his own way. The one good thing Feezy had going for himself, was that Shayla really liked the guy, and wanted to make a life with him. However, Feezy didn't believe in that type of love, and was a grimy nigga to the core; set on getting it how he lived, with no remorse.

"Shay, look. I feel some type of way about you getting money with that nigga Von and them, and want us to hustle together," Feezy said to his girl.

"Feezy. I'm sorry to tell you, that's not gonna happen. Unless you get your weight and your dollars up. I have been getting money with them long before you. And not only that, I know Von and Eunice. Them niggaz been putting money in my purse. And I'm able to smoke and pop pills like I want. As long as I have the money for them. They supporting Me and Tangee," Shayla responded. Her words seemed to irritate him.

Before the day, Shayla had talked a little too much about the business she had with Von and Eunice. Feezy knew the operation on how they did things. He'd been at Shayla's sister Cori's house and seen the heavy traffic flowing in and out and knew how much product they were provided each time. At all costs, he wanted to place a demand on Shayla, for them to get on the same page together, even if he had to force her to do what he wanted her to do.

"So you choose them over me? That's what you're telling me?" Feezy asked.

"NO! I'm choosing to make my money and put myself in a position to live my best life while I'm *with* you, if I'm able to. And I'm not in the mood to go back and forth with you too much longer, Feezy. Why do you have to give me so much hassle about things?" Shayla asked her boyfriend.

"I'm not giving you any hassle about this. I just need you to show me you're all the way down with me. The same way you down with them niggaz. That's my only issue," Feezy clarified.

"Feezy! I'm here with you. I cook for you. I clean up behind you. I suck your dick when you want me to. We fuck all the time; which that's about the *only* thing we do that you don't complain about. And, I spend *my money* on you when it's supposed to be the other way around. But you're the one with an issue about who I get money with. Man, go on with that bullshit, bro!" Shayla said, then got up off the bed and made her way to the bathroom to relieve herself.

Tangee entered the house at that point. She'd been over at Cori's house all throughout the day and brought home money to put away. She was looking to go back for a little while. Tangee was taking a break. The time was just after 8 p.m.

Tangee made her way to Shayla's room. They keep their money in the same location, in the closet inside a shoe box. There was also a large plastic bin in the closet where they had the pounds of weed they'd been supplied. She didn't know Feezy was there in the room. He took her by surprise once she'd stepped inside without knocking.

"Oh! Hey Feezy!" Tangee let out upon sighting him. "How you doing?" She was now at the door of the closet and pulling money from her pocket and purse with a few bills falling to the carpet.

"I'm good. You?" Feezy responded to the roommate and friend of his girl.

"Been good too. Just busy grinding out here in the world, doing hair and nails, and trying to be somebody, you know," Tangee said while picking up the cash she'd dropped.

Feezy's attention was locked in on what was holding it in that instance; the large roll of bills being stashed in a pot where anyone had easy access.

"I see. You and Shay been at it a minute now, huh. Hopefully, we all can do the same together at some point soon," he suggested in his own way. "Get money as a team. Except with a different product."

"Hmm! I don't know what to say about that one. Shay will let me know what our next move is," Tangee related, and began to walk to the room door now.

Feezy lastly spoke on the topic. "That's what's up. Only a thought for now. We've been talking over it."

Tangee simply exited and doesn't offer a reply.

Shayla finished up using the toilet and was washing her hands at the time. Tangee heard her in the bathroom.

"Shay! It's me, Tangee," she said, making her presence known.

"You home now for the night? Or you plan on going back out again?" Shay asked.

"Yeah, I am. I'm in for the night."

The time was 9:40 p.m., still somewhat a young night for a Wednesday, but not too tender for a female hustler to call it an early one from the trap house. Tangee did just that. She had no intentions to leave the house anymore.

Shayla came out of the bathroom and went to the kitchen where Tangee was located.

"Hey girl," Shayla greeted Tangee with open hands upon laying eyes on her. The two hugged.

"Hey Shay," Tangee responded with a smile.

Shay was relieved in the fact that her friend made it home yet another day all safe and sound. And Tangee felt blessed to be situated there herself. Although the two were now strapped with a gun to protect themselves with, there was still a sense of worry and anxiety they possessed over each other. They were elevating in a world where nothing but ruthlessness and viciousness heavily prevailed, and problems could arise along with tragedy striking at a moment's notice. This was known and maintained in mind.

"Everything good with you? Smooth day?" Shay asked.

"Yeah, everything good. Typical Wednesday. But hey, I wanna ask you something," Tangee responded.

Shay furrowed her eyebrows and slightly jarred her head.

Tangee pointed over her shoulder with her thumb in the direction of the bedroom where Feezy was located. "You mention anything to Feezy, about us three supposedly coming together to get money?"

"No!" Shay spat emphatically. "His ass said something to me about him feeling some type of way about me working with Von and Eunice and not him. Did he say something to you about that?"

"Not necessarily about *that*. He just hinted at it when I went into your room to put up the money I made, and the remainder of the weed and pills I had. It was more so a wishful thought than anything, I thought," Tangee clarified.

She saw that Shayla didn't like the fact of her boyfriend speaking to the friend in that way.

"Oh, Okay. But we're gonna continue rocking with who we rocking with. So long as they keep us supplied. Besides, we've known Eunice and Von for a while now, and they ain't shown us nothing but love, right?"

"Right."

"And, until that changes, or until Feezy gets his weight and dollars up, those two is who we staying with. Okay?" Shayla said to Tangee.

"Okay."

The subject changed briefly. Shayla then returned to the bedroom to entertain her boyfriend, leaving Tangee fixing herself something to eat.

Shayla didn't mention anything to Feezy so to avoid an argument. She merely kept it to herself.

Feezy didn't bother to go back down the same line of conversation. He simply committed it to memory all he'd seen and maintained a disguising smile to hide his true thoughts. Another day would come to manifest exactly how he felt and perceived things.

***

Von had a cousin he'd begun to hang out with. His name was Shamar Savage, aka "Monk" aka "Solo." Monk's grandfather and Von's grandfather were first cousins. Von's father and Monk's father were JBM and used to get money and hang tightly together.

Monk was heavy in the dope game under his brother. He sold heroin and had plenty of money. The Savages were always known to have a tight bond between family, especially the males. And Monk always had the desire to fix it to where he and Von would come together and do some things; the same as their fathers had. But Von was too young for Monk to do so with in the times of the past. But not now. Monk was 22-years of age, tall, dark-complexioned, fit and athletic, and loved to spend time chasing females, along with shopping for expensive clothes, shoes, and sneakers. He also loved to visit clubs, party hard, and tour the city in one of his many vehicles, in particular, the S-Class 500 Series Mercedes Benz. Von was now of mature age for Monk to take him in and hang out with him.

It was a Friday afternoon. Von had free time on his hands. He was home alone. Chloe and her cousin Rosa, went shopping at the Gallery Mall, in Center City Philly. He took a shower, got dressed, then checked his messages on his phone. Monk had texted.

MONK: Vonnie, what's good fam! It's me, Monk. I got a play for you. Hit me back when you get the chance to. One!

VON: What's good fam! Long time. Glad you still had my number. You got a play for me, huh? That's what's up. Call me. One!

Monk responded with a phone call. He and Von had a brief discussion. Von provided him with the address to his house. Monk made the trip to pick him up. The two began to ride around town to talk and catch up on the business of the day.

"I ain't seen you in a minute, Monk," Von expressed upon getting into the car. "The world has been treating you well, from the look of things," Von then complimented.

Monk had on a *Gucci* sweatsuit, two thick and heavy Cuban link chains, an expensive Swiss Army watch, a pair of matching Gucci shoes, and a hat. And looked like a celebrity. He was a music mogul in the making. The boy had his shit together for real, for real, Courtesy of the big brother he represented and worked for. *He* was the man.

"I ain't seen you in a minute either, little cuz. You done grown up too. We can now hang out. You ain't a young *boul* anymore," Monk let out with a smile while looking over at Von occasionally as he talked, then putting his eyes back on the street he drove down.

"Nah. I ain't young like that no more, fam. I'm on my way now. And I'm up."

"I see! Kidada been keeping me informed about you. Your sister knows some things too, Von. And she's hungry. She busts a move for me every now and then. When she needs to make a few dollars," Monk made him aware.

"Yeah . . . sis . . . sis is out there like that. She solid too. Ain't no doubting that. She's all about the money. And no wonder she seems to be on top now. You got her on the team! I tried to get her to fuck with me and what I got going on with the weed and the pills."

"—And what she tell you?" Monk quickly chimed in to say.

"She says it ain't enough money in that shit for her. It's too slow as well."

Monk laughed at Von, quoting the sister, "It ain't enough money for her! It's too slow as well!" he repeated.

"You done spoiled her, cuz. She only comes to me to buy weed to smoke anytime she didn't make it her business to up and take a trip out to Cali for a weekend vacation.

"If I've told you once, Vonnie, you've heard it a thousand times, fam. Ain't no money," Monk took a toke of the weed he was smoking, holding in the smoke for as long he could, then continuing with a famous phase he'd heard before, "Like *dope* money! All the paper from other shit don't even matter," he let out in exhale of the weed smoke. Monk then reiterated, "Ain't no money, like *dope* money. Never forget that, fam. And when you ready to get down, *I'm* ready to build you up! One brick at a time, you know," Monk emphasized with a serious tone of voice.

"Word!"

"Word!"Monk confirmed.

They then made their way to one of the commercial buildings Monk owned. It was a game room that had a recording studio atop it. The location was in North Philly, just off Giraud Ave, near where the Richard Allen Housing Projects used to be.

"What's this fam?" Von asked once the car came to a stop behind the space.

"My game room and studio. Reality Music Group is gonna be a big name in the industry one day. R-M-G, be the best!" Monk proclaimed.

"Oh shit! You making power moves for real with the paper."

"No doubt, I am!" the ambitious street boss uttered with confidence.

Monk then retrieved his pistol from the armrest console. It was a .45, black in color. He had a .44 Bulldog in a holster strapped to his ankle as well. Von had his gun on him too. They exited the car and made their way up the flight of stairs inside a door entrance alongside the building. The entrance to the studio had a thick steel door to it with a trio of sophisticated deadbolt locks. Monk opened and they stepped inside.

The studio was actually a wall-decorated one-bedroom apartment. There was upscale black leather seating (a couch, a love seat, a recliner, and a large square footrest). The TV was every bit of 80 inches. It was mounted to the wall. Monk had large oil painted portraits of influential black recording artists. There was Nina Simone, Miles Davis, 2 Pac, Thelonius Monk, Meek Mills, and the Notorious Big, Monk's five favorites.

"This is my favorite lounge spot, fam," Monk said. I'm here more than home, actually. My recording equipment over there," Monk pointed to the dining space area. A small booth cubicle was situated in the corner area.

"Nice man space, cuz," Von complimented.

"Have a seat," Monk said to him, then picked up the remote to the surround sound stereo system. It was connected to the TV. He put on music videos. Monk then disappeared to the backroom.

Von observed the dwelling with admiration as he tuned into the video playing. Monk returned to the living room with a money-counting machine and a black pillowcase stuff with something in it, more than likely, loaded with stacks of money. He took a seat next to Von and sat the machine on the glass table in front of them. He then dumped the contents onto the thick Persian rug beneath their feet. There were swollen folds of small bills of money that already had rubber bands on them. No $1 bills though.

"I need you to help me out for a moment, fam. You're cool with that, right? You don't have nowhere to go, do you? We're gonna hang out all day, cuzzo," Monk stated.

"Nah-Nah, I don't have nowhere to go at the moment. I'm cool with helping you. Not a problem. And also, I thought you said something about you having a play for me?" Von asked.

"Oh yeah. I do. A homie of mine asked did I know somebody he could buy a few pounds of weed from."

"Yeah, I can serve him. A few pounds like what?"

"Actually, the nigga is the brother of a female I've been fucking with for a minute now. Me and Shorty really feeling each other. She's one of the many that I can honestly say I like. But, her brother, a dude by the name Dreek, is the one trying to grab like fifty *elbows*. Can you cover that?"

Von thought over all plausible ways he could compile fifty pounds of bud, serve Dreek at a reasonable price, and still make a profit. He would be able to do so, but only under one condition: in the way he would want to go about doing this.

"Can you get his money upfront first, then let me do what I need to with it, and have the product later that day or the next day?" Von asked his cousin.

"Yeah, I can do that. He came to me, so I set the rules. You must don't have it all in one place right now?"

"—Nah, I don't," Von quickly replied. "I gotta go to my connect with both our money and bust a move like that."

"Smart thinking. His money with your money gives you more buying power."

"Exactly-Exactly!"

"But look. Let's count this paper up here, then handle the business," Monk said.

The two got busy running the money through the counter and re-wrapping it with rubber bands. The total was $190,000.

"This the money from one of the dope houses I got, fam. Two weeks worth of sales," Monk stated in boast. "It always pays when your people are the supplier. I go through my brother for everything. My mom and dad's oldest of us all. Damien."

"Talkin' 'bout, Drip?" Von asked.

"That be him. The one and only, '*Drip Savage.*' Pops had four sons and two daughters by two different women."

"I'm kinda familiar with your dad's history. It's very similar to my pops. But look, hit your man up who want the weed, and let him know we able to cover the order," Von stated.

"No doubt," Monk responded, then pulled his phone from his hip clip and made the contact.

Monk and Dreek discussed the business at hand and verbally agreed on a deal. Monk let him know that he'd be by in an hour or so, and to be ready with the money. He wanted Dreek to meet him at an apartment in Northeast. It was the residence Monk and his girlfriend stayed—Dreek's sister Ayonna—an additional location he laid low the majority of nights.

"You fam, my girl Ayonna, got a home girl she hang with damn near every day. She ain't got no man in her life either. A nineteen-year-old sweetheart. Shorty *bad* too!"

"Shit fam, I'm down to get to know somebody new. Tell *your* girl, I wanna meet *her* girl, and hopefully, I can make her my *girl,*" Von put together in wordplay.

"I know that's right, fam!" Monk cosigned and dapped up Von.

Monk then took the money machine back to the bedroom and returned with a designer-labeled backpack. One by Gucci. It too, was stuffed with bundles of cash inside.

"Let's roll, fam," Monk declared and the two departed the apartment.

Once inside the car again, Monk opened up in a conversation over a series of subjects at this particular point.

"Say fam, check this out, right? Who you know we could tap, to snuff somebody out for me?"

Von jarred his head at the question. The severity of it took him by surprise. He swallowed the air stored in his throat. At no point in his life, had Von ever been asked a question of that magnitude. Although he had no knowledge of who would be willing to go from weed and a pill dealer to a hitman overnight, two names got tossed around in his head. There was Ron and there was Eunice, the oldest two of the crew. The only thing to consider now was, exactly how much would it be worth? For the right price, a non-killer would convert to a hitter in an instant.

"I got a homie in mind who would love to make his bones in that world. The nigga is always getting extra aggressive behind the thought of being that type of dude. I do know he's about that issue though," Von responded.

"So that's a yes?"

"No doubt. But I know my nigga. Once I bring it to his attention, he's gonna want to know what the current ticket for a body. Or at least, what's being paid to drop *this* body that you want put down?" Von said convincingly.

"This nigga I want popped, he ain't no ordinary clown. He's one hell of a dude. I've got ten thousand to make him disappear."

"I'll run it by him and see what he wanna do."

"Do that, and we can go from there with the details. I'll let you be the one to facilitate everything from that point. A'ight," Monk said.

"That's a bet, fam,"

They rode and talked more about a little of everything. The conversation was interesting.

EIGHT

Monk and Von made it to the apartment he shared with Ayonna. Luckily for Von, Ayonna's friend Monyetta Laruens, was there as well. Von had the opportunity to introduce himself to her personally. There was no need for a middle person.

The two girls Ayonna and Monyetta, were seated in the living room talking and watching TV. They were making plans for a weekend of shopping,

"What's up baby!" Monk said and walked over to give his girl a kiss.

"Who is this, Monk?"Ayonna asked in surprise at her boyfriend bringing someone by the house who wasn't her brother.

"Oh, this here one of my cousins. He's another Savage. His grand pop and my grand pop first cousins. Both our dads used to hang tight."

"Oh okay. I knew he had to be somebody close to you," Ayonna responded.

"And Monyetta, just so you'll know, I mentioned you to my cousin too. His name is Von. Make yourself acquainted while me and Ayonna talk in our room for a minute," Monk stated. "Come on 'Yonna."

She got up and followed the boyfriend to the bedroom.

Von thereafter took a seat on the plush leather couch, separated from Monyetta by the cushion in the middle.

"Monyetta, huh?"

"Yeah. That's me. Von, right?" she responded.

"Trevon, actually. But Von will work. You look nice. I like what I see. Hopefully, looks don't deceive me. It won't will it?"

He humorized and made her smile.

"You don't look too bad yourself . . . Von . . . *Vonnie,"* Monyetta responded with the seemingly perfect comeback.

"My mom and my grandma refer to me by that name in their own affectionate way . . . 'Vonnie.' And the way you said it, had a certain sensation to it. I *like* the way you said it. You may have started something, you know . . . *Monyetta.* With your pretty ass," Von mesmerized her with his articulation.

Monyetta looked on at him with a smile on her face and sparkles in her eyes. She then offered something in reply to match his energy. "I may have started something, huh? Interesting choice of words Well put. But I'm sure you probably got a girlfriend and all, don't you?" she asked.

Von already had a ready made response for her. An honest one to tell the truth. "I'll be lying to you if I said I don't. I do. But I strongly believe that I'm worthy enough to have more than one. I've got too much promise and potential to not think highly of myself in this way," Von wooed further with his words.

Monyetta continued to glow and smile in admiration at the strength of Von's confidence. Her silky smooth chocolate complexioned skin radiated about the face. Perfectly structured white teeth beaming behind the opening of her wide lusciously glossed lips, and chinky eyes. She batted those thick jet black lashes of hers.

Through the brief exchange of words, Monyetta was convinced. She'd heard enough to feel comfortable to at least provide Von with her phone number. If this doesn't go so well, she could always change her number once she tells him to fuck off. If it gets to that point.

"Here, take my number. I wouldn't mind hearing you talk more often. Plus, you're easy on the eyes to look at. Such a handsome appeal about yourself," Monyetta said while poking her digits into his phone. He had an *Apple iPhone,* the very first of many to come." Nice phone too. I've got to upgrade at some point soon."

"Shit, you already have. Choosing me and opening the door to opportunity is an upgrade to it all. If you want a phone like this, I will buy you one. Just be patient and let love and prosperity dictate, " Von said in a tone of sensuousness.

Monyetta couldn't think up anything to say so to top those of his. She wanted what he'd said to be the last of it. At least as it related to the two of them hooking up.

Monk and Ayonna exited the bedroom. They took a seat in the living room again with their guest and joined in on the conversation between Von and Monyetta.

Ayonna's brother, Dreek, had already been contacted, and was now on the way with his money. Von would have additional funds to buy more weed from Tito, in line with what he'd be fronted. The more he spent, the more he'd get on consignment. With Von now having Dreek's money to go along with his from that point, once he arrived and initiates the business, this would create a stronger clientele base to Von's network. And, he felt it wouldn't take too long to reach a higher level in the game, to where he would only have to sell pounds, nothing less. He was on his way up with no worries of falling down. The mysteries of the underworld were unlocking for Von in a strange way. His cousin Monk, was the front runner in exposing him to it all.

"Ain't no money like dope money!" Those words stuck with Von, in the event he was to cross over in product to sell. That phrase was the seed planted in his mind to establish the contemplation of the move. Monk was very convincing. Very very convincing.

***

Two Weeks Later . . .

Boom!
The hired hitter let off a thunderous round from his .45 heavy metal pistol.
Boom-Boom-Boom!
He let off three more rounds while walking up towards the intended target. The girlfriend of the guy whom was being shot, screamed at the top of her lungs over the sound of gun fire. She was on the passenger side of the *Jaguar* when the boyfriend had just opened the door to take a seat again himself, prior to his name being called out to capture his attention, causing him to turn and face in the direction where he was made more vulnerable. The first slug struck him in the abdomen, knocking him down between the door panel of the vehicle.

Rashawn Johnson aka *"Playboy,"* was standing in the doorway of his car when the gunman pulled up. The shooter came to a stop in his vehicle, got out, and walked up to Playboy to deliver the be-all end-all barrage of bullets. He took aim at Playboy and pulled the trigger.

Boom! Boom-Boom!
The assassin shot Playboy in the forehead with the second round, then in the chest with two more. He then trained his gun on the head of the hysterical and shouting girlfriend.

Boom!
Although she wasn't included in the contract, she had to bear the brunt of a bullet as well, behind the lifestyle the boyfriend lived. Simply put, she was in the wrong place (with him) at the wrong time. The killer shot her in the head and she slumped over onto the dashboard. The gunman then hopped back into his car, and sped off into the night, back down Roosevelt Boulevard, en route to Philadelphia City.

***

Rashawn Johnson, aka "Playboy Johnson," was a high-level heroin dealer in Philly. He had several minute territories in North Philly and one in West Philly. Playboy was hated by many and loved by few, with those who held the most distaste, wanting him out the way more than anything. The same way that Playboy managed to gain the areas he controlled, was the exact same way his world was snatched from under his feet, by his life being taken.

Although young (only 28-years of age at the time he was assassinated) Playboy was a cruel ill-hearted Kingpin, who inherited the remnants of territory from a greater ill-hearted and cruel kingpin. He was passed on wisdom of the streets, and Playboy's father was a Philly hood legend. He'd died and left him in charge. All Playboy had to do was hold on to the throne, manage well, and allow everyone on the team the opportunity to eat. He failed in that regard and made himself vulnerable to outside powers that be.

Drip, the brother of Monk, gained the drop on Playboy on a chance-happening occasion. Like Playboy, Drip loved to party and have a bite to eat at the IHOP (International House of Pancakes) on the Boulevard, his favorite restaurant. Drip that is.

One night after a party in the Northeast section of the city at a diverse sports bar, Drip and a girlfriend of his, went to the IHOP mentioned. The girlfriend was tired and sleepy, and didn't bother to get out. Drip went inside himself. He'd already called and placed his order. Upon entering, he took notice of Playboy seated in the far back corner. Drip had on a hat to match his outfit for the night, and this also offered a way for him to disguise his face. Playboy had knowledge of whom Drip was and had heard his name more than a time or two, but was at a disadvantage, by not being able to put a face to the name, therefore unable to identify a potential threat, if ever was to come his way. Drip knew this and used stealth movement at all times while moving up the food chain of the underworld. Playboy was the top dawg out the hood in the dope game. A boss-nigga for real. He was the man who had the most lucrative trap houses in North Philly, and on and around the vicinity of Erie Avenue.

The only time Playboy had a bodyguard by his side was when he was in the city area, mostly while moving about through the hood. Not when out with his girlfriend.

"Who's that guy sitting back there?" Drip asked, already knowing the answer to the question. "He's dressed really nice."

The young black female cashier offered an insightful response. "I don't know his name. He's here every weekend though. Sometimes by himself. Every Saturday night. Sometimes he talks on the phone while he eats. Sometimes people meet him here. He tips well though. We are all happy to see him each time he visits," she related.

"Every Saturday night, you say?" Drip fished for confirmation.

"–*Every* Saturday night, from eleven to one. Sometimes until two," she said with a smile.

Playboy utilized the 24-hour eatery as an office of some sort, or a place of peace to get between his thoughts and away from it all.

"He has to be a celebrity, a sports athlete, or a rapper maybe? Seems like an interesting dude," Drip said, to make a lie of the inquiry and not raise suspicions.

He paid for his food and left, taking notice of Playboy's Jaguar in the parking lot. Drip knew without doubt that that was the favorite car Playboy loved to drive. It was there in his visual. It had a Small Playboy Bunny Sticker with reflective metallic colors in the lower left corner of the back window. The tag plate read **PLAYBOY** as well.

Drip was equipped from that moment moving forward with information on Playboy to use at will. He went to work in scheming up a plot that was to bear fruit nearly four weeks later. Drip contacted Monk for him to do the rest. Monk went to Von, and Von gave the contract to Eunice.

The next day after Playboy was murdered, his territory was taken over, and all the workers were issued an ultimatum . . . *Get Down or Lay Down!* The dynamic mantra of the **JMB** still had power and dictation in 2008.

NINE

Von was now hanging out with his cousin Monk more often than he had before. The game room Monk owned was a spot Von began to take a liking to. The atmosphere was exciting. The balance of the crowd made for an energetic experience. The many females who parlayed there, kept the boy around, and no problems or animosity occurred to the point where a resolution of bloodshed took place. Only a fight or two. Nothing more. The game room was basically a haunt for teenagers in the area to congregate and have fun. On making it a pastime, he seemed to never be home with Chloe anymore or spend time with her. She hated that, and wanted to communicate how she felt to him.

"Von, I wanna ask you something," she let out. Chloe was ready to express how he made her feel by them no longer sharing time together like before.

"What's up, Chloe? What's on your mind? What you wanna ask me?" Von responded.

"What's the reason why you seem to not want to spend time with me like we used to? What got your attention nowadays the way it does?" Chloe asked bluntly.

She was seated on the bed looking at him as he got dressed for the day. It was a Saturday.

"Chloe, that doesn't even sound like a legit question you asked. What do you mean, '*what's the reason why I seem to not want to spend time with you like I used to?*'" Von retorted, clearly annoyed by Chloe's line of questions. "You already know what I got going on. If I'm with you all the time, I can't be out there making money," he pointed towards the outside world at large beyond their house, "and doing what I need to do, to take care of us. And we do spend time together. I come home every night, don't I?"

"Yeah, you do. But then, just like that, you're gone hours later."

"That's because I've got business to attend to, sweetheart. And the game I'm in, along with me getting to the money, is what has my attention. I love money, Chloe. I'm always busy trying to make enough to create a better living for the both of us. What's hard to understand about that?"

"It's not hard to understand. I just get so lonely at times. I'm always here alone when I'm not with Rosa, or over at my mom's place spending time with my sister and brother," she said to him.

"Well, continue to spend more time with them whenever I'm out and about. And when my time permits, we can get back to spending time together, a'ight?"

"Since you want it like that, me and Rosa trying to get our hair done and go shopping today. I need some extra money," Chloe asked him.

"Just get what you need out the safe. And be sure to buy me something while you're at it," he lastly said, gave Chloe a kiss, grabbed his phone and the car keys, then headed out the door.

Von had a date with Monyetta that day. He hadn't seen her since the day at Monk's apartment three weeks prior, and he wanted the two of them to spend quality time together. They'd only held a couple of phone conversations between and were eager to see each other yet again. The moment was upon them.

***

Von's mother Lilly, and her boyfriend Bernard, hit a rough spot in their relationship. He'd begun to put his hands on her quite often now. They'd fight over just about anything.

On this particular occasion, they had it out because he felt some type of way about her going out to events and socializing with her two female friends at late hours of the night. Lilly had someone else in her life and was looking to get rid of Bernard at some point soon, if he were to ever find out about the other guy, or if the beatings continued. The only thing Bernard had going good with Lilly was, the way he made her feel when they fucked. His sex game was precise and on point. He knew exactly how to put the dick on Lilly in the way she wanted and liked it And she felt the ass whippings he gave her, weren't worth sacrificing the dick he was in possession of. However, Bernard began to take things a step too far. Way too far.

Whop!

Bernard slapped the shit out of Lilly. She fell backwards onto the floor of the living room of the house they lived. Her own damn house. She looked up at him in shock. Lilly held the side of her face and her mouth were agape.

"Where the fuck you been!" Bernard barked at her. He'd had too much to drink and hadn't long gotten in himself.

"Bernard! Why the hell you hit me!" Lilly let out in response. "And you drunk like always! I'm tired of this! I'm so sick of you!"

"I said, where the fuck have you been!"

"I been out with my friends, Bernard! And this my damn house! I ain't got no certain time to be home in my own place!" Lilly said in defiance.

Bernard staggered closer to Lilly. He positioned himself to administer more chastisement upon her. She scooted backwards on the floor, still holding her face with her left hand and extending her right to try and block him. Dude was a jealous wreck over her and completely incapable of controlling his emotions when she pushed against them at any time.

"This my damn house too! I been paying bills and shit, ain't I! And I don't give a damn about you being out with your damn friends! Not one of them sleazy bitches got a man in their lives and doesn't have any type of structure! Them hoes nothing but renegades!" Bernard barked, then returned to a grimacing demeanor as he had been.

"Bernard, my friends ain't no damn sleazy bitches! That's just like calling me one!" Lilly retorted with an angry tone.

She then hopped to her feet to stand up to her abusive boyfriend. Bernard grabbed her by the shirt and smacked her yet again.

Whop!

"Who you think you're talking shit to!"

Whop!

Lilly buckled at the knees behind the impact of the blows. He held her up and cut loose more.

Whop! Whop!

She attempted to fight back but to no avail. Bernard was too much for her physically. Her only defense was to go down to the floor once more and curl in the fetal position to protect herself. She knew eventually he'd stop, then either go to the bedroom to cool off, or leave for a time being and return with an apology. Lilly pleaded for mercy.

"Alright Bernard, all right!" she cried out. "I won't stay out so late anymore."

She felt the need to say whatever was necessary to make him stop. He did so.

"We shouldn't have to go through this, Lilly. I don't come into this mothafucka' at no two in the morning! So why you gotta do it to me?" Bernard worded.

"I said I won't stay out late like this anymore," she repeated herself.

He managed to come to his senses at that point, then turned and went to the bedroom. He had a bottle of liquor that needed to be finished off. It was *Crown Royal.*

Lilly got up from the floor and went to the bathroom. She locked the door behind herself. Once done relieving, she took a look in the mirror to survey the damage. The left side of her face was slightly swollen. She had a busted lip as well. *Nothing serious,* she thought. *We've been through this before. I pissed him off, and shouldn't have done that.*

Lilly actually took Bernard's feelings and emotions into consideration, even though he'd put his hands on her and had no right to do so. She knew exactly what type of man she had in her life, and what not to do to make him tick. It doesn't hurt to mention the fact that she antagonized the situation by coming in so late at night, and not thinking to call her jealous boyfriend to make him aware of what was going on. That would've been the better course of action to have taken. But she didn't. Lilly was too preoccupied with what she and Jamar were into. Her guilty conscience had the best of her in the aftermath of Bernard getting on her ass.

No doubt, Lilly could have called the cops and had Bernard arrested, along with a restraining order set in place. But the thought of that never crossed her mind. Von's father—Little Hound—use to beat her throughout their relationship, but they would always get pass the ordeals and move on about life. Little Hound had long taught and trained Lilly that, no matter what happened in their relationship or what they may go through, or how many times they may fight, or after any situation, she should never call the police and put them in their business. Under NO circumstances should she. Little Hound was a high profile high-level drug kingpin and member of a declared Security Threat Group (STG) identified by the FEDS and local authorities. He and Lilly had too much going on in the underworld and would have run the risk of them both being investigated and eventually arrested. With the fact of this, it prevented her from calling the cops on Bernard.

Lilly cleansed herself up, exited the bathroom, and made her way to the den area to get some rest. She would sleep on the couch for the remainder of the night.

I've got to figure out how I'm gonna get rid of this motherfucker! she thought to herself. Then the thought of his love-making abilities came to mind. *But I love him. And he fucks me so well. I don't want to let that part go. Now do I!* she further pondered.

TEN

Von contacted Tito. He was ready to re-up on supply. This would be the largest purchase on weed and pills he'd ever made. He had his own money and money from his cousin Monk girlfriend's brother, Dreek. Von was set to buy 250 lbs of weed and six thousand pills.

His homie, Eunice, put up the 10K from the Playboy murder pay off. Also, the money from the other homies—Ron, Kareem, Lonnie, and the girls—had all increased. Tito would match all he was to buy in fronting him. This would mean Von would get 500 lbs and twelve thousand pills. The order was made and the deal set. All Von had to do now was meet up with Tito and exchange money for the product. Tito wanted to meet that Saturday night at just past dark thirty at the shop.

Prior to going by Eunice's home to pick him up for the occasion, Von rounded up money from everyone else, with the house Shay and Tangee shared being the last stop, since they lived not far from Eunice.

While on the way to meet Tito, he called to let him know. Tito already had the order there at the stop for a quick exchange.

They arrived at the location. Tito had two of his men there with him. They stood to the side while their leader handled business. He was unaware that Von would have someone to tag along with him. He voiced his mind.

"Say homie, you never mentioned anything to me about someone else being with you!" Tito said, jarring his head, furrowing his eyebrows, and cocking his head to the side at the sight of Eunice exiting the vehicle with Von.

"My bad about that, dawg. But we here now. And that's all that matters," Von let out as he and Eunice began to approach to shake hands.

Tito's men quickly came to his side. Tension filled the garage area where they stood. Something had to be done to lessen it.

"We're here now, and that's all that matters!" Tito retorted. "Homie! I don't need no one other than you, knowing what we got going on," he further stressed.

"Tito! Calm down, homie. Relax. This my homie here, dawg. And my business partner. His money is in this bag with mine too," Von said, then opened the back pack to reveal the rolled-up bundles of cash stuffed inside. "And not only that, my homie is my security as well. A man moving up in the world like I am, definitely needs somebody to tote a pistol for them. You got 'em!" Von stressed the issue by pointing at Tito's two guys who now had their hands inside their hoodies. It was the first week in October and somewhat cool that night.

Tito eased up a little behind Von's explanation. "That's understood, homie. But look, next time, you be sure to let me know ahead of time, so I won't be taken by surprise when you pull up," he instructed. "You got me on that?"

"No doubt. Now that we go that out the way . . . Tito, meet this big, black, ugly, nappy-headed, cold-hearted motherfucka' here! He's my homie, my business partner, and the one to go hard when it's time to go hard. And homie (he turned to face Eunice), meet Tito," said Von with passionate energy and a smile. He failed to mention a name. Tito would provide one himself.

"*Cold Heart,* huh?" Tito's understanding of how Von worded things to describe Eunice was flawed in a way. So to simplify, he repeated what he'd last heard. The words that registered with him. He still had work to do with his English and the linguistics of the language.

"Yeah! *Cold Heart!*" Eunice accepted the new nickname and proceeded with it. "Nice to meet you . . . Tito," he stated as he approached to shake the hand of the Puerto Rican weed and potent pill kingpin.

Von then shook hands with his connection, and the business between the two sides began.

Von and Tito walked into the office area of the shop to discuss the business at hand, while "Cold Heart" and the two other guys unloaded the product from a minivan into the trunk and backseat of the Acura Von owned.

While in the office. Tito made a phone call. He spoke in Spanish. Von had not a clue what was being said. He simply sat in silence. The call ended. The two quickly made a brief count of the money. Von had it all in $1,000 stacks. He and Tito didn't even bother to break the rubber bands on the knots of cash that were there. They merely counted out a thousand dollar fold at a time.

"It's all there, homie. Trust between you and I shouldn't be an issue," Von said.

"The more businesses we do, the more things could change. The world we live is a strange universe to be in at times, homie. Nobody can be trusted. Nobody!" Tito emphasized.

Von looked on in surprise at Tito and his choice of words. He'd never heard him speak in that type of manner. Shit had gotten real. The feeling was in the air. Von had no words to throw back at Tito to combat the way he'd expressed himself.

Nobody can be trusted! Nobody! Von recollected over Tito's words to himself.

It wasn't so much about *what* Tito had said, but more so of *how* he'd said it, and the way he made Von feel upon saying it. There was a sinister undertone to it.

Tito escorted Von out of the office back into the garage area. He said something in Spanish to his boys. They confirmed what he apparently had asked with nods of the head.

"We good homie?" Von asked of Cold Heart.

"Yeah. We good."

"Word!"

Von then dapped up Tito, and he and Cold Heart, the newly accepted name of the man whose government was Eunice, got in the car, backed out of the garage, and pulled off, cruising down the road.

The two friends began to hold a conversation,

"That nigga Tito, just made it his business to give you a new name, didn't he?" Von let out with a chuckle,

"Oh yeah! He did, didn't he!" Cold Heart responded on cue. "I like that name though. It fits me. And also, when I popped that nigga Playboy and his bitch, I had a one-on-one with myself, and came to the conclusion that I *had* to be a demon, or some type of Cold Hearted motherfucka,' to do some shit like that. My thoughts were in those terms exactly, bro. For real!" he said. "I'm claiming 'Cold Heart' through. That's me now."

"That's some hell of a shit, ain't it?"

"Sure is. But look. I got to ask you, Von."

"What that?"

"What was the reason why you didn't mention my name to him to begin with? I'm dying to know," Cold Heart asked.

"Because bro . . . you're the silent unknown power who I got by my side. Me and you were the only ones to know who you are. We're on the same team. It wasn't that nigga's business to know your name, bro," Von stated, then raised his fist to bump Cold Heart's.

They were now maybe four blocks away from Tito's shop. A stop was made at a four-way intersection. A stop sign was on each corner. An SUV crept slowly in front of Von's car. Then suddenly . . . .

Wham!

The Acura TL was encountered by a truck from behind. Four gunmen hopped out of the S.U.V. with assault rifles in front of Von and Cold Heart. Someone from the truck behind jumped out and had smashed the passenger side window with a baseball bat where Cold Heart was seated. The four guys with the firearms had them set and thoroughly trained on them both. To add further insult to injury, the two friends had been caught down bad without there guns on hand and ready to shoot. Neither of the two had their pistol on them.

"Get y'all bitch asses out of the car!" one of the rifle-toting villains barked at Von. He was on his side of the car.

"FUCK!" Von vented.

Cold Heart was busy trying to identify who the masked goons possibly were, by voice or body posture. He wasn't able to.

Von was tempted to stomp on the gas pedal and plow into the S.U.V. But it was too close to allow any speed to generate. He abandoned the thought.

"Get the fuck out of the car, nigga!" the goon ordered yet again. "Don't make me have to let these guns talk for me!"

Von grabbed hold of the door handle and slowly pushed down on it. It opened. The assailant yanked it wide. He then punched Von in the face before grabbing hold of his shirt with his free hand and slinging Von to the pavement. Cold Heart was already out of the vehicle and laying face down.

Both the gunman on the driver's side and his partner in crime on the other, got into the luxury automobile and prepared to leave, the three men in front got back into the S.U.V. and sped off, burning rubber in the process. The new driver of the Acura followed suit with the truck tailing. Von and Cold Heart were nearly run over as the hijackers fled. They moved out the way in the nick of time.

"Fuck bro!" Von let out vehemently.

Cold Heart stood and didn't say a word.

"I know that nigga Tito, didn't just set us up!" Von insinuated.

91

"You know what. Let's go back around there to see that nigga right now, bro!" Cold Heart demanded.

"Bro, we ain't go no bangers on us to go back around there to see what the deal is!"

"I don't give a fuck, my nigga! Let's go back around there anyway! I wanna see what the nigga's reaction is to the situation."

"Fuck it! Let's go!"

They were there at Tito's shop in ten minutes. An additional problem occurred for them. No one was at the shop anymore. They'd left.

Von reached for his phone that was supposed to have been clipped to his waistline. It wasn't. He'd had it plugged into the charger in the car and situated in the console.

"I know for a fact now that that punk motherfucka' Tito, sold us our material, then had us robbed to get it back! I got a trick for that bitch-ass nigga! Real talk!" Von stated.

"He gave me the name 'Cold Heart.' Now it's time for me to *be* that! Against his ass! My money was part of that too. And I had to put in some serious work to get that paper. I ain't going out bad like that! On my momma, I ain't! Somebody gotta die. And I mean that shit bro!" Cold Heart now vented himself, venom seething from his teeth, lacing his words and empowering his evil intentions.

The two then began to walk in the direction of Cold Heart's house. He didn't live too far from the location.

Once there, Von used the house phone to call Chloe to come to pick him up. She had a lot of questions for him while on the phone. He told her he'd explain everything once she was there.

Cold Heart found himself still fuming behind the robbery. Probably more so than Von. He was ready to do something about it. Dude wanted payback. In blood! And was determined to get it. He and Von dapped up and Von went on and got in the car with Chloe.

"Von, what the hell happened?" she asked. She observed the swollen eye he had. The blow was a devastating one.

"Where your phone at? Call that bitch-ass cousin of yours, Tito!"

"What! Von! Why you speaking about Tito like that!"

"Where's your phone, Chloe! Get him on it now!" Von barked.

"Get it out of my purse. And why are you yelling at me! Don't be talking crazy to me like that!" Chloe said to him.

"Yeah, whatever! That nigga had something to do with me and my homie being carjacked and robbed!"

"Von, I know that's a lie! Ain't no doubt in my mind!"

"And ain't no doubt in my mind! That nigga set me up!"

Chloe called Tito. He answered. The two cousins spoke in Spanish.

"—Speak that shit in English so I'll know what the fuck y'all talking about!" Von demanded. "As a matter of fact, gimme the phone!"

"Tito, that's some foul shit you pulled, my nigga! Word up!"

"Dude, what the fuck you talking about?" Tito wanted to know.

"My nigga! Me and my homie, got four blocks down the road from your spot after we got supplied, then, a group of motherfuckas' pulled up in front of us and behind us, drew down on us, and snatched me and my homie out of the car. They got in and pulled off. You already know I had my re-up supply in the trunk and in the back seat. They got away with everything! The car and the product!"

"You gotta be bullshitting me!"

"Why you acting surprised, my nigga! You already knew what the fuck was up!" Von accused Tito personally.

"Yo, who the fuck you making allegations on!" Tito screamed.

Chloe quickly turned her head to the right in reaction. Tito had startled her. The phone was on speaker. She shook her head at Von, basically pleading with him not to piss off her cousin. She knew what type of attitude he could have. Tito could be a mean motherfucker when he felt he needed to.

"Motherfucka'! I'm accusing you! You the one who set up the whole thing! The fuck you mean!"

"I know one thing, homie! I ain't got shit to do what you are going through, and didn't have shit to do with! I fronted you a lot of work and you owe me money. I want my paper, Von! And I mean that shit!" Tito was now no-nonsense.

Von may was young, but he had a temper at the same time. The Savage in him came out at that point.

"And I know one motherfuckin' thing too, nigga! You can suck my dick, you bitch-ass nigga! And if I ain't got no product, you don't get no money! Now live with that!" Von vehemently spat, then disconnected the call.

"Von! You don't talk to Tito like that! What the hell is wrong with you!" Chloe said, now fearing retribution upon the both of them by Tito.

"Shut the fuck up, Chloe! I ain't trying to hear that shit! That fuck-boy sold me some product then turn around and had me robbed! I ain't got no respect for him no more!" Von barked.

Chloe didn't even bother to respond to him cursing her out. She knew he was mad and needed time to cool off.

Throughout the ride home, Chloe gave an occasional glance at Von, then put her eyes back on the road. He still had his face balled up, grinding his teeth, and jaw muscles flexing.

They got home and went inside. Von took a seat on a couch and turned on the TV.

Chloe went to the bathroom to relieve herself. While in the privacy of the rest area, she texted Tito. Her reason for doing so was to apologize for Von snapping uncontrollably, and disrespecting with his mouth. Tito accepted, then went on through in texting, explaining the business between the two and what had transpired hours earlier. Tito vehemently detested having anything to do with Von and Cold Heart being hijacked and robbed.

Without doubt, Chloe sided with her cousin over the boyfriend and promised she'd have a talk with him to assist in resolving the issue. Again, Chloe knew Tito very well and wanted to get ahead of things before Tito was to have someone send a message to the young buck by punishing him, or worse, whacking the boy.

Chloe came out of the restroom and took notice of Von seated, still brooding. She spoke at that point.

"Von, are you calm enough now for us to talk?"

"What's up, Chloe! I'm listening," he responded politely, but with an attitude.

"I texted Tito"

"—Okay. That won't solve shit."

"He told me to tell you that the both of you can talk once you pipe down and get a grip on yourself."

"Chloe! You don't seem to understand."

"Help me understand. Because I know my cousin. And he is not the type of businessman to do something like that."

"So you're saying I'm wrong? That's what you're saying?"

"Truth be told, yeah, you're wrong. The way you disrespected Tito was wrong, is what I mean."

"Please! Miss me with that bullshit, a'ight! My mind is made up, Chloe. I believe that that nigga Tito had everything to do with what the fuck happened."

"What proof you got on that?"

"Chloe look—"

She cut him off. "Just answer the question. How do you know for sure that Tito set you up?"

"Everything points to him. I gave him all my money to pay for the work he served me, and he fronted me the other half. Me and my homie get four blocks away and here come these motherfuckas' drawing down on us, yanking me out my whip. And not only that, one of them niggaz snuffed me! Right in my eye!"

"So the robbers were black?" she asked.

"I didn't say that," he responded.

Chloe kept silent as she didn't want to offend Von by sounding racist. She allowed him to speak, that way, maybe he'd make some type of sense to himself.

"Actually, I don't know what color was them motherfuckas.' They could have been a group of black niggaz . . . a mix of black and white niggaz . . . or even some Spanish niggaz! I don't know."

You sound so ignorant right now. But go on ahead and speak your peace, Chloe thought to herself.

She didn't want to offend Von by voicing exactly what she thought.

"So if you don't know the color of the dudes who carjacked you, how are you gonna blame Tito? Make some sense of that for me, Von? You got to," she urged.

"Chloe, I don't know. Shit just too fishy to me. That's all. I invested everything I had in the re-up. I lost out. I'm broke. My homie lost ten thousand dollars. And the brother of my cousin's girl, had *fifty* thousand dollars tied in with us. How the fuck I'm gonna come up with that type of paper to pay that man back! Not to mention the ten grand my grand pop gave me," Von expressed with a strong tone of anxiety.

Chloe jarred her head in an appalling way. A Look of anger and disdain was cast at Von. She had to speak out on something he'd stated.

"What you mean, you broke now?" she retorted.

"I'm broke! Tapped out! I ain't got no more money! That's what I mean."

"Von, we don't have but four thousand dollars to our name. And bill time will be around again soon."

"We ain't got shit to worry about on that end."

Chloe stared him down more. "*You* don't have nothing to worry about. *I do!* There ain't no way I'm going back to my mom's place! No fucking way, Von!" she expressed while shaking her head in disgust.

"No reason to panic"

"—Should've taken Tito up on his offer on my college tuition. But I told him I wouldn't be off to school until next year, because I wanted to wait around on you to graduate."

"Oh okay. I got it now. I see you're more on Tito's side than you are on mine?"

"That's because my cousin is a provider, and a boss. He takes care of family, and business."

"—So I don't know nothing about that?"

"NO! Not like Tito does."

"*Psss!* A'ight! Okay! Whatever!" he detested. "Look, leave me be. Go on to the bedroom and let me get some sleep. And you're gonna learn before long to believe in me more. I promise you on that."

"I'll believe in you more when you make better decisions. And I'm going looking for a job Monday when I drop you off at school. I've got to depend on me from here on out. Not you," she said as she got up from the couch and made her way to the bedroom.

The insult Chloe dished at him had stabbed Von directly in the heart of his soul. At no time throughout their relationship had she ever made him feel so low. He was stung in the ass, and the pain hurt like all hell.

"Fuck school! I ain't concerned about that shit no more!"

Von couldn't think of anything better to say. He'd been made to feel so small.

ELEVEN

Monk was contacted by Dreek. He wanted to know what was the delay with his product? Fifty thousand dollars was no chicken feed to be overlooked, and he'd came a long ways to simply fall short so fast.

"Yeah, what up, Dreek," Monk answered in observance of the number in his phone.

"Yo bro, what it do. I'm checking to know what's the delay on my material? Your people ain't hit back yet?"

"Nah. Let me hit him up now to see what the deal is."

"A'ight. Get back at me when you do."

"Word," Monk lastly stated and disconnected.

Monk then went into his contacts and called Von. He now had a new phone and transferred the number from the old.

Von recognized Monk's digits on the screen. He had him locked into the contacts.

"Yo fam. What's good!"

"What's good fam. You don't sound too up. Everything kosher?" Monk asked.

"Hell fuck no! Shit done got ugly!"

"How so?"

"I was meaning to tell you sooner. But me and my homie Cold Heart, got carjacked and robbed!"

"Cold Heart! Car jacked! Robbed!" Monk retorted. "Explain!"

Von gave a synopsis of all that took place. Monk was outraged. His face and name were on that money which belonged to Dreek. Something had to be done. A sit down was necessary. Monk made it his business to go and pick them up. The intention was to confront the problem head on.

Von, Cold Heart, and Monk, were all seated in Monk's Mercedes Benz, and headed to Tito's detail shop. All three had a pistol on them. For security purposes only. Things could get real crazy real fast.

Taken aback by the unannounced visit, Tito hopped to his feet in his office at the sight of them exiting the Benz. He recognized both Von and Cold Heart, but not Monk. They were viewed as a potential threat. Tito shouted out something in Spanish to his other two men present. One was his cousin, his mother's nephew and the brother of Rosa—Alfredo. And the other, was a close homie named Enrique. They ran up to stand guard next to Tito.

"Yo, what's up! Can I help y'all? And I hope you got my money, Von!" Tito spat.

Von was ordered not to say shit. Monk would do all the talking.

"Tito! I'm Monk. Von's people. I don't know if you've ever heard of me before or what. My pop's name is Izzy Savage . . . 'JBM' Izzy Savage.

"I heard of your pop before. Never heard of you though. But get to the point," Tito responded.

"Look, Von and the homie here, told me everything that took place."

"—Did he tell you he accused me of *backdooring* him too! Motherfucka' had the nerve to insult me like *I'm* a snake!"

"And I made sure to let him know he was wrong about that too. He wants to apologize. Don't we, Von?"

Monk nudged Von with his elbow harshly.

"I apologize about that, Tito. I was mad and not thinking rationally," Von uttered.

The apology seemed sincere. Tito accepted. They'd done too much good business in the past not to allow reason and compromise to take over between them at this point.

"Can I speak to you in private, Tito? Just you and me," Monk requested.

Tito didn't get a bad vibe from Monk and his energy indicated he wanted to come to a resolution of the problem. Also, Monk had a serious demeanor and had an appearance of a businessman, ready to get down to the business.

"Step into my office," Tito instructed.

He then spoke to his men in Spanish, basically telling them to stand down but stay on point.

Tito and Monk entered the domain and their conversation began. They hit on all topics related to the situation. An agreement was met. It would require Von and the members of the crew he was a part of, to now switch the product that they sold, and the money Tito was owed, would be paid in installments. Once the debt is to be paid, the business between Tito and Von, would be no more. This was a stern decision made by Tito. He had no knowledge Von was still a kid in school. He didn't deal with little boys. Only grown men. The Puerto Rican weed and pill Czar scolded himself behind his poor sense of judgment.

Silly me! Tito thought.

Prior to the talks coming to an end between the elders of the six, Tito yet again made it absolutely clear that he had nothing to do with the bullshit that happened to Von. Monk took him as being truthful. Tito displayed no signs of shadiness. Monk gave his word that Tito would get his money, even if he had to come out of his pocket himself to pay him. They shook hands firmly, established a deep level of respect and potentially a pact, then Monk exited, and they left, leaving Monk with the opportunity throughout the ride to articulate to the youngsters what the new game plan was, in the now grand scheme of things.

At the end of the day, everything managed to all work out. Monk was in charge, and looking to add on to the heroin empire his brother and him were building upon. Savvy savage business moves made by a Savage himself. Now how gangster was that. More gangster as gangster could get.

TWELVE

Within the same week of Monk working things out with Tito for Von, he'd met with Dreek as well, to make him aware of what the situation was regarding his money. There wouldn't be any product of weed and pills, Monk properly explained, then left him with an option: to either accept a half kilo of heroin each at a time until fully paid back, or accept $10K at a time? Although Dreek held a certain type of fear of being busted by the police for dealing such unrelenting hard drugs, reluctantly, he opted to be supplied with that over the slow pace of reimbursement in cash. Not to mention the fact he no longer had a weed and pill connection, and he was very eager to make money. He was behind on things, and Monk told him he'd hit him up with buyers to help build his clientele in the *dope* market now. No longer cannabis and MDMA.

Monk proved shrewd in the negotiations with Dreek. His empire was expanded by adding someone he knew would do the right thing, for the sake of his sister at least, Ayonna. Dreek's sister that is.

Monk's next move was to take the initiative to go ahead and lock Cold Heart up on contract, as a hired hitter, and someone who would go hard once the order was issued. He now brought Von and Cold Heart closer into the inner circle and made it his business to get together with them for a meeting at least three to four times weekly. He loved to tour the city in his big-body Benz. The conversations would often be deep.

"Yeah fam, these ghetto streets of Philly here, have helped to make our family rich. Our grand pops set roots here back in the fifties from Georgia. They made that Black Mafia shit a reality. Straight gangsta," Monk said, complimenting the groundwork put in by his father's father, and Von's father's father.

"I heard. My dad and pop-pop Hound, gave me bits and pieces on their upbringing. I want to live my life exactly like that. Only take it to a higher level," Von responded.

Cold Heart sat back and took in the moral of the story the two cousins related.

"And how you plan to do that?" Monk asked Von.

"I'm already off to a good start. A head start actually. I'm a Savage for one. And I've got connections with a family of bosses for the other. How can I go wrong like this?" remarked Von.

Monk smiled, obviously pleased by the words of his people. He then directed a few questions at Cold Heart to know more about him.

"What about you, Eunice?"

"—I go by Cold Heart now, bro," he corrected.

"*Cold Heart!*" Monk retorted. "How you get that name?"

"Somebody else gave it to me. I only embraced it. But my plan is to have no plan. I'm gonna continue to get it how I live and do it how it goes. And I wish you had some more work for me. I ain't got the patience to sit still and deal with dope-heads all day. I've got to be busy and moving," Cold Heart informed.

"Oh! You do! A live wire, huh? Well, since you let me know you've got an appetite in that area and are hungry for more, I'm gonna load your plate and let you eat all you want, my nigga. Goddamn sure are. Just hold tight. I was planning to turn you loose again soon anyway."

"Well, I'm ready. I need to make some more paper anyhow."

They continued in their ride. Monk showed them the different territories he had in operation and introduced them to the top homies running the spots. Monk's brother was the man who masterminded the entire group and the kingpin who called the shots. He would meet the two newly added pieces to the team later in the week. He was simply too busy at the present moment.

Monk laid out what his game plan was, and told the two to get with their people who sold the weed and pills, and let them know what the new agenda was, and give them the chance to choose what they wanted to do; to either roll with the crew with how things are now going; or, get left behind on their own. The choice was theirs to make.

***

Chloe and Rosa were doing some shopping at the *King of Prussia Mall.* They always had a good time when they were out together. The cousins were like sisters in many ways. Their height, weight, hair color, and skin complexion were all the same, and the figure of their bodies held similarities. They were often regarded as twins in many instances.

Chloe brought it to Rosa's attention the problems she was going through with Von, his lack of time spent with her, and the depletion of funds made it difficult to keep their bills paid. The situation Von had gone through with Tito, definitely complicated the relationship. And his choice of words towards the cousin who was basically a God-send to not only Chloe but the Dominquez family as a whole, made it to where she was forced to re-evaluate her commitment to the younger boyfriend, as he was proving to be a bad choice. Chloe poured out her heart to Rosa. She revealed it all.

"Rosa, how about, me and my boyfriend now find ourselves in a bad space in our relationship," she began on the topic.

Rosa jarred her head at the revelation. "No Chloe. What happened? How did it come to this?"

"He seems to have gotten deep in the streets now. Don't have a job. And not in the habit of trying to grow up and become a man from a boy. I told him to his face too."

"Girl! You didn't."

"Oh yes I did too."

"So y'all had a recent argument?"

"Hell yeah. He had the nerve to disrespect Tito over the phone in my face."

"—Tito!" Rosa retorted. "How the hell did it come to that?"

Chloe related what she knew about the robbery. She then mentioned the exchange of words between Von and Tito, which led to her and Von hashing it out at home.

"You definitely did the right thing by taking Tito's side over his," Rosa stated. "Boyfriend or not! Family is over everything, mami!"

"I know that to be the truth. And not only did Von get out of line by disrespecting Tito. We're broke now, girl, and may not have enough money to pay all of our bills came the first of the month," Chloe said.

Rosa stopped browsing then and there on the clothing rack and looked on at Chloe. She had a construed demeanor and was confused at the remark her cousin had made.

"Chloe, if you're not gonna have enough money to pay your bills, then why in the heck are you out here shopping and appearing like you living your best life? You know I'm gonna speak my mind no matter what." Rosa had always kept it real with Chloe, not biting her tongue in the least.

"I'm able to splurge a little. *Now*. I gave somebody a call and asked for his help."

"Who? Tito?"

"Nope. My ex. Raul," Chloe revealed.

Rosa smiled and gently shook her head. "I knew you weren't through with him. You still love Raul, don't you?"

"I do. I can't lie He's come into some money. *A lot* of it, somehow."

"How much did he give you?"

"Ten thousand dollars!"

Rosa maintained the smile she had and then offered her thoughts on the rekindling of the passionate flame between Chloe and Raul. "You already know, by calling that man and accepting his money, you are attaching yourself to him again, right?"

"I'm aware. All he wants is to go out on a date, and for me to suck his dick and fuck him good like I know how. That's it. I don't have to be back in a relationship with him to do that."

"So you gonna give him some?'

"*Mmm-hmm!* I gotta keep the money coming. Plus, he ain't never been bad sexually. Only a control freak and too impulsive. But if I can fuck him and keep him at a distance, that'll suit me just fine," Chloe declared.

"And what do you plan to do with your *boy toy?*"

"I don't know. I'm having second thoughts about him. I may need to give him back the money he paid to put us in the apartment, then go on to get my own place to live as a single woman. I can do what I want then, and see who I want."

"That makes sense. You see how I'm doing me, don't you? Exactly the same."

"And I learned from you. Not to commit myself to a guy, and make it my business to be in my own space. That way, I can see who I want, when I want, and how I want. By the way, Raul is still close to the family. He and Alfredo good friends. Is everything still the same?" Chloe asked Rosa of her brother. The two guys both worked for Tito at the shop and sold his products for him, the weed and pills.

"They still cool, and now that you mentioned it, Alfredo seems to have come up on some money too. He gave me three thousand dollars and bought our mom and dad and car.

You know he stays over at my house every now and again. Anytime he and the wild-ass bitch he's got as a girlfriend gets into an argument and goes through some shit. I can't stand that slut!" Rosa stated, relating to the turbulent relationship between her sibling and the mother of his daughter. Rosa adored her niece, Kylie.

"Baby Kylie," Chloe let out with a smile. "How has she been? I miss seeing her."

"She's been good. Growing fast like a weed in a fully fertilized garden."

"When will you be keeping her again?"

"Soon. Maybe this weekend. I'll be sure to bring her along with us next time we're out shopping," Rosa assured.

"Please do. I wanna see her. She's so adorable."

The two cousins continued to talk and shopped. They always had the best of time when together, doing what they loved to do. Companionship of the family on a strong level was something they believed in. However, the cardinal rules related to the *do's* and the *do not* that females are to respect regarding their personal business were violated in more than one way. Bad seeds was planted between them, and the fruit that was to come from such poisonous tree, was subject to make the whole affair a dirty rotten mess. If only they knew.

PART TWO

THIRTEEN

Von and Cold Heart, now had the duty to bring all members of their crew together at one location. They needed to explain to them what had happened, what was now in process, and which way the team was going from that point. A meeting was set, and a lot would be put on the table in discussion.

The day was a Thursday, and the seven hustlers to make up the squad were there at the house of Shayla and Tangee. This was the first time they'd had the opportunity to lay eyes on one another. It was now known what each other looked like. No longer a mystery or in name only.

Cold Heart, the perceived leader, began in a monologue. Not long at all. Short, simple, and to the point. He was the only one who stood while everyone else remained seated in the living room.

Past the point of what happened and when new product would be provided, he informed them not in the know, of a different character brought to life.

"Oh yeah, I almost forgot. I go by the name *"Cold Heart"* now, y'all. The code of the streets made it this way," he let out with a smile and slight chuckle.

Von stood and began to speak. It was his turn to elaborate on the business.

"A'ight y'all, look. Here's the deal. We're done with selling weed and pills. No more of that. It's now time to get money in the dope game. Heroin is the new cash-cow for us. Why? Because . . . ain't no money . . . like dope money. And I want some of it. I know y'all do too. Don't you?"

The two females were the only ones who had concerned looks on their faces. Shayla expressed what she and Tangee thought.

"No doubt, we wanna get some money, Von. But what we supposed to do about all the customers we got, who are looking for the normal product they buy from us?"

Her question was a legit one.

"Shit Shay. Ain't but one thing to do. If you want to keep them as *your* customer, find a way to get them to buy the new material you got for sale," Von answered.

They all smiled and laughed at his witty suggestion. It was actually not a bad idea at all. Practical even.

"But on the real, Shay, I'm sure it won't take us long at all, to build up a clientele base with dope. Philly has a big appetite for H. Damn near everybody in the underworld is always looking to get the monkey off their back in some type of way. This shit is big business. And that's why we are here together to discuss things. The *new 'JBM'* begins with us," he pointed a finger and waved his hand at them all, then towards himself. "Us seven right here."

Von motivated them with his words. He saw the passion in their eyes become a reality in their ambition. Their involuntary nodding of the head confirmed the loyal hustling spirit they possessed. He provided them with more to believe in. An assurance to their minds that they had next in line to be the top hustlers. A street team put together and was now ready to compete for the top spot in the game.

"Also, I'm sure y'all know who my family is. We have their backing. My cousin Drip and Monk, are the ones who are putting us on. We work *for* them for now. But in due time, we'll be working *with* them."

Kareem and Lonnie looked at each other in a questioning way. They had no knowledge of who "Drip" or "Monk" was. They then looked around at everyone else, silently asking to be informed. Cold Heart understood what they asked silently through the body language on display. He offered something brief in explanation

"Drip and Monk are both brothers," he said while looking over at Kareem and Lonnie, one to the other. "Their dad—the old head Izzy Savage—was one of the head dudes of JBM," he related.

They then knew immediately who Izzy Savage was, from the legendary stories of the past they'd heard growing up. And with Von and Cold Heart now tying them into the particular movement, they'd began to feel a sense of comfort, because they knew that the business would be taken care of.

Cold Heart spoke again. "Everybody still got the bangers we gave y'all, right?" he asked.

Everyone answered they did.

"Okay. Good. Once we make more money, we're gonna buy more weapons. And remember, with good dope being put out on the streets by a team nobody knows about yet, this is gonna cause other motherfuckas' to get out and ask questions about who is doing what. They might even want smoke. And we can't hesitate to blast first, if it comes to that."

"We sure as hell can't!" Ron spoke up for the first time.

"So when we suppose to get supplied?" Tangee asked. "Because I'm ready to do what I gotta do and run it up again."

"Tomorrow," Von confirmed, "We're gonna have to slow grind our way to the top, selling twenties until we reach the point of offering weight. At all cost, loyalty and team work, gonna be the only way to make the dream work. And anything less, is beneath us."

Von had gotten really good at repeating the words he'd been indoctrinated with by Monk (most recently), his father, his brother, grand pop, and other cousins, who had many years in the streets and in the game. The wisdom they'd conveyed upon him, managed to situate itself deeply within his mind, spirit, and hustling ambitions. He was hungry and ready to eat. Cold Heart also was hungry and ready to eat. And so were the other five. They all planned more.

The crew exchanged phone numbers and went on about their day, anxious for the next one to come. The day the dope to sell would be delivered.

***

One Day Later . . .

Drip was contacted by his brother, Monk, and was made aware of all going on with the new additions to the crew. He now knew that the son of his cousin—Little Hound—was in the streets and going about doing things the same way as them. Von owed Drip a great depth of gratitude, being that he was the leader over Monk and the product they were in the process of supplying to Von and company. Everything belonged to him, more so than his brother.

Drip wanted to meet with Von, as he hadn't seen the teenager since he was a little boy. Monk was told to come by the house with him. He lived in the next town over from Philly, in Norristown, Montgomery County Pennsylvania.

Monk called Von.

"What up cuzzo," Von answered.

"What it be like, fam. Got some good news for you," Monk responded.

"Oh, you do! What's that?"

"Big bro ready to see you again. He wants me to pick you up and we meet him at his house over in 'Naughty-*Town*' PA, where the bitches are thick, pretty, and ready to fuck on site. You up yet, nigga?"

"Yeah, I'm up. I'll be ready by the time you get here."

"The spot in northeast, right?"

"You know it, fam."

"I'm on my way."

The call concluded.

Nearly an hour later, Monk was pulling up in one of his other vehicles. It was a *Jeep Grand Cherokee*, black and gray in color, He texted Von:

MONK: I'm outside fam.

VON: For sho.

Von exited the row house and got into the S.U.V. The weather was windy, somewhat cloudy, and at sixty-two degrees. He had on one of his favorite outfits. It was a black Adidas sweatsuit (throwback) with the bucket Adidas hat, and shell top sneakers. He looked and felt dope, while eager as ever to be provided the work from his people and hustle his way back to a bank roll.

"What's popping fam," he greeted Monk then they dapped each other up.

"What's poppin'!" Monk responded with a smile of admiration at how fresh Von was. "Dope boy clean today, ain't you? I see you. I like that. Just my style."

Monk had on something similar, only by *Puma*, and made of fleece material.

"Check that. But you on point too, cuz. I like your style," Von returned the compliment.

They rode off.

Monk arrived at his brother's home. Drip had a luxurious mini-mansion in a well-to-do gated community in the town. It was a six-bedroom, two and half-bath bachelor's pad, and sat on 1.8 acres of land. He texted and let Drip know he was out front, with Von. Drip came to the door. He opened to welcome them in. The two youngsters got out of the vehicle and made their way towards the dapper kingpin.

"How you doing bro?" Monk greeted.

The siblings embrace brotherly. Drip turned his attention to Von.

"What's good little fam," the six-foot-six, slim, dark-skinned, clean-cut, well-groomed, aspiring property developer said. He smiled and displayed a set of glorious white teeth. Drip appeared to be happy at the sight of Von. Perhaps a thought of the boy's father flashed through his mind, He leaned over to give Von a hug.

"Long time no see, Drip. I see you living like a real boss out here in the world," Von complimented.

"That's because *I am* a real boss, little cuz. And I care about my family," Drip responded confidently.

The three then stepped inside.

Von immediately took notice of how magnificent the interior of the home was. It had a high ceiling to it, a very large and expensive chandelier, high-quality tile flooring with an exquisite Persian rug in the center of the living room, and many other accommodations. The sheer opulence of the $1.5 million rest haven was enough to make Von gleam in admiration as he never had before. Although his grandfather had the riches to live in the same way, not even the legendary Hound Savage, had it going on like him—-Damien "Drip" Savage—managed to build himself up to be.

Von continued to look around in awe at the prestigious architectural structure and contours of the home. His cousin inspired him in a major way.

"Damn! You living large, fam! Large and in charge! How the fuck can I get on this level? I need to know," Von remarked.

"You're already on this level, Vonnie. Your bloodline runs deep, and rich with money-making genes. Just be patient, and continue to keep loyal to the family. Everything is gonna come to you in due time. I promise you it will," Drip stated, doing very well in motivating and strengthening Von's morale.

Von nodded in agreement, then worded his compliance. "No doubt, fam. No doubt."

They all took a seat and began to delve deep into discussion.

In addition to being a potent dope dealing and savvy businessman, Drip was heavy into major white-collar activities. But on the surface, he had a fleet of legitimate business ventures dotted in and around Philadelphia City. He had a net worth north of $20,000,000 and just south of $30,000,000. An eight-figure boss, and had his tentacles far-reaching into many facets of Philly's organizational societies.

Although not a married man, Damien was known in the legal spheres by his government name, and as "Drip" throughout the ghetto. He loved women, young ladies in particular. Young girls who'd just graduated high school and were fresh in college or on their way to an alma mater.

The Savage cousins held their conversation and business talk for two hours. Drip basically laid out the rules to Von and vehemently let it be known that Von, was not to try and take advantage of him, Monk, or none of the family, simply because he was family. Von swore with his life that he wouldn't. Drip designated him the leader of his crew he was apart of, the six others who were already in lockstep with him (Cold Heart, Ron, Shay, Tangee, Kareem, and Lonnie). Basically, Von would be the lieutenant who would report to the Capo—Monk—and Monk to him, Drip. He wanted to also now meet Cold Heart, to personally thank him, for the hit he carried out on Playboy Johnson. But on the opposite end of that, little did Drip know, Playboy's crew, may had a lot they wanted to get off their chest in retaliation to avenge his murder. But they had no knowledge of *"whodunit"* ("who done it" with Swag) or why.

Drip pulled out a thick photo album that was flooded with pictures of the Savage family. Von's father was in a lot of these images with Drip. Then there were those of their grandfathers and grandmothers. Drip and Monk's grandmother—Josephine "Mama JoJo" Savage—was also there alongside Von's father's mother. Those photos of the ladies were taken in the '60s' and '70s.' The heyday of their grandfathers.

"Black Mafia in the beginning days, Von," Drip said with passion at the photo of the OG's Mickey and Hound Savage. He shed a tear in expressing his zealous mind set to be exactly the same. But in a contemporary more sophisticated way.

"I see. We are now responsible for upholding their legacy," said Von.

"No doubt, we do. Black Mafia Incorporated (BMI), has begun to fill that role. That's who we are; the third generation unit, I so declare," Drip dictated.

They then placed their right hands over one another's with Drip's as the foundation. He changed the slogan.

"B-M-I till we die! Grind hard with a purpose!" he proclaimed.

The other two repeated loudly. It was on from there for them.

FOURTEEN

Drip instructed Monk to lay four bricks of heroin on Von, to be divided amongst his crew. He also was sure to let Von know seriously, to report to Monk, for any and everything he needed, that Monk was Capo, and he was Monk's lieutenant. A chain of command was established.

Von and Cold Heart took two of the kilos and broke them down into quarters. Every member would get one each, and the basics of dope dealing was now in effect.

Pairs within the group was formed, with Ron, the only one of the seven to handle his business in the way he was accustomed; by driving around in his car to make sales. Von and Cold Heart, would alternate from one location to the next—from the Erie Ave vicinity to that of Darien Street— pumping dope and getting money. Kareem and Lonnie dug in deep on a spot over in West Philly. And the girls, simply did their thing between the apartment they lived and Cori's house. Once enough money was to be made, the two ladies had plans to get a spot in another area. A car as well. Everyone was off to a good start with the different product. A clientele base was gradually being built, and things flowed smoothly.

***

The two love-birds—Lilly and Jamar—were laid back chilling and relaxing in the hotel room they'd reserved. The day from work was taken off by them both. They worked at the airport, the same place they'd met. This was the second time in thirty days they'd had the opportunity to spend intimate time together. Getting away from Bernard to be with Jamar, proved more difficult than she'd originally thought, and taking too many days off, would get her and him fired from their job. So, a great deal of caution had to be taken, to balance out the two, and needed to be played well, so to not be in trouble with Bernard or their boss.

Lilly let Jamar know about the ass-beating Bernard put on her. He didn't like the fact of this happening. Jamar wanted to do something to him for putting his hands on the woman he was now looking to have situated in his life. Lilly made light of the incident by making jokes of it. They were seated on the bed naked after the first round of fucking they'd done. Something they couldn't hardly wait to get to. Ooh, how she craved the dick. Lilly was a thirty-seven-year-old freak. Von's mom loved to fuck. One dude at a time though.

"But back to what I was telling you, Jamar. I blame you, for getting me smacked around. It was all your fault," she let out with a smile and a laugh.

Jamar returned a smile of his own. One very pleasing in the eyes of Lilly.

"'I'm laughing along with you, but best believe it, I don't like that shit one bit. Not at all. I wanna do something to that nigga's ass! Lord knows I do!"

"It ain't necessary, Jamar. I got Bernard under my control. I know what to do to get rid of him. I just gotta do it in the way I know how. He'll be gone before long. Then we can go on about life together. Exactly how you we see fit," Lilly assured.

"Well, do what you gotta do. Just please, don't have me on hold too long. A'ight."

"All right. But in the meantime, don't you keep me waiting too long either," she said sensuously while locking eyes and tenderly palming his manhood, passionately caressing to bring it back to life. It didn't take long for that to occur. His dick instantaneously inflated in girth and length. Lilly held back no more.

She went down on Jamar, taking him into her warm moist mouth. Her hot pink medium-sized lips wrapped tightly around his shaft. The sensation caused him to tilt his head and lean back against the headboard on the bed. He then stretched out his body and had his dick vertical in pole-position. Lilly maintained both hands securely on Jamar's meat-stick, working up and down simultaneously with a bob above and an upward jerk from below, both meeting one another in the middle.

She loved to get extra sloppy and wet anytime she pleased a man with oral sex. Lilly drooled and spit on the dick at every moment she came up for air, while at the same time, she twirled the tip of her tongue around the head of his love pistol. He was overcome with passion and ecstasy. Jamar wasn't ready to blow his load, and neither was Lilly. He used his hand and placed it on her left shoulder, causing her to ease up for a moment, signaling he was now primed to fuck. Lilly did so, then lay on her back. They both loved the *missionary* position and were eager to get to it.

Jamar mounted himself over Lilly and cupped her legs in the pocket of his arms, between the bicep and forearm. He raised them high and grimaced at her while penetrating the pussy. She cooed in pleasure, wrapped her arms around his waist, and pulled him in with a strong sense of urgency to feel the dick deep inside her. Jamar's manhood stuffed her hole. His thickness expanded the entrance of her walls. Jamar then found a rhythm, grooving to the vibe of her energy, and stroked in and out her love nest to the tune of music playing. It was the song, *Say Yes* by the duo female vocalists, *Floetry.*

Although Jamar loved to fuck at a steady pace between high and low gear, Lilly craved for him to bang her back out in an aggressive and rough way to match the physicality that his body presented. He was athletic, muscle-bound, and full of sexual vigor. He began to fuck her hard and convincingly just as she liked, producing grunts here and there, with the slapping of his pelvic against her hind side, splattering love juice wildly on the both of them.

Jamar's moment of truth had arrived. His climax point was there at the tip of his dick. He then pulled out, squeezing his manhood tightly so as to not blow the moment and eased up to Lilly's caramel complexion breasts, then let loose. His cannon had blown a thick plentiful and robust load. He'd plastered those luscious titties and lips of Lilly's as she open wide to take his dick head into her mouth, to clean him up well, and then swallow all that was left.

Round two down and maybe one more to go, prior to the 9:00 p.m. hour being upon them, and they having to go for how many ever days between before having the chance to come together again. Neither had total control to hold back until the next escapade. They wanted it more than ever. The time shall come again.

***

Unexpectedly, Shay and Tangee gained a customer base faster than any of the others. The neighborhood they lived was a prime area to sell their product. The majority of the people who bought from them, preferred to snort the heroin with the exception of the others who shot up. And not to mention the fact that they were females—young and attractive at that. It brought about a sense of calm for the people who they dealt with, especially other females. Everyone was comfortable buying. Shayla's boyfriend now had more complaints to vent about. He voiced his mind.

"Damn Shay! You went from hustling the weed and pills with them niggaz to now selling dope! So just fuck me and all I had in mind to do, huh!"

"Look, Feezy! I'm not up for this shit with you, bro! Like, for real, I'm not! So don't start," Shay fired back.

"Shay! I'm supposed it be the nigga in your life. I'm the one who suppose to be leading the way in what we have. If anything, you was supposed to bring your ass to me and let it be known the offers them niggaz made to you. Not doing shit how you see fit, when you see fit. Or how you see fit! What the fuck you on!" Feezy spat.

At a total surprise, Shay allowed him the time to get his long line of words out of his mouth before blasting in back talk.

"You finished!"

Feezy jarred his head at her insubordinate and fucked up attitude. He definitely had something else to say about this.

"Shay, who you think you're getting smart with!" he let out in a harsh but easy way.

"Who you *think* I'm talking to, *Feezy*? And before you decided to try to dictate to me and tell me what the *fuck* to do, it'll be a good thing if you begin paying bills and shit on this side of the relationship!"

"Didn't I make it my business to pay all your shit for you when them niggaz you think you getting some money with, let you down for those two weeks? And before you even got going with selling the weed and shit, I held you down. And now, it's fuck me!"

"Nigga! You ain't done no major shit! I been taking care of myself by doing hair and all else over my sister's house long before I stated fucking with you!" she spoke in an ugly put down type of way. Her words were very condescending. Shayla's intention was to chomp Feezy off and make him feel worthless. Like he was a nobody. To her or anyone for that matter

Feezy snapped.

"Bitch, who the fuck you think you dogging out!" he spat, then rushed in and smacked the shit out of her.

Whop!

He'd slapped Shayla so hard, the sound effect of it was like a gun had been fired. She went down to the floor in a daze. Feezy leaned in and mean-mugged his girlfriend. He was full of anger and rage. Every nasty, ugly, fucked up thing she'd said or done to him before the day came out then and there. The toxic energy that had built up within him caused the boy to lash out and get on her ass. Shayla's mouth got her in trouble with dude, and the consequences that came to be, began that day. He smacked her again.

Whop!

"Huh! Who you talking to Shay!"

Whop!

Shayla now had a bloody nose and a busted swollen lip. She slowly rocked from left to right on the floor trying to regain her composure. Feezy had heavy hands.

They were the only two there in the house, in the bedroom. A thought was triggered within Feezy. Something he'd seen and known. On impulse, he jolted and headed to the closet. His intention was to take all the money and product Shayla and Tangee kept there. The girls hadn't changed the protocol they had in place from the weed and pill dealing.

Feezy knocked over everything and yanked down the shoe boxes and pieces of clothes in the closet in search of the dope and loot. He knew they still had ounces of *dirty sugar* left and a couple thousand in cash. Dude wanted it.

"Since we can't do our thing and get money together, I'mma just take your shit and make you submit, bitch!" he spat. Feezy was serious.

Shay managed to get a grip with gaining composure. She looked around the room in search of her purse. It was located on the nightstand next to the bed. She made a break for it, dug in, and pulled out her pistol. Feezy still had his back to her and stuffing his pockets with their money and work.

Shayla cocked her gun and took aim to blast. She'd gotten his attention with the sound of a bullet being set in the chamber. Feezy paused. He knew what that was all about.

Pow!

A round was let off. She missed him as he made a break for the front door. That motherfucker was doing all he could in scrambling towards the exit, trying to get up out of there.

Pow!

Shayla shot again, missing once more. Feezy was now in the living room almost out the front door. She got up and ran behind him.

Pow!

He'd made it out the door just in the nick of time. Her last shot fired had missed as well. There was now a heavy beef between the two.

Feezy got away with $4,000 and two ounces of H. Risk and reward, the games people play.

***

Shayla grabbed her phone and sent a group text to Von and Cold Heart.

SHAYLA: 9-1-1

Cold Heart was the first to reply. He called.

Shayla explained what happened. Cold Heart was now on his way to her house. He wasn't too far from where she was.

Von then called and was told the same. He and Cold Heart were both there in less than twenty minutes.

The three of them then got into Cold Heart's car and she showed them where Feezy's mom lived and his sister, the two places he was known to stay. The trio then returned to Shayla's apartment. Tangee was called and told to come home quickly. They had to go over the format on what to do and who to call if the nigga Feezy, was to come back causing more problems. Cold Heart told them to keep their guns war ready and their trigger fingers tweaking to blast. No hesitation and no remorse. And at the same time, the boys of the crew would now themselves get out on the hunt to track down Feezy. He was a marked man. Dude had to be got.

Nobody could get away with taking shit from them! Not even the boyfriend of one of them.

Tangee was a single girl. She had no desire for a man at that particular time, especially not so with the fact of the bullshit that Shayla and her now *ex-boyfriend* went through. Tangee's feelings and thoughts may change at some point in the future. But currently, a dude was off limits in her world and in between her legs.

Shayla gave Von and Cold Heart physical pictures and text message images of Feezy to help them know what he looked like. No mistake could be made once they were to get the drop on that clown. The need was to hit him as quickly as possible, so to keep Shayla and Tangee out of harm's way. And not only that, Cold Heart of them all, had a thing for Shayla she knew nothing about. He liked her and had felt that way for the longest, but didn't want to complicate things with the business they had going on. Maybe in due time, he'd communicate his feeling for her to her. The time then wasn't right. He didn't even know if Shaya trusted dudes anymore. The girl had been violated and attempted to chastise the motherfucker who'd done it with a few pieces of lead.

If only Feezy had known how bad he'd fucked up. He'd never had done it. Too little too late now. They had it out for him.

FIFTEEN

Lilly was told by Jamar to go to the police and take out a restraining order on Bernard. His intent was to move him out of the way as fast as he could. That way, Lilly was his to himself, and he didn't have to share her with another man. She told him she would do just that, but it turned out to be a lie she'd told, to keep him in the frame of mind that the process was in place to move Bernard to the wayside, then eventually, out of her life. That was a far cry from the truth. She despised cops as well.

Lilly originally lied to Jamar by telling him Bernard had his own place—which was partly true—and didn't stay with her full time. Bernard had long moved his belongings into her house. And although he beat on her from time to time— no punches or other harsh blows—he was good to her, and Lilly had love for him. Or maybe it was lust? She was confused.

Bernard knew that Lilly and her son Von, would travel down to Florida to visit his father Little Hound mostly every three months. The mother and son would stay the entire weekend. Von's father was housed at Coleman Federal Correctional Institution. He anticipated their visits.

"Bernard, me and Von planning to go to Florida Friday to see his dad, okay," she made him aware. Basically asking him permission to do so, as she didn't want him to not be in the know and then feel some type of way. Lilly wanted Bernard to continue to think he was still in charge of the relationship. He wasn't. The day she talked to him to reveal her plan was on a Wednesday.

"That's cool, bae. I know and understand you gotta take the boy to see his daddy. Thank you for considering how I may think and feel about it. All I ever asked you to do was let me know what's going on, haven't I?" Bernard responded.

"Yes you have, baby," she responded. The two of them were there together in her house that evening, situated on the bed watching TV. It was Lily's favorite, *Girlfriends* on *BET*.

Normally, the two would make it their business to have sex a day or two leading up to three days away she'd be gone. But that wouldn't be happening this time around. Lilly wanted to rid herself of Bernard and the strong feelings she still had for him by depriving dude of any sexual activity; the best way for a woman to indicate to a man she didn't want shit to do with him any longer. And Lilly knew it. She made it her business not to go for anything strange from him. Their relationship was now pedestrian to her. Unusual and strange ass fuck.

Bernard placed his hand on Lilly's thigh in an attempt to caress and get her in the mood.

"No Bernard. I'm not up for it," she responded to his actions, then took hold of his hand and removed it from her leg.

He crept her out now. No longer having the ability to stimulate her in that way. Bernard spoke out.

"You know how long it's been since you last decided to give me some, Lilly?"

As if on cue, she chimed in.

"—Not hardly long enough! And you made it this way. You're responsible for being in the dog house sexually."

"How so?"

Bernard seemed to not know, or at least didn't care to know, that just three weeks before the day. He'd physically beat on Lilly. He really didn't give a fuck.

"So you don't remember putting your hands on me, huh," she said. "You're getting more and more out of control,

Bernard. If you must know. I'm a small woman. I Can only take so much," Lilly uttered in a sorrowful tone.

"Lilly. You know I'm crazy over you and how I get when you ignore me and my feelings."

"So that makes you *beat*, me? Because you feel like I'm ignoring you?" she turned her head sharply towards him and said.

They were seated upright with their backs against the head pad of the bed. Bernard exhaled and lowered his head. He was at a loss for words. Not Lilly.

"And the sad part about it is, you didn't even offer an apology. As good as I've been to you." She maintained a stern look at him, obviously angry and saddened all at once.

Lilly then went to the living room to rest on the sofa. She would continue enjoying her show on TV there.

***

Chloe opened up to her ex more so than she should have, being that she was in a relationship, and held no remorse behind her ill actions. She and Raul were together in a hotel suite. They'd been fucking like jack rabbits. He wanted to talk and reaffirm his love and how he felt about her. She wanted to listen. And if it sounded like something she could consider and agree on, the possibility existed that everything he brought to her attention, would come to reality.

The two lay in the nude under the cover, touching, smooching, nibbling on one another necks and body, and vibing passionately. He on her breast and she on his chest and dick. They faced each other, locking eyes, and glowing with affection. He wooed her with words.

"Chloe, I didn't know what I was gonna do without you, baby. I love you and miss you so much."

"Aw, sweetie. That's so nice of you to think of me in that way. I love you and miss you too," she responded.

They tongue-kiss intensely, and had to pause to catch their breath. The intimate talking continued.

"I'm curious to know, we broke up again for what now? I never knew," Raul asked.

"Raul. I don't want to spoil the moment, sweetheart. I only want to enjoy you for the time being. That's why I'm here. And had I *completely* left you alone, you wouldn't have me here now," she stated, maintaining in mind her one and only reason why she was there to begin with, to simply keep the money coming he'd provided her.

"That's fair. And I understand you basically needed a break from me at the time. I could be a motherfucker when I wanna be," he let out wittily.

They both smiled and laughed like they were young and out on a date for the first time. The kissing continued, then, they got back to the fucking part.

Through the time they'd spent together, Raul was sure to question her in an easy but in-depth type way, about the relationship she and Von carried on. Chloe broke down the differences between the two, and provide her likes, her dislikes, the ups, the downs, the highs, and the lows of it all. Chloe basically made Raul aware that she really wanted to go on about life by herself, and not be in a committed affair with no one. Her ambition was to go to college and have a career in public service, or as an economist.

Although in love with Von, and didn't want to let him go so easily, she depended on Raul, but knew the importance of keeping the distance between the two. Her intent was to be with him when she needed money and when *she* wanted, on *her* time. Not his. He couldn't have it both ways. No-no! That part of what they had was over. It'll never be the same any longer. However, Raul thought totally different. He felt the need for something that would bond them together for the remainder of their lives. Chloe would be taken by absolute surprise. Will his plan work, or won't it? The question was in the air.

***

Cold Heart hit Tangee up. He wanted to talk with her to see what she may knew about Shayla's boyfriend Feezy, and hear her view point on the relationship they had.

Tangee was picked up by him in the new car he had. It was a Pontiac Firebird, black cherry in color, and clean as ever.

Cold Heart began in conversation.

"Yo, Tangee, how you been lately?" he asked.

"I've been good, big homie. Just been keeping it steady and copacetic out here in the world, man. A bitch gotta do all necessary nowadays to survive. Shit be trending in the wrong direction at times," Tangee responded.

"Everything gonna be alright, you know. We got you. Don't worry."

"I trust y'all do. That's the only reason I stayed down for the cause. You and Vonnie came through."

"No doubt. But look, keep in mind that anything we talk about—you and me that is—-it's gotta be kept strictly between us. No one else. And the conversation we have will never be about nobody in the crew in a fucked up way. I'm the main man over our security, and will only be trying to get down to the bottom of something. A'ight," Cold Heart emphasized in his elaboration.

Tangee was drawn back in mind to the day she and Shayla were given the guns they had. It was Cold Heart who gave over to them and spoke about a few things. Also, on the day of the meeting when they all came together, Cold Heart's speech was all about security and protocol, and them not holding back to shoot if need be. She clearly comprehended his intentions at that point.

"Oh, okay. I'm taking it all in properly now, big homie. I'll be sure to keep everything between you and me. I don't assume you trying to come onto me in that type of way anyhow. It's business first with you. You do look good though. But go ahead with what you wanna talk about, bro," Tangee complimented then urged him on.

Cold Heart smiled, took her kind words in stride, then proceeded with what he had to say.

"What you know about the situation between Shay and the dude? The reason I ask is because, I'm trying to determine how I wanna punish that nigga's ass once we finally do catch up with him!" Cold Heart stated as he clenched his teeth and gritted.

"Dude always been a lame, bro! He stayed trying to force Shay to do shit how he saw fit. I never was the one to try and be in their business or anything like that. But Shay would say things to me about how aggressive he would be about everything, especially in trying to make her stop hustling with y'all, and them two do so together," Tangee related.

"Word!"

"Hell yeah, bro! That nigga was a hater, for real!"

"And what type of product is he serving?"

"He a coke dealer. The nigga Kam Rich, is his brother."

"You talkin' 'bout the nigga Kam who got it popping down on Carpenter Street? The Hit Squad, right?" Cold Heart needed clarity.

"Yeah. Them niggaz. Feezy part of that crew."

"Okay, that helps me somewhat know exactly who I need to look for."

"Oh yeah. How 'bout that nut-ass nigga, had the nerve to say something to me like that! Talking 'bout, did Shay mention anything to me of us being in the process of lining up with him, and we three get to the money together," she brought to his attention.

"What!" Cold Heart jarred his head and furrowed his eyebrows in reaction to what was said. "Dude a real clown, ain't he!"

"A *world-class'* Bozo, my nigga! Dude a noodle!"

"And when was this?"

"Probably around the time when we had that last bomb of weed and beans."

"I'm sure he really had something to say once he knew y'all was banging diesel on the block, didn't he?"

"That's probably why he flipped out and put his hands on her, then ran off with our work and money. Shay blasted at his ass though!"

"And I gotta teach her ass how to shoot too. My uncle taught me everything I needed to know about guns and fighting. He was in the military, the Marines."

"Oh yeah. Hopefully you gonna teach us both, because I can use the lessons. And I'm sure to learn a thing or two," Tangee said with a smile and eyeing him in admiration at the same time.

Cold Heart continued to steer the vehicle. They toured the city for a while. He made it his business to ride through the known territory where Feezy's brother Kam, controlled. An attempt was made to spot the violator. He was nowhere to be found. Something had to be done, and fast. It would make it to where Shay and Tangee were no longer in a state of panic behind the threat of him. Dude was bad for business, and could retaliate against anyone he knew from their squad, beginning with Shay when she tried to take him out when he pulled his stunt by taking their material. And now, they were short a couple thousand, along with a few ounces of *Boy*.

I'mma make sure I spank that nigga Feezy real good!" Cold Heart thought with malice in mind. *I might even murk that bitch-ass nigga! Nah! I am gonna whack him! That's the only way to send a message and get my point across! I gotta let niggaz know, BMI is here to stay! We ain't backing down or going anywhere! Period!*

The two made a stop at a *Starbucks*. They both loved Frapps. Also, the night was set in and it was late October. Chilly season was on its way. If all went well, they had intentions to take a Winter vacation to the Poconos. A very beautiful place to see around this time of year.

SIXTEEN

Von got in touch with Monyetta, after a long hiatus between the two. She was happy to hear from him, and he from her. Monyetta wanted to see him. She had an apartment not too far away from her homegirl Ayonna, Monk's sweetheart. Von now got around town in a rental. It was a new model *Dodge Magnum.* That motherfucker could scat like a jet too! It had absolute horsepower. Von had lead in his foot and stayed heavy on the gas pedal. He loved to drive fast and reckless.

He arrived at her place and tapped on the door. She opened to let him in. The sensual voice of the lovely *Mary J. Blige* played at a mature level from the sound system inside her place. The two hugged then tongue kissed like they'd been in a relationship for years. Her body and energy instantly conformed to his touch and tender lips. Von ignited a flame in shorty. One like she'd never had the pleasure to experience before. She closed the door and led the way to a space to sit, holding his hand going towards the direction of the loveseat in the living room. The lights were dim and scented candles burned. Monyetta created a pleasing atmosphere. Not a word had been spoken between the two. They communicated perfectly through silence.

The plan was for them to go out on a date that evening. A dinner and a movie. Monyetta had other things on her mind. She made that obvious upon answering the door with a pair of extra thin female soccer shorts and a see-through top, putting those pretty 34C cup titties of hers on display. Her nipples were hardened and stuck out buggy-eyed through the material of the blouse. They were about the size of the tip of a pinky finger. Her ass-cheeks bulged from beneath the shorts. She had a nice round butt.

Monyetta whispered sweetly into his ear. She was seated to his left.

"Von, can we stay home tonight? Here? And try something new, maybe? My drink got me feeling right. And I wanna get loose, and lose my mind tonight, boo," she expressed, then leaned in to kiss and suck on his neck. His dick stood through his fleece material garment.

Von smiled in delight. "Damn! You are on one, ain't you," he responded.

"*Mmm-hmm,* I am, baby. And ready to let you have your way with me. It's your world, Von. You're the King. '*King Von'* that is."

He continued to smile. The compliment and her willfulness made him feel really good. Something Chloe had seemed to lose sight of was how to cater to him. If not but with words and easiness.

"By the way, what you sipping on?" he asked.

She pointed towards the small bar-like stand at the bottle of *Grey Goose* that sat atop it. Monyetta then reached over to get her tall glass drinking flute. She gave Von a taste, holding and tilting for him, taking a sip herself in the process. Baby girl was really feeling it. The mood was superb.

"A'ight. Cool. We could chill here tonight. I'm with that. But I got one question. How do you plan to keep my attention the whole time I'm here? Because I got **ADHD**, baby! And that shit for real, shorty!" Von let out with a smile and a gentleman's chuckle.

Monyetta lit up with excitement. Her eyes and face glowed. She offered her best response.

"With pills, Grey Goose, and me grinding on top of you in a pleasing slow motion," she related on cue, returning a smile.

"I'm definitely with that. Let's get to it."

Von stood, then began to get naked. Monyetta was faster at it than he. She was already out of the two pieces of clothing. No panties or bra. Her smooth rich chocolate skin looked like the finest of satin the world over. The small waist, thick thighs, and matching titties of hers, fit the height and weight she was in possession of. She had an exotic appearance and unique qualities about herself. Monyetta was top of the line in feminine features.

Von was now naked and stood directly in front of her. His erect dick poked her in the belly. She cooed behind the touch. His plump dick-head was firm and juicy, full of blood flow. It looked like a seasonally ripe tomato. The color, texture, and all. Pre-cum drip. Monyetta giggled at the sight. She leaned over and licked the tip for him.

"Talking about being '*Young and full of cum!* Oh my! Don't worry though. I'mma get as much of the shit out of you tonight as I can, boo. Beginning right now," she assured, then placed her hands on both his arms, indicating for him to take a seat once more. He did so.

Von was half on the couch and half off. Monyetta knelled between his legs on both her knees, grabbing hold of his manhood with both her hands, flipping her hair prior to, and went to work. She took his beef sausage into her mouth in deep throat and held it there in that position. The 19-year-old sex appealing sensation, had enough experience sucking on a dick to please the 17-year-old ambitious street thug. She knew what to do, when to do it, and how to do it while in the act. Practice made improvement.

She then eased up slowly, thick full lips of hers locked around the shaft and pulling, going back down without breaking the rhythm or flow. Monyetta picked up the pace and bobbed up and down, slowing in between with the pulling, and lowering back down the shaft in the same way.

Clutching with both hands continuously and squeezing to inflate the head, she rapidly agitated on the dick up and down while jerking with thorough intensity along the shaft. Monyetta spit on Von's cannon to get it slick just the way she liked it. The both of them locked eyes momentarily. Von then leaned his head back into the cushion of the seat to continue in enjoying the pleasure he was receiving.

Monyetta took the tongue and swiped upward, from his balls, along the line of his urethra, and arriving at the tip of the head. Shock waves of sensation shot through Von's body. He was at his climax. His dick erupted cum, sputtering his release all about her lips and in her mouth. She attempted to catch as much as she could of his love juice, swallowing what was inside already.

"Ooh, Von! You do good, boo-boo. You taste good too," Monyetta said between swallows. She was beginning to blow his mind.

Being the more sexually aggressive of the two, Monyetta mounted Von's lap and situated her knees on the seat. She grabbed hold of his dick and held steady, placing the head at the entrance of her love nest. She was already extra wet. His entry wasn't difficult whatsoever. Monyetta was determined to keep Von's gun up and strong. That proved to not be a hard thing. He was a young vigorous wolf and built to go. And go, they'd done, all throughout the night. She made him cum three times on separate occasions. And her, she kept her count a secret from him, only telling him to *"use his imagination"* to guess how many times her spring water flowed.

The two were now locked in and ready to take things to the next level, then higher with what they were set to build upon. The chemistry was unique between them. The sky was the limit. Not the everyday struggles of life.

***

Von did something he had no intention of doing. He'd stayed all night over at Monyetta's. When he finally did wake up, he found himself all alone and still naked in her Queen sized bed. She was gone. But left him a letter and a plate of breakfast in the microwave. Her letter read:

Dear Von,
Good morning King! (smile). Didn't want to wake you, as you're so handsome in sleep the same as awake. I made you breakfast. Hope you like my cooking. Anyway, I had class. I'm a student at Temple University. I take journalism and also trying to be a Public Service Worker (Municipal Politician). Hopefully you'll be there when I return at 3 p.m. If not, I understand. Do what you have to do. Just don't have me waiting too long before you call again. Last night was amazing. You satisfied my desire. Scratched that inner itch I had. Nothing like the second time around shall be, I'm sure. Take care!

He smiled behind reading her words. She was different. A special type.

Von got dressed and exited. He headed home, to the house he shared with Chloe. She wasn't there. Her work day had begun. A bit surprised he hadn't gotten a call from her blasting him for not bringing his ass home the night before. He'd fucked up and forgotten to turn his phone back on. No doubt about it, Chloe was due to give him an ear full the moment she was to lay eyes on him. There was no rush to power his phone at that point.

He had remembered something. *Damn!* he thought to himself. *Me and mom are supposed to go see pop this weekend, I almost forgot. I've gotta get in touch with sis too to see if she wants to go with us.*

Von pulled out a second phone he had and was intent on using that to call his mom and Kidada. No matter what, he was not ready to face Chloe. Not just yet. Dude wasn't up for the bullshit that early in the a.m.

He took a shower, got dressed, and headed out the door, en route to the other mom's house, Big Momma Edna. He had money and work stashed there.

During the drive, he called his mother.

"This is Lillian," she answered.

"Mom! This Vonnnie," he responded.

"Boy! I didn't know who you were. What happened to your other number?"

"I still got it—"

"—*Okay!*" she let out, waiting to know why he wasn't using it.

Lilly had a general idea what was going on. She knew her son and had played the same game before herself.

"Okay, what?" Von let out with a laugh. He was still a little boy in certain regards. "I'll turn it back on later today."

"After you lie to that pretty girlfriend of yours about where your ass was last night, huh," Lilly said in response and laughed. "I'm not gonna lie for you with this one, Vonnie."

"You won't have to, mom. I got a good one already set and ready to go."

"*Mmm-hmm!* I bet you do. Anyway, what you want?"

"What time we leaving tomorrow?"

"At our regular time, son. Our flight leaves at ten in the morning. We gotta be there by nine. You know how TSA be," Lilly said to her son.

"Oh, okay. Kiki going with us too?"

"Yeah. She coming over tonight."

"A'ight. I ain't seen her in a while now. Can't wait to see her again."

"Well, you will in the morning. Now momma gotta get back to work. I'll talk to you later, son. I love you," Lilly last said to her only born before ending the call.

Von smiled to himself yet again about the truth his mother called him out on. Lilly basically revealed her honest thought about Von's girlfriend, Chloe. She admired Chloe's beauty and felt that she and Von made a nice ideal couple. They had gone through a stretch of high school together, and now live under the same roof. However, Von had other things on his mind, and worked hard in the streets and between the two women he juggled, to have the type of life he wanted. One the same as his father and grandfather. Big and Little Hound.

He arrived at his granny's home in the Germantown section. Mrs. Edna was there in the house tidying up the place. Her and her cat, Prixie, a thick fur female Persian, who was treated and taken care of as if she was a child by the elderly lady.

"Hey, Nana. How you doing this morning?" Von greeted as he approached, and gave his grandmother a hug and a kiss.

Mrs. Edna was draped in a full apron from neck to knees. She was wiping down the coffee table and other objects.

"Hello, Vonnie! Grandma been okay. I can't seem to remember where I sit things down nowadays. But I'mma be better, I'm sure. Good Lord willing," the grandmother responded. "And where have you been lately? I ain't seen your behind in a couple of days now."

"I was at my girlfriend's house. I'm between her and here throughout the week."

"So you got a girlfriend that's too good to pay your Nana a visit, to let me see what she looks like, huh," Mrs. Edna expressed her feelings.

"Why you say it like that, Nana? I've brought her here before. You were asleep though. It was after eight that night. But, since you mentioned it like that, I'll be sure to bring her by to meet you personally. Next week."

"Please do. Lilly spoke about how good-looking the girl is. She likes her," she said and smiled at the gleeful look Von had dashed about his face.

The old lady continued in her duties with Prixie looking on. Von went to his room in the house. He began to pack up for the trip to Florida that was upon him. While doing so, he took a pause long enough to power up his main phone.

Others from the crew may had called or texted. He knew for sure Chloe had. But he was ready to lie his way out of ii. Something any young dude would do.

SEVENTEEN

Two Days Later . . .

Now down in the *Sunshine State* and at the federal Correctional Institute of Coleman to visit his father, Von, his mother, and sister by another, sat in the multi-purpose area of the facility to await the man of the hour, Little Hound Savage.

He appeared, dressed in federal garb, starched and pressed in brown khaki pants and shirt, then moving himself in the direction of his kids and ex-girlfriend. He and Lilly maintained a platonic relationship and vowed to keep in touch for as long as need be. But Little Hound had intention to get a young lady once he were to be set free in the next five years ahead. He wanted someone who was half his age (he was 41) and full of energy. The former kingpin wanted to do nothing but have fun and live life to the fullest once released. Lilly didn't want to be left out, and had in mind to do all necessary to have Little Hound pay her some form of attention, no matter the amount.

"Hello-hello-hello, my lovely and handsome people," Little Hound said, displaying a bright smile and full of flair. He had his arms spread wide to hug them all, beginning with Lilly, then Kidada, and finally Von, in that order.

Hound and Lilly kissed as they embraced. A level of affection was present between them.

"Hey daddy," Kidada said, upon her turn to hug.

"Hey baby. Daddy miss you all."

"What's up, Pop," said Von. They dapped up each other as they hugged tightly.

"You growing fast, son. Almost my height," the six foot-four Little Hound expressed.

They all took a seat at that point, and went deep into conversation over all that were currently going on in their lives. Von had a lot to talk about with his father, but needed to do so in private. Hound let him know he was in the process of buying another cell phone. They'd became a valuable piece of contraband in the prison system around the time. Hound had to have one.

The family trio carried on gracefully throughout the time they enjoyed together that day. The following day would be the same but probably more or less in-depth.

**

Meanwhile . . .

Chloe had only gotten a text message from Von before he'd left for Florida. She hadn't had the chance to see him or talk to him since that Wednesday afternoon, three days prior. But she held no anger about it, nor did she attempt to call or reply by text. Chloe simply allowed him the leeway to continue and show her what he had intentions to do. This was the thing she wanted. At least on a temporary basis. The necessary space to think, breathe, have a look in hindsight, and even see other people until they were to come to the conclusion on exactly what they wanted to do. She spoke to Rosa more about the drama she and Von were experiencing. Chloe went to visit her cousin at her place.

"Rosa, how about, Von didn't come home Wednesday night. He had never done that before," Chloe said, now seated on the couch.

"Well, boys are gonna be boys, Chloe," Rosa responded. "He may not mean anything by it. Probably was out hustling all that night. They did lose a lot of money, didn't they?"

"He never told me how much was lost. But it had to be a lot. You might be right. He probably was out trying to make some money, because we need it."

"Did you at least ask him where he was?" Rosa asked to make her reason.

"No. I didn't. I should've though."

"No harm, no foul, Chloe. And I honestly don't believe Von got anything going on other than trying to rebuild from the loss he'd taken. He's a good dude, Chloe. Give him a break. Besides, your guilty conscience may be getting the best of you," Rosa stated.

"Guilty conscience!" Chloe retorted. "Why you say it like that?"

"I'm only stating the obvious. You know I gotta keep it real with you, no matter what."

"I know you do. And I respect that. We all need somebody to tell us the truth, no matter how harsh it may sound."

"And I'm that 'somebody' you got to do that for you," Rosa replied quickly.

The two Latina cousins laughed at the remark Rosa bluntly made as Chloe knew she was the one to speak her mind. Rosa never held back in her words nor bit her tongue.

"Just do you, Chloe. And don't worry about what your dude got going on. Don't ask. Don't tell. If you don't see anything, don't go looking for it."

"I got you on that. But look, enough with the small talk. Let me tell you about the time I had with my ex, Raul . . . ."

They continued to talk a little longer before getting into Chloe's Car her dad blessed her with as a graduation gift and went riding. The both of them were ready to smoke some weed and drink a little alcohol. It was a Saturday and the clubs were calling their names. It was time to party and have some fun.

Raul had Chloe on his mind heavily and wanted to spend more time with her. He would make it his business to contact her the same day. The more they were to stay in touch, the closer their hearts would be brought back together. Things always seemed to go that way.

EIGHTEEN

One Week Later . . .

Shayla and Tangee were busy getting to the money over at Shayla's sister house, Cori. There was a lot of foot traffic through the streets; mostly kids that evening, due to it being Halloween, and trick-or-treating going on. The girls were posted on the stoop and not in the house dealing product. They didn't want the aggravation of having to get up and open the door each time there was a knock. So they'd done the logical thing and gone outside to know for certain if or not it was a kid or a customer.

The weather was cool. They both had on a jacket and other proper clothing. Their guns was close by too. Situated in their purses and strapped to their shoulders. The reason to fear robbery was in air as well. There were a lot of people draped in costumes and masks terrorizing the city all day, and doing capers or even hits like it wasn't nothing. The majority of the action being committed was being done by various crews and cliques. But the two felt there wasn't a thing to fear, so long as they were on their own territory.

"Shay, I'm hungry. You?" Tangee asked.

"Hell yeah. I'm hungry myself. What you wanna eat?" Shayla responded.

"I can go for some Chinese food. You know I love my hard fried wings and shrimp fried rice."

"Mmm-hmm! Me too bitch."

"—And it's your turn to go this round Shay. I went to the last time," Tangee reminded.

Shayla exhaled, but then knew she had no choice but to give in to making a run to the Chinese cafe they often ordered food. It was only a block down the street, walking distance from where they were.

Little to their knowledge, they'd been the topic of a conversation. A target was put on them. All that was left to do was to track them, catch them down bad some type of way, and run down on them in robbery, or if need be, a hit. The two had pissed off someone who was looking to make waves themselves, and felt offended by something that happened to have taken place. Halloween was the perfect cover-up to get back at the two females, the angry person thought. Others had been paid to do the job.

"I'mma go for us, Tangee. I was hoping you would, but fuck it. It was on me anyway. Hold it down while I'm gone, a'ight. I'll be back shortly," Shayla said.

"No doubt bitch. I'm out here."

Shayla stepped off and headed to the eatery.

Once there, She placed the order and waited. It was a small place. Standing room only. No seating. One other person was present. A female. Older than Shay. Looked to be in her late thirties, possibly coming down from a high and hungrier than a grizzly fresh from hibernation.

Not even a minute after Shay had entered and placed the order, in walked three costume-clad individuals. They were dressed from head to toe as "green goblins." The faces of them all were covered as well. Each had a purse and a sassy walk. They were female maybe, or feminine homosexuals posing as such. Shayla didn't know. A few things stood out to her. Everyone had on sneakers and they all were tied tightly, while posturing in an aggressive way with body language. One blocked the door and the other two ran up to Shayla.

It was a stick-up.

"Give that shit up, bitch!" The apparent leader of the trio spat while drawing down on Shayla with a Glock .40 black in color.

The other of the two had also pulled out a pistol and then slapped Shayla side the head with it.

Whop!

It was a metal .380 with a black handle. Shayla went down on one knee from the blow. She then scrambled with her hands trying to reach inside her purse to withdraw her gun.

Whop!

The partner in crime to the lead female goon smacked Shayla once more, but this time, with a sock that had heavy objects in it. Lead ball bearings tightly secured by a knot on the sock. Shayla went down to the floor face first. She'd been dazed badly by the blow.

Shayla planted both hands on the floor and was now on all fours struggling to get to her feet. The lead green goblin then yanked Shayla's purse away from her and kicked the girl in the face. Shayla went back down once more and tried to recover. The robber had enough time to dig in their purse and withdraw another object. A razor.

Upon raising up high and coming down at an angle forcefully, the assailant hit Shayla across the face, producing a deep ugly nasty gash. Blood instantly spring forth. She bled badly.

"That's for Feezy, bitch! And you better be glad I ain't popped your ass and put you away for good behind shooting at my people, hoe! Next time, stay in your lane before you end up dead!

Whop!

The second of the two doing the robbery, whacked Shayla on the head yet again before they turned and walked out quickly.

Shayla dropped face-first to the floor for a second time, in a pool of her own blood. Her ex had clapped back before she had the chance to get at him again. There was nothing she could do to even things out. Feezy bombed first.

***

Thirty minutes passed and Shayla hadn't returned.

Damn! It ain't never taken Shay this long to go the Chinese cafe! What the fuck she got going on! Tangee thought to herself. She then pulled out her phone and called Shay's number. Straight to voice mail.

Tangee tried yet again. Same results. She texted. No speedy reply as Shayla would normally do. Worry begin to set in at the point., especially so with the sound and sight of an ambulance now passing by, headed in the direction where the cafe was located.

What the fuck! Tangee's pessimistic mind-state caused her to claim. She got to her feet and fast-stepped towards the place, calling Shayla's number yet again throughout the walk.

Once there, she spotted the medics patching Shayla's face and applying pressure. Blood seems to be everywhere.

"Shay, what the fuck! Who did this to you!" Tangee said loudly as she approached her friend.

"Three bitches dressed as green monsters, Tangee. They got me. Took my purse, hit me on the head with something hard, then cut me. Stinking bitches! Feezy sent them. The hoe who sliced me said he was her people."

"You didn't see who they were?"

"Nah. I couldn't. They all had on a mask and their faces were blocked out."

Tangee then called Cold Heart to notify him of what had happened, being he'd last told her he was over their security.

He answered. Tangee then explained. She was in a hysterical fit while doing so. The call ended.

Tangee then got into the ambulance with Shayla and was about to ride to the hospital with her. Then suddenly, she came to the realization that she had a gun and bundles of heroin on her, and they would likely be questioned by the cops once there, being that a crime had occurred. Tangee got out and made her way towards the apartment they lived. She would get Cold Heart to take her there once he arrived, then the both of them—-Shayla and Tangee—would make it their business to inform Cold Heart who was responsible. They would be in a need to up the ante in trying to track down Feezy , so to finally put his lights out to prevent him from causing more collateral damage. Dude had to be stopped.

***

Three Days Later . . .

Shayla was now out of the hospital and healing from the face slashing she'd suffered. There were well over hundred and fifty stitches sewn in to close the deep wound of her face. The cut stretched from her left earlobe to the area just above her top lip, and it was about a half-inch deep. A permanent scar was sure to take from her any and all of the remaining self-esteem she hadnonce having a look in the mirror. She broke down into tears in doing so and had to be consoled by Tangeee.

"I hope that punk motherfucka' Feezy, die, Tangee! That nigga ain't shit! He deserves to be killed for the shit he has done and had somebody do to me! Look at my motherfuckin' face!" Shayla cried out, tears streaming down her cheeks. Shayla had anger in her mind and hatred in her heart. She knew life would never be the same.

"We gonna get that nigga, Shay! I promise you, he's gonna slip up and come out of hiding, and then, we'll have the chance to get his ass. Don't worry. We tied in with the right people. And our homies 'bout that issue too. I know they are," Tangee comforted. She remembered Von mentioning to them that they were in business with his people. Dudes whose names held weight in the streets, in infamy and legacy.

No matter how grim and unpleasant Shayla's realty was, life still had to go on, and product needed to be sold to keep the movement flowing and money coming in. Tangee was up in sells and nearly out of product while Shayla was behind. Indeed, the customer base had expanded and a craving for the particular product they sold was in demand. All there was to do for them was to be present there at Cori's house and deliver. Tangee took up the slack for Shayla, and Cori worked a pack off when not doing hair. Shayla had time off to get herself together. However, when emotionally strong and not ashamed of the scar, she would be required to return to work banging packs.

Von eventually made his way to see Shayla to show his support an assure her that he stood by her side. She appreciated the love and kind words he expressed. The two spoke privately. Shayla had malice in mind and felt the need to tell Von exactly what she thought should happen to Feezy or *anybody* in his family, for that matter. She truly wanted that nigga dead!

Von couldn't take his eyes off the scar that had now altered the beauty that Shayla once possessed. He'd once seen her as a very pretty girl who was simply caught up in the streets. That was no longer a thing. The sympathy he'd developed for her grew with each and every thought of how he'd feel had his sister (his dad had one daughter) suffered a cut that serious, and what he'd do about it. Von related the thought to Shayla. The two talked.

"Von!" Shayla, let out while intently staring him in the eyes as they sat on the edge of the bed in Cori's house.

Von shook his head in disgust at the despair he observed in Shayla's eyes and at the pain in her voice.

"We can't let that nigga get away with this. I want him dead, bro! Y'all need to find that nigga and pop his ass! On sight! No matter where he's at, he needs to get it!" Shayla vented, now clutching the handle of Tangee's gun they both shared to protect themselves. He can't live to brag about this, bro! On my dead baby that I miscarried by him, he can't! And I mean that shit!"

"Calm down a little, Shay. I don't need you to get all worked up. We gonna handle the business for you. My word. Just give us time to find him. He can't be that hard to locate, I'm sure."

"Look if y'all can't get him, make his momma or sister pay instead," Shay declared

Von gave her a look like he never had. He knew how serious she was and how badly she wanted blood. But going out to harm innocent people wasn't on his agenda.

"We can't do that, Shay. The mom and sister did no wrong."

"—Yeah they did! By giving birth to the motherfucka' and by being a sibling!" Shayla quickly responded.

Von shook his head once more to express his thoughts behind her words. He wished like hell she didn't speak in that way. If Shayla were to go out and do something to Feezy's people on her own accord, then that would be on her. It wouldn't fall on no one else if her outcome don't turn out the way she perceived it would, or if she gets harmed or killed in the process, but if she was able to, he would do his best to talk her into letting them handle the situation. He had it in mind to run it by Monk, to see what he has to suggest should be done.

Cori then walked into the room to be a part of the conversation the two had going on. She'd just finished doing a client's hair and had a moment to speak with them. She saw the worry and anger on the face of her sister and then offered a hug to try and comfort her more.

"Von, we gotta find that clown-ass nigga Feezy, and make him pay for this shit, bro," Cori said.

"And we will. Ain't no doubt about that. We gotta find him first," Von responded to Cori.

"I told him we need to go to his momma's house to look for him and if he ain't here, make that bitch pay instead," Shayla vented more.

Cori looked on at Von to imply that she was in agreement with the idea her sister had in mind.

Von returned the same expression. Neither said a word. He felt it was time for him to leave and come back when the two weren't so pissed. He was there to pick up the money they had for him, in addition to checking on Shayla.

"I'mma holla at my people about this, and do what he says to do from there. But I'm more than sure that the nigga Feezy, gonna show his face at some point, and then, we do him on the spot. A'ight," he said to them to bring some sense of calm.

"Just do something, Von. Because Shayla is not gonna be right in any type of way until something is done," Cori let out.

"Again, my word, we on it. Y'all please let us do what we do and allow the time to make it right. Now, I gotta go. You two be easy," Von spoke, gave the two a hug and a kiss on the forehead, then walked out.

When he and Cori hugged, she slyly caressed him on his manhood and smiled. She'd done it without Shayla noticing what was going on. Cori didn't want to offend her sister with her lustful advancements on Von. And he didn't make any noise about it. Only let her have her way. She was attractive to Von, but a little too loose and wild in her ways for the type of taste he had. However, she could be useful. At least that's how he viewed her. Use her for something.

NINETEEN

Four Weeks Later...

It was the day after Thanksgiving, the national shopping day known as *"Black_Friday,"* and a day Lilly loved to go out and spend money like she didn't have any sense. She and Von enjoyed time with Mrs. Edna all the day before, as the three of them ate dinner and enjoyed one another the entire holiday. A week prior, the they'd went to Atlantic city to celebrate Von's birthday. His girlfriend, Chloe, was there with them as well, and they had a good time in the gambling haven along the eastern seaboard of the United States. Lilly became attached to Chloe throughout the trip and wanted the two of them to spend more time together. What better way to begin than by a full-day shopping extravaganza through the city on Black Friday? Lilly contacted Chloe. She'd gotten the new number while in AC.

"Hello!" Chloe answered. She had Lilly locked in the contacts by name.

"Hey Chloe! Good morning. How you doing?" Lilly greeted. The time was 9 a.m.

Von had already dressed and left for the day. He and Cold Heart had to get with Monk, and they were to have lunch with Drip.

"I'm doing good, Miss Lilly. What about you?"

"I've been good myself. Ready to get out and do some shopping? Are you up yet?"

"I am. Just need to get dressed. I've been expecting your call."

"Oh, you have," Lilly responded. Now flattered in a way. "Well, I've made it. And I'm ready to get out and shop girl, before we miss out on everything. What time you want me to pick you up?"

"You can come on now. I'll be ready by the time you get here," Chloe informed.

"I'm on my way."

"Okay. See you soon, Miss Lilly."

"Okay baby," Lilly lastly let out, concluding the call.

Twenty minutes later, she was out front of the house where her son and Chloe lived, in northeast. Lilly texted to let the young pretty teenage sensation know she was there.

The weather was chilly and required winter wear material. Chloe had on a pair of tan colored tight fitting thick fabric stretch material pants, brown boots made of a wool-like hide that had fur around the top and went halfway up her shin, a thick wool coat to match the boots, a scarf, and a knitted toboggan hat to match the coat and boots. The pants conformed to the figure of her body. She had a *Coke* bottle shape, with thick thighs and cat eyes. Very pleasing to look at, to say the least.

Chloe got into the car. "Hey Miss Lilly," she let out with a smile then hugged her new friend.

"Hey girl. You look nice. I'm hoping my son got what it takes to hold on to you because you gonna have all kinds of men trying to snatch you from him," Lilly complimented, then added a smile to further express her admiration. She then pulled off.

Chloe smiled herself, as she were provided a boost of confidence to her already near the level of arrogant attitude. "Von has what it takes. I just don't believe he wants me like that any longer. That boy doesn't pay me any attention and offer no more quality time," she related to Lilly.

Lilly was taken back to the beginning phases of the relationship between her and Von's father. She thought maybe it would be cool to offer some counsel and advice to

Chloe, being that it was apparently clear, that the only thing which could possibly have Von's attention more than the sexy big booty naturally long-haired Puerto Rican bombshell, was the game itself. All Lilly needed to know now was what product her boy sold. And if anything, she knew Chloe had to know. If so, Lilly had no intent to interfere with what Von had going on. She would continue to let him make his own decision and live his life how he saw fit.

"Are you for real? What in the world that boy got going on, Chloe. Is he dealing?" Lilly asked.

Chloe looked at Lilly, unsure if or not it was okay to answer what she'd asked.

"You can talk to me, baby. I've been you before. Me and Von's father started out the same way as you two. That was the reason why I asked. That way, I could coach you to the best of my ability. I know for a fact Von likes you. And, if he is not paying you attention, that only means he's too preoccupied with the streets. Don't let that bother you. He introduced you to me for a reason. That has never happened before."

"You not gonna tell Von what we talk about, are you?"

"No! Why would I want to betray that trust so fast, baby? If anything, the both of us gonna have to stick together to protect him. From himself more than likely. The cops or whoever else for that matter. It's best that we talk to establish a solid rapport. I don't have but a very small circle of friends anyway. Two to be exactly," Lilly related.

"He's dealing, Miss LIly."

"I should've known that. The apple didn't fall too far from the family tree. His father's family that is."

"I'm aware. Me and him went to meet your mother already. I've never met anybody on his dad's side of the family."

"That was similar to the way his dad treated me. He then eventually took me to meet his father and that side of the family. So I'm sure Von will do the same with you. But, Vonnie is taking care of y'all bills and everything, right?"

"He was the one who gave me the money to have us move into the place where we live now. Von does his part. He just isn't as affectionate as he use to be. That's what I want him to get back to. That version of him I love most."

"I know that's right, because ain't nothing better to a woman than being with a man who she loves and knows he loves her," Lilly stated in a convincing way.

The two continued to speak the each other in a comfortable fashion as their acquaintance began to gain strength. Their conversation involved a few things related to past relationships. To Chloe's surprise, Lilly mentioned the reality of the situation about what she was experiencing with Bernard and her wanting out of what they had. Maybe that was a play to get Chloe to reveal what she possibly had going on with her ex, which she made known, but only spoke about Raul giving her money and nothing more. Lilly wasn't slow by no means, and she knew there was more to it, but did not dig in.

"Boys will be boys and girls have to be girls, you follow my drift, young lady," Lilly said to Chloe.

Chloe herself had heard the phrase from Rosa in times past.

"I'm looking to be your friend and somebody you can talk to. Von loves you and speaks highly of you. This is one of the main reasons why I'm making it my business to connect with you."

"And I appreciate you too, I needed this type of bond with somebody from his family. And I love Von as well. I only need for him to be mature about what we have, and about where we're trying to go in life together, if this be something he wants," Chloe said in relation to how she felt about their relationship.

"Your ex-boyfriend must be older than you?" Lilly asked.

"He is."

"That explains the reason why you have a need for the type of security in a man you're familiar with. But, you have to give Von some time to come to that realization. I'm sure he will. You may be the first serious girlfriend he's ever had."

"I believe that I am. At least that was how he put it to me. So, I have to be."

"And I want to help you come to know that it's a process. But eventually, you'll have it how you want it. Just continue to do what you do and be who you are. Ain't no doubt in my mind if or not you mean well. I know you do. And I'mma be sure to let Von know how much you do as well."

"Please do. Because it's like I don't exist to him any longer until he wants to have sex. And I hate that, Miss Lilly. I really do."

"That's all of our boyfriends, Chloe. I can relate. But I'll make it my business to get through to him to do better by you. Okay."

"Okay, Miss Lilly. And thank you."

"Absolutely."

The two made it to their first stop. It was at the Franklin Mills Mall in northeast Philly. Not too far from Chloe and Von's house. From there, Lilly hit I-95 and headed to downtown Center City Philly. Their shopping then intensified, and also became more high-ended.

Chloe was sure to buy Von a few items she knew he'd like. Lilly did the same for Jamar, not Bernard. The mention of her personal dealings to Chloe was more so how she was busy trying to do away with one boyfriend (Bernard) and replace him with another (Jamar), by ignoring the first and denying him the pleasure of sex, while showering the second with gifts of affection, and giving him the pussy at every opportunity available.

Chloe took Lilly's words and behavior to be a sign of what was going on with Von, by him ignoring her, and not seeming to be interested in having sex with her of late. Little did she know, Monyetta had worked her magic, and Von's attention shifted. Chloe now had stiff competition. She would have to re-prioritize what she thought and felt for both the guys in her life. She had serious work cut out for her.

***

One Week Later . . .

Chloe was hanging out with her cousin Rosa again on this day. The two was invited to a party held by another Puerto Rican female they both were cool with. It was the girl's birthday, and the celebration was held at a local Spanish club that catered to a pop and reggaeton theme of events for Latin Millennials. The Dominguez chicks loved to be apart of this type of crowd and environment. They were determined to have drinks, smoke a little weed, and let loose in having fun. It had been a few months since they'd enjoyed a chance to parlay and socialize, but now, the time was at hand, and there they were, on a Saturday night, doing their thing.

Now two drinks and one blunt in, both Chloe and Rosa were approached by two dudes they know from the neighborhood; two Puerto Rican cats who'd been down for a while as friends, and now on the prowl, looking to fuck something and get their dicks wet. It was Chino and Peppi.

Chino appealed to Chloe now in mature age than he had in the years prior. He dressed better, had a five o'clock shadow of a beard, a nice haircut with a part in it, and money now. He'd made something out of himself in the world. He owned a clothing store and was doing good business-wise. He was an athletically gifted guy, and held a brilliant mind. Chino cared about his body and was into health and nutrition. He stepped to her while Peppi went to Rosa.

"Well, what you know! If it ain't the lovely Jennifer Lopez, two-point O," said Chino. He spoke in their native tongue.

Chloe smiled pleasingly at the compliment. It felt good to be recognized and admired in that way, and by a guy she could consider. If not but on a one-night stand. Von neglected her romantically. And romanticism was a vital element necessary to have the keys to her heart.

"Hey, Chino! You always know the right thing to say to me, don't you?" Chloe responded.

His smile had longevity. She was mesmerized by the change he'd grown into.

"Always baby. Always. You know you're the candy of my eye. The sweetness I can never get enough of. Can I have a hug or something? Damn."

He spread his arms and Chloe was the one compelled by his appearance and energy to step forward and wrap her arms around him. She then kissed him on the neck. He had a tattoo of a pair of red-colored lips there. Chloe's matched.

"How was that?" Chloe asked. "You now have an actual pair of sexy lips planted on your neck to go along with that tat, Chino. You're a lucky guy."

"Indeed, I am. Indeed I am, pretty girl. If only you know how happy I am to see you. I feel like it's *my* birthday." Chino expressed.

Chloe blushed, then kissed him on the neck once more. The alcohol and weed definitely had her feeling good that night. The intoxication behind both—-cocktails and Purple Haze–gave her a sensational effect like she never felt. Chloe's eyes sparkled and her face glowed. Her body language and way of expressing the feeling experienced inside told Chino all he needed to know. But simply getting the pussy and having a sexual affair with her, wouldn't be enough to satisfy the long pinned-up infatuation he had for Chloe. The difference was, he had control now, and the upper hand.

Chloe was all up close and in Chino's face, gleaming like she was starstruck and in love with him. She viewed the guy as if he was the man who was supposed to have been her future husband who'd gotten away from her to be with some other female. Chloe was determined not to let such happen for a second time. It'll be over her dead body before she does.

"So, who you got in your life now, Chino?" Chloe asked. "How *many* females you got, I should ask?" she corrected herself.

"I'm not necessarily in a committed relationship. That's on purpose, so I can see who I wanna see, and do what I wanna do. I love being single. It's better for business this way. What about you? Raul still there?"

"Actually, we broke up nearly a year ago."

"—So you're single now?" Chino asked.

"I'm about like you, not necessarily single in that sense. I'm involved with someone. A younger guy I'd met before graduating high school.

"Congratulation to you on that," Chino complimented, then dug into his pocket and pulled out a roll of money. He gave Chloe $500 in cash and told her to come by his clothing store down on South Street, a high-traffic tourist destination many go shopping, and he would allow her to have $500 in clothing to go along with the money he'd given her.

"Thank you, Chino. You're such a caring guy," she said, then leaned in to kiss him on the lips. He tilted his head to the side and posed so to be pecked on the cheek instead,

"Nah-nah, Chloe. The only person who'll have the pleasure to kiss me on the lips will be the woman I'mma have in my life I'll be looking to marry. But no matter what, me and you will always be good friends. I'mma always have a thing for you. Will that change and evolve into something deeper? I don't know. I Can't say. Only time will tell. And we'll have to spend time together to come to a conclusion about which direction we may be able to go. You understand what I'm saying to you?"

I do. And everything you're saying makes a lot of sense to me as well. But what I wanted to say was, the guy who

I'm with, we going through something at the moment. And hopefully, you and I can go out on a date sometime soon, and explore the possibility of what *we* could have," she stated, pointing back and forth between him and herself. "And on the type of life that could be established between us."

Chino smiled at how well Chloe articulated. "You still have a way with words and on how to communicate your feelings, I see."

"My language arts classes paid off. And hopefully, reconnecting tonight will too," she said with a high level of confidence.

They continued to carry on their in-depth conversation. Rosa and Peepi did the same. From the looks of things, it was headed in the direction of all four of them possibly checking into hotel rooms that night and getting their freak on, an occasion Chloe could definitely go for, being she was now hot between the legs and wet in the panties behind the sex appeal Chino gave off. She wanted to fuck, and began to throw the pussy at him in the erotic and sensual dance moves she groove to on him. Chino played his part and let the energy lead the way to wheresoever the two were to end up that night, and that wasn't a difficult scenario to figure out.

The four kept each other company throughout the time of the party. The 11 o'clock hour was upon them, and Chloe had let Von know she'd be back home by 11:30 no later than 12. She maintained her word in mind and didn't want to do anything to shift the blame on her regarding the problems of their relationship. Chloe did have a little room in-between to cheat on her commitment she had with Von though. And the best part about it was that, he wouldn't know a thing if she so chose to fuck another dude.

And what he doesn't know, won't hurt him, Chloe thought to herself.

"Chino," she called out his name and whispered into his ear.

He had his head over her right shoulder as she grind on him.

"*Mmm-hmm!* I'm listening. Talk to me Chloe," he responded, then nipped her on the neck with his lips.

"I'm trying to be with you tonight before we go our separate ways. How do you feel about that?"

"I feel good about it. What are we waiting on? And what exactly are you trying to do? For how long, I meant?"

"I'm trying to fuck! And I can't spend the whole night with you. So a quickie would have to work," she said.

This clarified what Chino wanted to know from her.

"Now *that* part . . . Is how I like for you to talk to me from here on out, okay."

"Absolutely."

Chino then held Chloe's hand and headed out the door. He had a Chevy Tahoe in the parking lot, black in color. There was no need for him to have Peppi know what he had going on or what he was up to. Peppi had a vehicle himself and arrived at the party alone. Chino did have Chloe to let Rosa know she'd be back shortly.

There was no need for the two to get a hotel suite for what they had the intentions on doing. Chino's S.U.V. was good enough to handle their business in, enjoy each other while at it, then return to the party. This became exactly what they would do.

Once in his ride, the two drove off and went to a location not too far away. Chloe had familiarity with the location. Chino kept condoms on hand, towels, and other freshening materials in one of the gym bags he had available. And Chloe, had baby wipes and other feminine products in her purse, to properly clean up with, if the need came up to relieve herself using the bathroom there at the party. It all worked out to the advantage of them both. She got what she wanted, and he took advantage of all that was offered to him. All is well that ends well, and everyone benefited the most by connecting once more that night. However, Rosa kept her composure and didn't give in to Peppi sexually as he hoped. They did exchange phone numbers and had intentions to keep in touch with each other. Rosa had someone else and other things in mind. All she was waiting on was the opportunity to pursue the guy whom she wanted to throw herself at. The moment was nearing.

TWENTY

Drip was in the city again away from the home he owned over in Montgomery County. He and his real estate team and property developing partners were out and about reviewing and surveying sites. He himself was also busy handling business, making moves, and collecting money from the four distributors who sold his heroin product for him. His brother, Monk, was one of the four. Monk's territory was North Philly, and the other three capos had south, southwest, and one was located in the suburbs, a white dude by the name Harley.

The day was a Monday, and the time was nearing 4:00 p.m. Drip had his driver and bodyguard-chauffeur steer the new modeled Range Rover about the city. His name was, Bruce Dillion, but also went by the name, *"Body,"* short for *"Body-Boy,"* a moniker he'd earned in the military, the Marines. Body did a tour in Somalia in *Operation Gothic Serpent*, and Iraq. He and Drip had been good homies since fifth grade.

Drip wanted a meeting between his four distros first; then with Von, and he also wanted to finally meet Cold Heart, so he could make a personal assessment of the young hitter who'd done such a nice job taking out a problem he faced in Playboy Johnson. Everybody except Monk, Von, and Cold Heart, would all meet at different times in the same location; Drips penthouse he owned in downtown Center City Philly. He paid 1.3 million for the rest haven, over a five-year period of mortgage payments. Drip was a serious-minded Savage boss, and had it going on in multiple layers of his enterprise. His foundation was solid.

Monk had already contacted Von earlier in the day to let him know what the lick read, and for him and Cold Heart to be at his spot above the game room at a specific Time. They were there.

"What it do, fam," Von greeted upon Monk opening to let the two in.

"What's good, fam. How you? You and Cold Heart?" Monk returned, then dapped them up and let the duo inside.

"Nice crib, Monk," Cold Heart complimented. "You living good homie. I wanna have something like this one day. Damn sure do," he let out upon his observation of the apartment converted to a studio.

"You like this spot, Cold Heart?" Monk asked.

"Hell yeah, I do! This motherfucka' all that, homie! It looks like a studio in a way."

"Shit, it *is* my studio, bro. You spit bars or something nigga?" Monk responded with a smile.

"I do a little something. I ain't *Beans* (Beanie Sigel) or *Black Thought* (from the Roots) or one of the main steam-rapping niggaz who made a living doing their thing. But, I know how to flow," Cold Heart stated.

"Well . . . when we get back from seeing bro, I'mma see what you can do, my nigga."

"A'ight. We can do that. No doubt, I'm with it."

"Word. But look. Back to the business of the hour. Bro Drip, wants us three to meet him. So look, y'all gotta leave your bangers here, then we can go. Bro got a spot downtown in Center City.

Von and Cold Heart passed off their guns to Monk and he put them under the mattress of the bed there. They left out, got in Monk's Benz, and made their way to see Drip. Monk had $300,000 in cash on hand in a backpack he'd put in the trunk. It was money for Drip from the sales of product.

Traffic was heavy that day due to rush hour. It took them nearly thirty minutes to get to Drips penthouse. Monk parked, they exited and now stood in the lobby of the high-rise. The female receptionist called Drip's suite to notify him he had visitors. He made her aware to allow them access. They took the elevator. Drip waited for them at the front door.

"Family-family-family! What's good fellas! How y'all doing? Come on in," Drip greeted each one individually, beginning with his brother, with a hug and a kiss on the forehead.

Monk handed Drip the backpack with the money in it.

"Welcome to my player palace, fellas," Drip said with a bright smile, waving his hand from right to left then left to right, for his newest visitor to have a look at his posh second home.

Body stood at a distance near the pool table. He had on his signature black suit, red bow tie, and shiny dress shoes. He smiled and saluted Drip's guests.

Drip was dressed in a pair of slacks, a white dress shirt, a vest, and a plaid bow tie. He continued in speech.

"I'm glad to have y'all here, fellas. Let's get down to business, shall we?" he said, then led the way to the pool table where he wanted to initiate the discussion of all he had in mind to speak with them on.

Drip had his eyes locked in on Cold Heart, as he admired how the young gunner conducted and carried himself in the presence of power. He knew how to play his role in a better way than Von. Maybe due to age and more years of experience in life and on the streets. He was nineteen, while Von was seventeen.

Drip sat the backpack on the table and went into his monologue.

"A'ight fellas, here we go with what the business is. If you don't already know—Von and Cold Heart—the chain of command for you two is, Monk as Capo over the unit y'all part of. Von, little family, you one of his lieutenants. It's three of y'all Monk got as Lieutenants. And Cold Heart," Drip looked him square in the eyes, "You're a special kind of dude, homie. You really are. I personally take a liking to you and the potential you have. In due time, I'mma bring you into the fold a little more than you are now. The more trust you earn. But for the time being, I've told Monk to tell you that you're head of security over y'all team."

Cold Heart nodded his head to indicate *yes* to the high-profile street don, Drip.

"Okay, now look. The main reason I wanted to meet up with you two is because, I wanted y'all to know that I trust you two to the fullest, and wanted y'all to have a deep understanding of what it is I've made y'all a part of. You're in the big leagues now, boys. '*Black Mafia Incorporated*' is a movement. And if any mothafuckas' get in our way, guess what? We're gonna roll right over their asses and keep our shit going that way," Drip stated and emphasized by pointing upward to the ceiling, indicating the sky being the limit.

"Now bro there—Monk—told me how well you two did—you and y'all crew—with getting off those four units of work he laid in y'all hands. I was impressed. That let me know y'all know how to handle responsibility. So, with that being said, I want y'all to know, I'm looking to increase the amount of product I want y'all to work off, from four bricks to eight . . . or maybe ten, then so on and so forth. A'ight."

Von and Cold Heart both nodded in agreement together. They knew that they were in the process of becoming rich in due time, from heroin deals, and would move up the ladder in the underworld just like Monk and Drip were, then go into the areas of life as legitimates.

Drip continued. "Okay now look," he said, then took a stack of the money from the backpack and held his palm flat atop it. It was $10,000. "Cold Heart, I've got another special mission for you, little homie. Here is ten thousand to start you off again, and I've got another five for you when it's done," Drip stated, then awaited for Cold Heart to signal if or not he was in agreement to do another job for him. No doubt, it was another murder for hire.

"I'm with it, Drip. I'm on your team now, bro. Me and my nigga Von here—your people—belong to you and do all you want us to do. No questions asked! I ain't never made this type of money before in my life! I ain't never even so much as *seen* that type of dough before in my life, let alone, have the opportunity to make it."

Drip dumped all the cash on the pool table at that point.

Cold Heart spoke more. "Why the fuck would I tell you no to anything! On my momma, Drip . . . how many ever motherfuckas' you want me to put down, I'm gonna do it! Just say who and when!" Cold Heart let out with a lot of passion and enthusiasm.

Drip smiled at his obedient soldier, then eased the money in front of Cold Heart for him to get a hand on and put into his pocket. Cold Heart thanked him for the bread.

"Okay, so, the situation with the guy Tito y'all had, Monk, Von?"

"I've been paying him fifteen thousand every two weeks, bro. I only owe him two more payments," Monk made Drip aware.

"Okay. That's what's up. And just so you'll know, Von, the reason you and your people paying sixty thousand a unit instead of fifty—the regular going price—is because your debt to Tito is being taken care of. But I'm sure it's no pressure on y'all end, since y'all making seventy-five to eight a brick selling breakdown. But once the situation is taken care of, then y'all pay the basic ticket. A'ight, little fam," Drip said.

"For sure, fam. And I appreciate the love. I really do," Von responded.

"Oh yeah. I had a chance to talk with your Pop the other day too," Drip mentioned.

"Oh yeah."

"No doubt. He told me you, your mom, and your sister made it to see him a couple of weeks ago."

"Yeah, we did."

"I took care of something for him."

"The business about the '*jack,*' right?" Von asked, forming his hand in the shape of a phone in gesture.

"Yep. I also had one of my lawyers take on his case to have a look at it. Family said something about there was possibly a few errors that were made and they could get him free a little sooner rather than later."

"Okay, good. Everything is taken care of for him. And hopefully, Pop will be home, then we can go on about life as we so choose."

"That's right. Here's the number to call your pop, fam," Drip let out, then went to the contacts on the secondary phone he had along his belt.

Von gave him his phone number, and Drip texted him the contact information.

"Say, Body," Drip called out to his homie for him to approach.

Body stepped to the pool table next to Drip and he put his arm around his neck.

"This my homie, Bruce here, aka "*Body,*" Drip said to Von and Cold Heart specifically. Monk already knew who he was and all about him.

Von and Cold Heart greeted him personally.

Drip continued. "Body and I been homies since way back when. Long before I became who I am now. He's my driver, and personal bodyguard," Drip related while still hugging his friend. "A man of status and rank in the world should never have someone close to him to protect his life who he doesn't know or can't trust. Security should also be skilled and trained in combat. Body done did a tour of duty in Somalia and in Iraq before he got out that shit. But, my homie learned what he needed to know, and now applies it to the work he does for me," the leader of the group stated.

"And from here on, I want you—Cold Heart—to keep in contact with Body, for him to teach and train you to know what he knows, do what he does, and move how he moves. The both of you are two of a kind, and I take security of the family very seriously."

"Whatever you need me to do, big bro. I'm here," Cold Heart declared.

The other three distro men of Drip already had bodyguards by their side and had no reason to fill that role. But Monk was in need to do so, and had been pressed by Drip to make that happen. He recognized the potential Von had and knew at some point, he'd possibly be a distro, and would more than likely keep Cold Heart close by to be security for him. Until Monk was to hand-pick one of his homies to be that, Drip wanted Cold Heart to be the *bodyman* for both of the younger Savages, and what better time to make that known than at that point?

"Cold Heart, I need you to hold down Von and Monk with the pistol, a'ight lil bro," Drip directed.

"Not a problem, bro."

Body then gave Cold Heart a contact to him and a business card. The two then began to discuss in private a time frame to set up workouts and training sessions. Drip owned a small farm up near Williamsport, Pennsylvania as well. He had a gun range and outdoor training courses on the site too. The young bucks were being incorporated into the fold of Drip's underworld enterprise, rather they knew how deep they were being recruited or not.

They talked a little further. Drip went to his bedroom to put the money away, leaving the others there to shoot pool and listen to the sound system while enjoying a drink or two. They were now a dynamic crew of young hustlers looking to someday make it big in the world like Drip turned out to be. Monk, Von, and Cold Heart that is. Drip was a made man, and an outstanding example whom they wanted to live like.

***

One Week Later . . .

Rosa, worked for a nursing agency that made visiting rounds to their list of patients. She was a CNA and in preparation to elevate to an RN at some point soon. The particular patient Rosa had to go attend to, lived in the Philly suburb of Doylestown Pennsylvania, located about forty-five minutes to the northwest of the city. The time was right at 6:00 that night, in the month of December, and darkness was setting in. She was headed home down the highway, then something not thought of happened. Rosa's tire blew out on her Honda Accord. It was cold and she seemed to be in the middle of nowhere as she was passing a wooded area near the Bucks County-Philadelphia County line. She was pissed.

"Fuck!" she yelled to herself as she pulled the car to the side of the county road in the rural area.

Rosa had no idea how to fix a flat, and didn't know who to call to come out and repair her tire. She gave it no thought to call 9-1-1 for any statewide sponsored towing agency. The Dominguez family wanted nothing to do with five-o. However, she did know one person who she could call to come to pick her up with no problem. Chloe. She contacted.

Chloe's phone rang twice before being directed to the voicemail service, clearly indicating Chloe hit the ignore option on the screen of the phone.

A text appeared.

CHLOE: Hey Rosa! I can't talk right, now. I'm chilling with Chino (smile). What's up?"

I know damn well this bitch is not with that boy again! Not this fast, Rosa thought to herself.

ROSA: Bitch, I need help! I'm broken down and stranded. Come pick me up!

Chloe replied with a message Rosa absolutely didn't take a liking to:

CHLOE: You better call a tow-truck! LOL! Chino's going out of town tomorrow and I'm trying to spend every minute with him I can before he does. So, I'm not able to come, sorry.

Rosa fumed with anger now.

ROSA: Chloe, how could you! You better come get me! And now, bitch! I'm outside the city and in the woods side the road!

CHLOE: No bitch! I told you! I'm not able to. I'll call Von and tell him to come get you. I told him I had to work late anyway. I'mma give him your number and tell him to call to get directions where you're at.

ROSA: Whatever bitch! Just tell him or tell somebody come get me ASAP! And I don't appreciate this shit either, Chloe! I thought I could trust and depend on you. But now I see you let a dick get between that! It will never be the same!

CHLOE: Yeah yeah! Whatever! Miss me with that bullshit, Rosa! It ain't even like that, so don't come at me with that! Von gonna call soon. Bye!

Rosa didn't bother to reply. She simply maintained an angry frustrated look on her face and awaited a call from Von, if or when he does.

Moments later, Rosa's phone rang. It was from a number she didn't recognize. It had to be Von.

"Hello!" she answered.

"Rosa. It's Von. Chloe told me you needed to be picked up. Where you at?" he responded.

She provided directions and he was now on the way to help.

Once there, Rosa got in the car with Von. He still had the *Magnum* rental. Dude liked that car. She admired how nice and clean the vehicle was. Her thoughts were expressed.

"Thank you Von, for taking out the time to come get me. I *thought* I was able to depend on Chloe. But she had to bother you from what you were doing. Dope ride by the way. Good choice. How long have you had this now?"

"Oh this. I'm renting it. I do plan to buy one just like it in due time. Maybe in the next week or two," he said as he pulled off.

"This type of car fits you though. I highly suggest."

"Thanks. And what the hell going on with your car?"

"I had a flat. My tire blew out."

"Why you didn't call, Tito? Not saying I got a problem with helping you or anything like that. I'm just asking."

"Didn't even think of that. I ain't ever had a flat. I just knew to call who I *thought* I could depend on. But now, I know better. At some point, we all will come to know the ones we think are the ones, are really not. What was so hard about Chloe making it her business to come get me? *Whatever* she's up to, ain't *that* important!"

Von turned his head to have a look at Rosa over the emphasis she placed on two words. He noticed the maddening features she had about her face. Something wasn't right. It was detected. He had it in mind to draw more out of her as he could.

"Why you say it like that, Rosa? She pissed you off that bad to make you feel like this? Chloe had to work late, and I was out and about when she called."

"It ain't shit. But we're gonna switch the subject for a moment. You say you gonna buy one of these nice rides in the next week or so, huh? How do you plan to do that, and you broke?"

Von immediately jarred his head at the remark.

"That's according to Chloe. Not me," Rosa piled it on.

"Chloe said that about me!"

"That and more. Let her tell it, y'all don't even have enough money to pay the bills. That you didn't have but four thousand to your name after the robbery that happened. But what does she know about what you got going on, right?

She's not trying to advance your cause or help you get to the money for the both of you. But that's another story."

Rosa opened a can of worms with what she slyly exposed. There was a lot of truth to what she said, being that only Von and Chloe knew the exact amount of money they had at the time, and he hadn't said a word to Rosa about the robbery. Chloe had. But why would she reveal their business to her cousin? And speak ill of the boyfriend in the process? Von had to know.

"Rosa, what the hell are you and Chloe mad at each other about? Because it's clear to me you're busy trying to tell on her about something?"

"Why do I gotta be telling on her about something? Why I can't just be keeping it real with a good dude I know you are, about somebody who does not do right by you? Good guys deserve to be treated right, Von. And you're smart enough to know how to understand what I'm saying, without me specifically saying it. I don't want to cause trouble in paradise or anything like that, but you're a young man with a bright future, and you need somebody solid by your side to help you achieve your goals. Chloe my people, but Chloe is still who she is," Rosa said, with a hint of sarcasm to her words.

"And who is that?" Von asked in relation to whom his girl was perceived to be.

"I'm sorry for you, Von, if you don't have any idea of who you're in a relationship with, or what type of female Chloe truly is. That's really sad on your behalf," Rosa responded. "But you have my number now. And anytime you wanna talk, exchange ideas, or even get a couple dollars together, please, don't be afraid to hit me up. I can use the companionship, and you could use the advice. How you feel about that and Chloe don't have to know a fucking thing about what we talking about, or potentially gonna have going on. A'ight?"

"I won't tell if you don't," Von remarked.

"Who did what? When? Where? I don't know shit about what you talking about, Chloe!" Rosa humorously confirmed to Von that their acquaintance was safe with her.

They both laughed and continued to talk until he reached her place.

Rosa had it in mind to call Tito or a towing service to go out and change her tire the next morning to come. Von gave her a helping hand with $350. She was very grateful and appreciated the money. There was something in the making between the two. But the question remained, was it something of benefit, or something to tear down a beautiful thing that was already in place? Rosa took her shot, and Von accepted the advance. Which way do they go from there? The world may never know.

PART THREE

TWENTY-ONE

Shayla continued to burn with fury at each and every time she took a look in the mirror and had to come to terms with the ugly nasty scar that stretched across her face. She hated it! Her patience had run out with Cold Heart and Von so calling themselves going out and putting the nigga Feezy to rest. She wanted instant gratification. And immediately. Shayla had another gun now, courtesy of Cold Heart—a Glock nine millimeter—and was eager to take action herself this day. Her blood boiled. Seasoned with malice. And ready to fire shots to cook the beef that existed between her and her ex. She'd set out on her own. Something had to be done. That day.

Shayla had a loyal customer named "J-Dub" who owned a fairly decent car he got around in. Normally, he wouldn't rent it out to nobody in order for him to get high. But, on this day, he made an exception for Shayla. She gave him $80 worth of heroin to borrow his car for a few hours. She'd lied to him by saying that the car was needed to make a few stops at department stores to do a little more shopping for Christmas gifts before the holiday a week away. J-Dubb let her have her way. It was a Saturday.

Shayla only had the intention to drive over near where Feezy's mother lived once it was dark enough outside, park across the street, and await the mother to appear at the door to greet a visitor, then hop out, and walk up gunning at her. If fate was to have it in her favor, Feezy would show up, then she could jump out with mask-on and blast at him, get back in the car, remove the mask, and drive away in the darkness of the night, having got the revenge she long wanted.

Shayla set out on her mission with her twelve-round small-size pistol. She parked on the opposite side of the street out from Feezy's mother's home on Cecil B. Moore Avenue and awaited. Her gun was cocked. A bullet was in the chamber ready to blast away. Ten minutes passed . . . twenty minutes . . . thirty minutes . . . almost an hour. And then, a car pulled up to the house. One she recognized. Feezy had driven it before. It Was his sister's Toyota Camry. A dude was behind the wheel. It was Feezy himself.

He got out, went to the trunk to retrieve shopping bags of clothes and shoes, walked to the passenger side door of the car, opened, and was doing something Shayla couldn't quite readily see what. By the time he had the opportunity to look up and realize what was going down, Shayla was already up on him at a speed from the back end of the car. It was too late for him to make break for it, and she'd committed to shooting to suddenly stop.

"Hey, Feezy!"

Pow! Pow! Pow . . . !

Feezy danced, dodged, bobbed, and weaved with all he had, to avoid being hit, but not hardly enough. And there was nothing he could do to save his five-year-old daughter from being struck in the line of fire. The little girl had just taken a step out of the passenger seat onto the pavement, and stood in the doorway when Shayla began blasting. There was no way a five-year-old would survive a hollow point, let alone more than one. She'd been hit multiple times. The father—Feezy—was hit in the arm and the leg. Shayla got off nine rounds before turning to run back to the car, cranking and driving away. She would return home, pack an overnight bag, then retreat to a motel to lay over and tune into the news for the end results of her actions.

I got that mothafucka' back! Ol' bitch-ass nigga! She thought to herself. Shayla felt good about what she'd done.

That was before finding out that the little girl was wounded and died as a result.

While at the hospital, Feezy suffered a nervous breakdown. He'd lost it upon being informed his little girl Dedra, didn't make it. He had a strong reason to believe Shayla was the one who had done it, but wasn't one hundred percent for certain, due to the shooter having on a mask. Not only that, at the moment his name was called out, the gunshots rang and muffled the voice so he wasn't able to recognize the person it belonged to. There were enemies in the street as well whom he had issues with, and in the mean vicious streets of Philly, there was nothing or no one off limits. When the beef is being aired out from the barrel of the guns blazing, not even innocent five-year-old girls were excluded.

Homicide detectives made their way to the hospital to interview Feezy. They'd already reported to the scene of the shooting and collected the shell casings that had been spun from the pistol. Feezy drove the car to the medical center himself. The door was dotted with bullet holes. Prior to the DT's approaching Feezy to hear what he had to say, they'd had the car temporarily seized, as it was part of the investigation now, and needed to be photographed, scanned, and tagged for evidentiary purposes.

The lead detective, William Edward Hilliard ("Bill Hillard") and his longtime sidekick, Valente Canelo ("Valco"), had jurisdiction over the case, as the neighborhood where the crime occurred, was in an area of the district they held authority. The six foot even stout body African-American police veteran—Bill—lead the way into the examination room where Feezy was being treated. Both policemen had yellow paper writing pads and ink pens at the ready to commit for the record on all the surviving victim might have to say.

"How you doing, Mister Richardson? I'm homicide detective, Bill Hilliard, and this is my partner, Detective

Canelo. I'm very sorry for your loss, and I want to assure you that we are going to do all in our power, to get down to the bottom of this, okay. It ain't no way I'm gonna allow a dangerous child killer to continue to run wild, and not have justice in a court of law doled out upon them. And in order for us to go out and make an arrest, we're gonna need your help, to be able to identify the shooter."

"Truth be told, detective, I don't know who it was. They had on a mask, and I didn't get a chance to see their face," Feezy responded.

"So you didn't see their face. Where were they standing when the shooting began?" asked Bill.

"They had to have run up on me from behind the car, because I was standing inside the doorway of the passenger side helping my little girl get out."

"We noticed all the bullet holes in the passenger door. There were nine casings found at the scene as well," Valco said.

"*Goddamn!* I wonder who the fuck wanted me dead that bad!" Feezy exclaimed.

Bill shrugged his shoulders and flipped his hand palms up. "That's what we are now trying to help you figure out. What enemies you got out there?"

"Shit, I don't know. I have done some foul things in my past, but not nothing to the extent that would make motherfuckas' come gunning for me while I got my daughter by my side."

"The person who did it didn't think in that way," Valco remarked.

"Tell me about it," responded Feezy . He then lowered his head and shook it from side to side slowly. The tears began once more. He was distraught all over again.

"I know you may not consider this to be so, Mister Richardson. But you were lucky to walk away with your life," Bill related.

"Why you say that?"

"For one, the bullets that were fired, were *'Cop Killers!'* *Rhino* tip lead assassins," informed Bill. *"Black Rhinos,"* are the official name."

"Say what!" Feezy was shocked by the revelation. *"Cold Killers!"* They definitely wanted me dead, I see!"

The thought of Shayla being the perceived shooter was pushed back a bit further. He felt that there was no way she had any connections to get her hands on a box of fucking *"Cop Killer"* bullets, let alone, take aim and blast at him while his daughter was there by his side and could potentially be hit too.

Feezy felt that, although Shayla indeed had shot at him at her place, she didn't want him dead. And definitely didn't want the little girl murdered in that way.

However, the fact of the matter was that he did tell his three female cousins to go out and rob Shayla if they caught her down bad, because that's what they did. They were stick up chicks. But on the other hand, he didn't tell them to slash the girl's face and disfigure her for life. They'd taken that upon themselves to do such an act. And in return, the grotesque permanent scar became the main thing to make Shayla wig out and snap the way she did, to want to shoot and kill without mercy.

Bill continued, "They damn sure did want you wiped out. Those Black Rhinos ain't no joke. One went through your bicep, and the other clean through your leg. An eyelash away from hitting that main artery."

Bill then dug down into the pocket of the leather jacket he had on and withdrew two items; a casing retrieved from the site of the shooting, and a bullet that was taken from the panel of the car door. It had blood on it. Tests were recently run to know which of the two victims it belonged to. He held the articles of evidence high above his head into the light.

"That red dot of the back on the shell casing, and the one on the tip of that piece of lead there, clearly indicates, they're *'Black Rhinos'* aka *'Cop Killers'*! So, not only do we got an outlaw hitter on the loose whose killed a little girl and tried to put you away. We've got to worry now about them going out and shooting other people with these extremely lethal-ass bullets in their possession. You need to help us, Mister Richardson. We've got to track this fucker down immediately! Who could you think of that might want you dead?" Bill asked.

"Any arguments, fist fights, unfinished business, etcetera?" Valco chimed in to ask as well.

"And we're sure you not gonna tell us if you've robbed, kidnapped, or shot anybody yourself to cause the other to retaliate in this way. We're not even gonna ask that. But *if* you'd like . . . you can share that with us too, so to help us get a step closer to capturing your daughter's killer, Stephon. At all cost, this person has to be stopped, and those bullets taken off the streets," Bill said with a sincere and concerned voice.

Feezy thought over their words carefully and pondered which of his enemies posed the gravest threat who he could put the cross down on to get out of the way the fastest. He also contemplated mentioning Shayla's name to them for her taking those shots at him.

*I really don't want to believe Shay was the one who did this, but I have no one else to point the finger at. And now that these cops got bullets in their possession, they could go to that bitches house and get the others out the wall she missed me with. Let's see what's really going o*n, Feezy thought to himself of the options he had at his disposal.

"You know what officers . . . y'all are right. They do need to be stopped, and those bullets do have to come off the streets. Here is what I could tell you . . . ."

Feezy had strong reason to also believe he could go and deal with Shayla himself. He was now eager to track her down, take her hostage, and beat whatever truth out of her she may have held concealed, and then kill her. He plotted on a way to cancel Christmas for her, for good.

TWENTY-TWO

Three Days Later . . .

Shayla was still laying low inside the motel room she'd booked over in Camden, New Jersey. She was pissed at herself for not killing Feezy, but instead, the daughter. There was now reason to fear that he and his people would go all over the county in search of the shooter. Feezy 's brother was a high-profile coke dealer and had resources and hitters out there who could be tapped to hunt her down and kill her. Shayla's back was against the wall. There was a need for her to do something. She had her phone off and contacted no one. The others were busy trying to find out where she was and what the fuck she had going on to cause her to not call or get in touch with anyone, especially Tangee.

Finally, Shayla powered on her phone and immediately went through the channels to change her number. She then called Tangee. All of her important contacts and customers were locked into the phone.

Tangee didn't recognize her new number. She ignored. A text was sent.

SHAYLA: You there?

TANGEE: Who dis?

SHAYLA: Tangee, it's me, Shay.

Tangee then immediately called.

"Tangee!" Shayla answered.

"Shay! Where the hell you at? What the fuck you got going on!" Tangee responded in a hysterical way. She was really concerned for her friend.

Shayla gave her the whole run down. Tangee couldn't believe what she was hearing.

"I told you that that nigga was no good, and that you should've gotten rid of his ass a long time ago. Then you got cut, and now this," Tangee exclaimed. "Cold Heart and Von know?"

"No! Not yet. And I need you to grab our money, and the product, and get the hell out of there, ASAP! Today Tangee! Because I know Feezy gonna come there looking for me, and I don't need you getting hurt or shot behind me. I'mma call J-Dub and have him come by to pick you up, then bring you here to Jersey where I'm at. I gotta call Cori too, and have her get the fuck up out of her place for the time being until this shit blows over. I don't know what *Feezy* may know, and I don't know what the *cops* know. And until I do, y'all gotta get ghost, to keep out of harm's way," Shayla stated.

Tangee took in all the friend had said, then began to brainstorm to think of any possible avenue she could suggest to bring an end to the extreme drama they all now faced. A child shot dead was a serious issue, not to mention the fact of those highly illegal military use only cop killer bullets Shayla had no knowledge about. Or, the severe penalty that they carried if a person is caught with them, let alone murdered somebody with them. A kid for crying out loud. Shayla's intention was not to shoot little Dedra. She honestly didn't see her at the moment of firing away at Feezy. However, it was too little too late at that point. What has happened couldn't be taken back.

Tangee spoke again. "Shay, how the fuck you let this get so bad like it is! I'm scared as shit now!" Fear was detected very clearly in her voice.

"Tangee. If I could take it back and make a better decision, I would. But I can't. So, it is what it is. And you need to go ahead and get the fuck up out of there before Feezy shows up, or the cops! Okay. I'll talk to you when you get here."

"And I think you need to call Cold Heart and Von to let them know what's up so we could relocate and get back to getting money."

"I am. When I'm done talking to you. Now see you soon. Bye," Shayla concluded then disconnected the call. She pulled up Cold Heart's number in the contacts. He had to be notified.

Tangee immediately contacted J-Dub to come by and pick her up ASAP. She was grabbing all she could while talking to him and preparing to be taken away.

Shayla next called Cori and told her to not ask questions or bullshit around, but to simply pack an overnight bag and be ready to leave, Tangee and J-Dub was on the way. They had a lot going on.

Cold Heart and Von made it to the motel where Shayla was before Tangee and Cori got there. That was a good thing, because she needed to have a private moment with them to let it be known the exact details of what she'd done, the parts she'd left out from telling Tangee.

"Damn Shay! What the fuck! You just couldn't wait to let us find the nigga and handle that, couldn't you!," Von vented. "Now we go this shit to deal with! A fucking kid done got killed! That's some serious shit to the police!"

Cold Heart just looked on at her and shook his head in disgust. "Why the fuck you couldn't let us do our part, Shay!" he spat. "That's what we're for. Now we gotta regroup somewhere else and get it poppin' all over again for you and Tangee. That spot y'all had was doing good numbers too."

"Where the money and the rest of the work y'all had?" Von asked.

"My sister and Tangee are on the way with everything now as we speak," Shayla informed.

Von still felt the need to stress the seriousness of the situation they'd been put in by Shayla being part of the crew. "Shay, I'm still busy trynna figure out why you didn't let us get the drop on that nigga and put him down on our time?" he asked.

"Bro! Take a good look at my motherfuckin' face!" she said, getting up to her feet off the bed and standing face to face with Von. Her nose touched his. She'd never shown that side of her to them. Shayla was a mad bitch.

Von jarred his head at her up close and personal demonstration of aggression on display.

"Take a *good* fuckin' look at me, Von! You remember how pretty and attractive I used to look? How I ain't ever have no problem getting a second turn of a man's head?" A tear streaked down her face, on the same side as the slash. It passed over like a car in slow motion over a speed bump. "You know how terrible I feel every time I look at myself and realize I'm a mess. I fit the description of a fuckin' monster, Von! I had to go and take action, bro! Y'all were taking too long," she spat with a lot of emotion. "He took my beauty, and in return, I tried to take him out, but got his daughter! An eye for an eye, and a tooth for a tooth. An even exchange! So fuck everything else!"

Von continued to lock eyes with her and began to internalize all she'd said. Shayla managed to touch him in some type of way and caused him to empathize with her grim reality. He didn't let out a word. Just stood in silence.

Cold Heart spoke up again. "Von, she's good bro. I understand her point. She had every right to do what she did. We took too long. I would've gotten impatient too, bro. So, you good, Shay. Just continue to lay low until we work this shit out," he said.

Shayla turned her head back to Von from Cold Heart then took a step back and sat on the bed again. She rarely smoked *Black and Milds,* but fired one back up she'd puffed on for the last couple of days.

"Yeah, Shay, relax. Be cool, okay. We're gonna find that nigga and eliminate all the problems he got attached to him.

A'ight. Now give us a hug to calm you down a little more," Von said.

She did so. They all sat and talked a little while longer awaiting Tangee and Cori.

Twenty minutes later, they arrived. Von and Cold Heart laid out to them what the next move was, collected the money that they had available, and assured them that all would be well in due time. Von was to get them a rental to get around in, and told them to keep out of Philly as much as possible. Shayla especially, as that went without saying. They told them explicitly to NOT let no one know where they were. Under no circumstances. Not even their mama or daddy! The girls vowed that they wouldn't.

J-Dub was hit with a stern dictation, to not say shit either. They gave him $200 worth of his favorite love, to keep his fucking mouth closed, and to run errands for the girls when necessary.

The boys then left and told the females to call at any time they needed them. Von and Cold Heart had a lot of shit to discuss. They knew it was necessary to bring it to Monk's attention to get his take. The crew was now on a chain of command and had structure to it. Breaking rank and not making it known could bring about trouble from the supreme leader on the throne, the big homie Drip. And they didn't need no static from the top. Drip took care of the problems they had with Tito; fronted them kilos of his heroin product; and made them a part of his team; which became an opportunity for them to make a lot of money and move up in the world in a major way. So, they had to let them know about it and also, get busy carving out a new location for Shayla, Tangee, Cori, and those who got money with them, to trap their dope. Possibly over in West Philly away from north. At least until Feezy was dealt with. That became part of the plan.

***

Tangee and Cori managed to pack and get out of the way in the nick of time prior to Feezy getting grimy and launching a strike attack in two different ways. He did the unthinkable, yet the thinkable, all to work out to his advantage. His timing was bad though. He was too little too late. So were the cops he'd ratted to.

What he'd done was, told the police—Bill and Valco—that the house Cori lived, was a place where an enemy he'd gotten into with sold heroin, and the guy could possibly have the gun there that was used to kill his daughter. This was the only person he could think of who wanted him dead behind the problems they had. That was a story made up which was so far from the truth.

The cops executed a raid of the house on his statement, they found nothing. On the same day of the raid, the day Shayla had the other two meet her in Jersey, Feezy and two of his boys went to the house where Shayla and Tangee lived, and were looking to rob, kidnap, torture, and murder them both. He hadn't been timely on that either, and now operated from behind the eight ball. Dude was pissed, because he didn't know what to think or do at that point. The cops got nothing and neither did he. There was good reason to believe that in fact, Shayla was the shooter, or had something to do with it, so he felt.

Why else would she, Cori, and Tangee, all of sudden get up and get ghost at the same time like that? he thought to himself. This was after the fact.

Feezy now had to lay low and remain out the way once he buried his little girl, and strike when he'd had the opportunity, if that was to occur. He needed to get her before she got to him again. But this time, there may not be another miss on his life. Shayla failed on two separate occasions.

TWENTY-THREE

Von and Chloe were at home together chilling, watching movies, and trying to gain a peace at mind from all they had going on outside of their place of living. This was something they hadn't done in a while and felt the need to do so, to at least talk, and figure out which direction their relationship was headed, to the right or the left. They wanted each other but had an interest in other people as well. What they had was not on solid ground. And they were too young and undecided to know how to identify the thin line between love and hate. Von maybe, but not Chloe.

"Von, let me ask you something. What are we doing? Are we in this to win this? Or are we in it just to be in it, per se? Because of our history together in my last year of high school and our dealings during the prom? What are we doing?" she asked as they sat atop the bed in their night clothes. She had on a fitted T-shirt and purple panties, and he was in his boxers with a wife-beater on.

The heating system of their place had the entire inside area warm as ever. It was cold out, a light snow, and a two days prior to the Christmas holiday. They were watching one of Von's favorite shows for the season *"A Christmas Story."*

"What you mean, *'what we doing,'* Chloe?" he retorted. A commercial was on. He had taken his attention from the monitor and towards her.

"What do you mean, *'what I mean'?* I'm trying to know where do we stand with our relationship? You don't seem like you're into me anymore like you used to be. And if you are not, you need to let me know, so we can go on about our business in a peaceful agreeable way,"

Chloe didn't hold back. She let it out just like Chino told her to do. Because that was the only way he would entertain anything further than a sexual affair with her. And man, they were so good to each other.

Von sharply exhaled and smirked at the same time. He thought about all of his available options. Monyetta. Rosa *potentially. Tangee if I wanted. And the many bitches that's gonna be on my dick when this money pile up.*

Chloe was ready to speed up the process and get it over with. But at the same time, she liked Von, the potential he possessed, and the idea of what they could have together. However, it was clear he didn't think in the same way as she did. And that part, she couldn't live with. To her, it was best to let go and move on, and not continue to play mind games with each other.

Von was now ready to respond. "How long you had that on your mind to say, Chloe?"

"For a while now, if you must know."

He looked down at her and held the stare. Not even a blink of an eye occurred.

You know what. If this is what she wants, I'mma go ahead and give it to her, he thought.

He looked her up and down, then up again at a slow nodding of the head—from head to waist, then her head once more. Von spoke again.

"Sounds to me like you have already moved on, Chloe. Is that true?"

She avoided the question altogether. "And it looks to me, you already have done so yourself. I was always told to not believe what a person says, but definitely do so with what they do. Now is that true? Have you moved on?" she asked.

"Look, Chloe, just be straight with me, Okay? Tell me right now, what you wanna do?" Von demanded in a mild tone.

Chloe was looking for him to become hostile, get angry, and raise his voice at her. He didn't. Dude kept it very cordial and didn't give her any excuse to use to support her argument. Rosa was right about what she let him in on. It didn't take many words from him to get the picture.

"You wanna know what I want, Von?"

"Well damn Chloe, I did ask, didn't I?"

"Yeah, you did. And this is what I want. I love you and care for you, Von. But you made it to where I don't see a future with you like I had before. And I don't want to let you go because I do believe in you. And I and your mom have developed a nice bond together, but I don't want to be with you any longer," she expressed.

"I'mma make it easy for you, Chloe. Because I know what you want."

"—An open relationship, Von. You can see who you wanna see, and so can I," she went ahead and let out.

Von smiled. He had a good idea that that was what she wanted to say. He was about to spit it out. She beat him to it. He agreed to what she wanted by a gesture of the head. And then, he spoke on it.

"A'ight. I'mma give you what you want. Just remember, this is what *you* want, and *you* said it. Not *me*." he responded. "And what about the house here?"

"Everything still can stay like it is. We're just cut buddies now. And the only people who we are to have sex with in this house, are the both of us. Okay?"

"Shit, fine with me. But what makes you want it this way? I gotta ask?"

"Because, I feel like we can be better, more open, and honest with each other like this, as friends, than we can in a committed relationship. I enjoy your friendship more so than I do you as a boyfriend." She spoke truthfully to him.

He smiled at the way she worded her revelation, "I respect that. And I ain't got no choice but to accept it. No love lost. No hard feelings. I got to give you what you want."

"This is not a breakup, Von. I actually think it'll bring us closer as we progress," she advised, then leaned over and kissed him.

The feelings was mutual between them on equally terms. They continued to talk, watch TV, and enjoy each other under the new status they had. Chloe's period was on the way. She spotted. So they couldn't fuck. She did suck him off really good though, to assure him that they were still on solid terms.

"Remember now . . . *you* said it, *not* me. This is what *you* want," he said to her for a final time.

Von clearly had Rosa on the brain now.

Chloe may had fucked up and didn't know it. She'd unleashed a beast in him.

***

Meanwhile . . .

At police headquarters, Bill and Valco were provided troubling revelations pertaining to the evidence obtained from the scene of two additional homicides that occurred in the city. Black Rhino bullets were retrieved from the bodies during autopsy. They matched those Feezy and his little girl were hit with. The two new victims whom lost their lives from the cop killers, were both black male heroin dealers, with criminal pasts. Bill feared that if they weren't able to identify the source of the lethal ammo and the possible hitters, more Black Rhino-riddled bodies would turn up, and more than likely, law enforcement would soon number among the casualties that were being put down by such vicious pieces of lead.

Bill's partner, Valco, stepped inside the office space of his with pages of documents he'd been faxed from the crime lab. They were in relation to ballistics.

"Bill, prepare yourself for this," Valco said upon being granted entry into his supervisor's domain.

"Oh no, Vally. What now? Every time you lay that phase on me, I know what to expect next," Bill responded.

Valco sat down the ten-page report on the desk in front of Bill. Bill lifted up the documents, put on his glasses, and began to read.

"Fill me in while I scan, Valco," Bill said.

"How about, we got a ballistics match from two murdered victims who were slain a little while back, at the I-Hop over on the Boulevard," he informed. "A boyfriend and girlfriend who was shot multiple times each."

"A match you say? How?"

"Black Rhinos too! Those fucking cop killers, Bill."

Bill shook his head and continued to read on. "What's your take on it all?" he asked.

"My take is that, those two victims from the I-HOP slaying, were the beginning of the storm. The male of the two—a Rashawn Johnson, known on the streets as '*Playboy*'—was a high-level heroin Kingpin, who I believe had more than likely, pissed off somebody at the top, and had to pay with his life. The girlfriend was a bonus, to keep her from reporting anything."

"And how does that shooting and those two bodies relate to the three additional ones that piled on afterwards?"

Valco went into his monologue to fully explain his theory. "Because, each of the victims was shot with Black Rhinos. All the males killed, had some known history of dealing heroin, and more than likely, was taken out for territory, or for a cause to be advanced, per se. Is there a connection to them all? It may be. I don't think so, though. Playboy Johnson, had his feet dug in the ground in North Philly while the two after him were West Philly residents, and did their dirty deeds on the opposite side of the river. You follow me."

"Yeah. I do. But you left out the father and daughter. The Richardson boy and the little girl? Where do they factor into the equation?"

"I really don't think Richardson fits into the puzzle anywhere. His history says, he, his brother, and his family, deal coke . . . crack that is it. Not the big bad boy, heroin, as did Johnson and the two Ballard cousins, Tyrell and Anton. By the way, the FBI, had Playboy Johnson under watch and was looking to arrest upon indictment. He'd been a subject of theirs for the past three years, until his unfortunate demise."

Bill completed reading the first page of the documents, and now had his head tilted, both hands palms flat atop his desk, and began to brainstorm. He then spoke up once more.

"Give me the order of the killings once again," Bill requested.

"Okay, we had, Playboy Johnson and the girlfriend to go first."

"—And they were killed on the Boulevard at the I-HOP. Clearly out of our jurisdiction, correct?"

"Correct. And that's the reason why we didn't get briefed or handed the case, because it wasn't on our watch," Valco responded.

"I figured that to be the case. But go ahead, continue," Bill urged.

"My pleasure. Okay so, Tyrell Ballard and the cousin Anton, were murdered shortly after Johnson. Again, they dealt heroin, and lived in West Philadelphia."

"—Two more not on our watch," Bill let out.

"—Exactly. No briefings. No case files to sift through."

Bill tapped his fingers now on the desk like he was playing piano. He brainstormed more and were desperate to come up with crucial evidence which would get him an arm's length closer to slapping the cuffs on the loose assassin who executed with overtly dangerous bullets in his arsenal.

"And Richardson and his daughter's case fell into our lap because of our jurisdiction. But the bigger questions now remain . . . who done it? What's the motive behind it? Where did they get those bullets from? And how many rounds might there be in circulation? We've got to get this bastard, Valco! Or *these* bastards, if there's more than one."

"I agree. But, I still have a hunch that Richardson is holding on to more than he's letting out. He had to really fuck someone over for them to come back in the way they had. I'm telling you, Bill. He seemed to be troubled, but not *deeply* troubled, as a father would be, who'd lost a child to gun violence, with bullets that had *his* name on them," Valco stated.

"You wanna know something, Valley. I feel the same way as you. That fucker holding on to something. But what? And who might he be protecting?" Bill let out.

"His brother maybe? He *is* at the top of the crack-slinging food chain. And maybe Richardson probably did a job for him or something to that degree. And an act of retaliation was had."

"Maybe so. Let's press our C-I's a little harder to see what they may have caught wind of in the streets. We mention *Feezy's* name to them, and the street name of the brother, to see what we churn up. We also do repeat visits to *Feezy* Richardson *wherever* he may be, to update him on his case and about our progress—if we get any further—and his daughter's killer. Maybe he'll hold it in place in the heat of our approaching him, maybe he won't. And if something deeper *is* going on, he'll bail. If not, he'll stay in place and won't have a problem helping us."

"How can a man say no to helping the cops find the killer who took a child away from them?"

"That's my point exactly. To work him from that angle. We can't go wrong in that way," stated Bill

"We absolutely cannot. Not at all," responded Valco.

***

Weeks Prior . . .

Ronald Waldon, the 19 year-old homie of Von and a member of the crew, also heavily connected with two other dudes from their squad—Kareem and Lonnie. They needed to come up with a plan to take hold of a particular area over in West Philly, where heroin product was greatly sold. Kareem and Lonnie were already in active duty on that side of town, and if lucky enough to take the turf they thirsted over, they all could be at the advantage to get more money by moving more product. The three knew exactly how it worked; the more product they sold, the more money they make; the more the supplier provide to them all with product; and eventually, he would be dying to meet them personally. The territory they had their sights set on was in *"the bottom,"* from 42nd to 44th Streets. An undisputed king of dope had his flag planted firmly on those blocks, and triple-dog-dared any mothafuckers to try and come for him and his crown. His name was Tyrell Ballard, a late thirties brown skinned six foot one plump fella, who had bricks of dirty for days, but not nearly enough hitters or go hard mothafuckers to protect him and the product. His right-hand man was his cousin, a cat by the name Anton, and they ran things together. The Ballard family were many and stretched from Philly to the suburbs of Bristol and Levittown, Pennsylvania. But not everyone had something to do with the underworld or with what Tryrell and Anton had going on, creating a wedge between those two and family, making them vulnerable to a certain degree, because they had to dip into a pool of other people outside the family, to move the work and tote the pistol for them. And that's NEVER a good thing.

It was really Kareem and Lonnie, who were looking to run down on Tyrell and Anton but brought Ron in to go along for the ride, as they needed hitters from another section of the city, to come over and eradicate those two fucks—Tyell and Anton—to clear the path and set up shop.

Cold Heart bought more guns and ammunition from his cousin, Herb. He'd gotten fancy again, and bought 700 more rounds of those *"Special Bullets"* Herb bragged heavily about as being *"Cop killers"* aka *"Black Rhinos,"* to fit the many different guns and rifles he was supplied with. Ron bought six *P89 Rugers* from Cold Heart, four AR-15's (223 Calibers), two .357 Magnums, and two Glock Forties. Ron equipped his cousins Khaddafi and Khalil, with two P89s each and two extended clips. They also got 100 rounds of Black Rhinos and 300 rounds of hollow points. It was those two—Khaddafi and Khalil—who'd been contracted to hit the Ballard boys. They were damn near running over each other to be the first one to get to them! Because of a bonus promised. Them two niggaz were on it.

Lonnie knew many things about Tyrell and Anton, more than the others. This was so because he was a die-hard West Philly Street nigga himself, who knew some of everything about everyone that was worthy of the mention.

Tyrell owned a corner store he utilized the back room for as an office. He also played poker there, hid product and money, and also entertained females there as well. He had a pool table, a flat-screen TV, and a plush leather couch to outfit the place.

Lonnie gained information on Tyrell. He came to know the days Tyrell would be at the store, the times, and also certain parts of his routine. He then set out to watch the guy and paid close attention to how he moved. Lonnie even went so far as to buy product from Tyrell specifically, beginning with $4,000, and gradually increasing to build rapport that led to trust. Before long, Lonnie no longer had to buy from the middle man Anton, as Tyrell now felt comfortable selling him his supply, and dealt with him personally.

Lonnie had $15,000 he wanted to spend with Tyrell. It was a Thursday night, and he knew the two Ballard cousins most often played around with the girls at the man cave in the back of the store on this day. They were there. Lonnie was at a distance down the block looking on at the store through a pair of binoculars when he made the call to Tyrell. Khaddafi and Khalil were with him and strapped with their P89s with Black Rhino bullets along the waistline, ready to rundown on those two ducks once they had the drop on them. The opportunity was almost within reach.

Lonnie was told by Tyrell to meet him at the store, to *"knock on the backdoor as he had a time or two before, that he and Anton had a couple bitches there, and were about to fuck! But before they do, he would serve him the supply as he had before, and was ready to make it happen. It was only those four there."*

"I'll be there shortly, bro," Lonnie said to Tyrell.

Lonnie waited fifteen minutes then they went to do work. He knocked on the door. It had sturdy thick burglar bars to it and a steel frame panel, completely impossible to kick in. The devil is only able come into your house when you let him in. And by Tyrell peeping through the eye space to know exactly it was Lonnie who was there and ready to shop with him, he unlocked the many bolts and security features that protected him and his guest, and made himself vulnerable as ever at that point.

"What up, L," greeted Tyrell.

Kaddafi and Khalil were up against the wall on each side of the door and couldn't be seen by Tyrell. Once he eased the door open, the twins took action.

The three stormed in with Khaddafi leading the charge.
Boom!

Khaddafi shot Tyrell square in the chest.
Boom-Boom!

He hit him with two more rounds for good measure.

"What the fuck!" Anton exclaimed.

"This what the fuck, nigga!" spat Lonnie, the only one of the hitters who didn't have on a mask.

Boom!

He shot Anton in the forehead while running up on him. A Black Rhino exploded inside it.

The trio then waved their guns from one female to the other, daring them to scream, so they could knock them off too. The girls simply sat in their seats on the couch with their hands held high, mouths wide open, and completely petrified out of their fucking minds. Those bitches were scarred.

"Y'all two sluts see anything?" Lonnie asked calmly. "Because if so, we can go ahead and do something about that *now!*" He'd gotten loud at the last word.

The two young ladies shook their heads from left to right to indicate *No.* They went back to being completely motionless at that point.

"Good. Now let me get this!" said Lonnie, then grabbed the brown paper bag out of the seat where Tyrell likely sat. He knew the dope was packaged in it. That was Tyrell's way of serving people while in the store.

Khaddafi and Khalil were busy running the pockets of the two dead dudes sprawled out on the floor. They took everything the Ballards left behind. They couldn't take it with them to the other side no way.

"A'ight you two whores! If I hear anything about y'all saying something of this here, I'mma come back for you, and do you dirty like these niggaz right here!" Lonnie declared while turning and pointing at Tyrell and Anton with the tip of his pistol. "As a matter of fact, where your ID cards! Gimme them shits right now!" he barked.

The girls frantically opened their purses and brought out their identifications.

"Just like Cleo said in *Set It Off* . . . these here are my insurance policies on you bitches! I know you won't say shit now," he said upon taking the cards into his hand and slapping them in the palm of the other.

Khaddafi and Khalil eased backwards in preparation to exit.

"Y'all be safe now, you hear," Lonnie last taunted, then back stepped until he'd gotten to the door.

The three ran off towards the get-away car, hopped in, and sped away. A new territory to pump their heroin product had been conquered. With Tyrell and Anton being assassinated, no one was there to challenge. Lonnie and Kareem would report the progress to Von and Cold Heart, and they to Monk, with Monk taking it to Drip. This was around the time Drip up and laid nine bricks of product on Von when they had the visit at the penthouse in downtown Philly.

TWENTY-FOUR

Presently . . .

Von was in his man cave he'd made for himself at his grandmother's house. He was counting money and breaking down bricks of H to quarter kilos. There were four left from the nine Drip last supplied. Von was calculating his options and being sure he could take out enough bread to make a $20,000 down payment on the new car he was intending on buying, a Dodge Magnum, same year and color he rented. Mrs. Edna would put the vehicle in her name for her grandson.

The thought of a person's smile and sweet words passed through his mind: Monyetta. The two had only texted between the time. Von craved another shot of that sweet pussy she had on her. His dick tingled and throbbed. The sensation felt so good to him. He texted:

VON: Monyetta. What's good boo. How you been? (smiley face emoji)

He sat his phone down and continued to count money. He felt a certain type of infatuation in doing so by hand. The practice made him feel important. A sense of power would overtake him. The young Savage dope-dealer, would even go so far as to iron his $100 bills. He loved crispy non-wrinkled cash. This would be the down payment money on the car—fresh from the streets, to the bottom of the iron heat, and into the car dealer's hands. A dream of his he always wanted to fulfill.

Monyetta replied,

MONYETTA: Hey Von! I'm so happy to hear from you. Had you on my mind. What you up to?

VON: Here at my Nana's crib chillin.' Wanna see you (smiley face). Had you on my mind as well. With your sexy chocolate self.

MONYETTA: (smiley face) I'm home. Had a long day today in class. Exams. You coming over?

VON: Hell yeah, I am. That goes without saying.

MONYETTA: (Smiley face). I'll be waiting.

VON: Naked? (Smiley face with tongue out).

MONYETTA: If that's how you want me to be. You get to have it your way. Remember, I'm trying to be number one in your life. Not the side piece any longer.

VON: Actually, me and her agreed to an open relationship. We have each other's permission to see other people. Just not in the house we have together.

MONYETTA: For real, Von?

VON: Yep. I'll tell you more about it when I get there.

MONYETTA: Ok. Because I need to hear this for my own good.

VON: No doubt about it. And it's all good, sweetness. You and me now.

MONYETTA: You and me, baby (smiley face). All the way to the top. See you when you get here.

VON: (Heart emoji)

Von completed what he needed to while at his grandmother's home. He let Nana know that next, he would like for her to cosign for him on the car he badly wanted.

"That's a nice car, Vonnie," Grandma complimented, upon looking on at the Dodge in the driveway. "It fits you. Your father had bought your mother a car like this before he went away. Same color," Mrs. Edna said.

Actually, the vehicle Little Hound gifted Lilly with was a black Mercedes Benz station wagon. Somewhat similar to the Dodge.

Von left the house and made his way to see the lovely Monyetta. He was becoming attached to her. The chemistry between the two was undeniable and very compelling. They had a lot in common, and Von was so ready to explore everything about it, to bring out the best of what they had, and establish what it were that they wanted. Their companionship was becoming so amazing, being that they were off to a good start.

***

Meanwhile . . .

The housing market crashed. The financial world was in a crisis. The country and much of the globe were in a downturn called a *"recession."* Damn near everybody was now broke and out of a job, or going broke while struggling to hold onto a job. The pain and emotional distress were felt by all people and many companies. The government had its hands full. And the new President-elect—Barack Hussain Obama—had his work cut out for him come high noon January 20th, 2009, the day he would be inaugurated as the 44th President of the United States of America. African-Americans —it seemed—had it the worst. And all their hopes, dreams, and prayers, were greatly invested in the nation's "first black president" with their vote on a ballot. Could he deliver? That became the question.

Under Lilly's roof, her and Bernard had a conversation. One he wasn't pleased to have, but had no choice. They were seated at the front of the bed watching TV. It was supposed to be their date night: *"Taco Tuesdays," "Ruby Tuesday," "Apple Bees's Tuesday's,"* or some other restaurant Tuesdays. But unfortunately for Bernard, work drastically slowed, and he was a broke-ass nigga trying to wash his problems and misery down his throat with the next bottle of liquor he drank. Lilly never had a dude in her life who was that pitiful and down on his luck. She could withstand a light ass-whipping from him here and there, but a beating by a broke motherfucker who had no money and couldn't pay the bills like he once had, Lilly wasn't going to go for on no level. What the fuck was he thinking!

The two normally alternated how they paid their bills, with Bernard fully paying on all the odd-numbered months, and he and Lilly went half on all the even number months, No exceptions. They had worked it in this way for the past year he'd been living there with her. The month of January was upon them one week away, which meant, it was ALL on Bernard. Lilly wasn't trying to hear shit different. This would be the thing she could use to bop his ass on out the way and continue with Jamar.

"So we don't do date nights because you ain't got no money now, huh? And you wait until the last minute to let me know, after I had gotten fully dressed and ready to go once you got off work. Explain that to me please, Bernard. I'd like to hear this," Lilly said to him. She was still dressed.

"We not getting much work lately, Lilly. This recession shit hit us hard. Me and my brothers are not getting any building contracts. And the work we do get, is only for a few hours at a time , one to two days a week. But I'mma make it up to you, Lilly, once the storm blows over," Bernard responded.

"Okay, what about our bills? It's all on you come that first of the month. Ain't no such thing as making that up to me," she put out there, looking to bring him to grip with reality.

Lilly was brutal on him in her attempt to crush his spirit.

"You don't have to remind me, Lilly. I know. I *should* have everything in place by then, okay."

"You *should*, or you *will*? Because the bill collectors only want specifics. Not '*maybe*,' '*should*,' or '*I don't knows.*' Nor any other vague terms to explain, I don't have the money, or I don't have the money if you—"

"Lilly! Give me a break! A'ight! You don't have to beat me down! So stop!" Bernard barked. He'd begun to get pissed.

"Bernard, mind you, this my house. I can talk like I want to in my place. I'm not disrespecting you, and I'm not raising my voice at—"

"Lilly, let that shit go now! I'm telling you! You're pissing me off!" he cut her off and said.

"I couldn't care less about you getting mad, Bernard! If I don't call you out on your shit, who else will? I can do bad all by myself. And if you ain't got no bill money when it's time for you to have it, guess what you can do?"

Whop!

"Shut the fuck up!"

Bernard smacked the shit out of her. It sounded *loud!* Like a car tire had blown out.

Her face reddened from the open hand chastising. She sat with her mouth wide and held her face while remaining seated in silence. Lilly then stood to her feet slowly and turned to walk out of the room to go rest in the den area of the house.

"Bernard, I want you to leave my house, dude! You have hit me one too many times now. That ain't love. That's abuse!" Lilly said to him before exiting.

"You my woman! Whenever you get outta line, I got the right to put you back in it. And I ain't going no damn where! What the hell you talking 'bout! Bernard responded to Lilly as she scurried out of the way from receiving another blow. He was ready to pain her ass yet again.

Lilly didn't sleep in the bedroom with Bernard that night. She just stayed in the den and slept on the couch. The next morning, she went to work as usual and left the issues along with Bernard until it was time to jump on his back again come bill time. That was soon to come.

TWENTY-FIVE

Body contacted Cold Heart. He hadn't done so since giving him the phone number and business card the day they were together with Drip. There was a mission in place that had to be taken care of. A High-stakes execution Drip wanted done, on a property developer who Drip was seeking to beat out in an auction for a contract stake on the renovation of the *Gallery Mall* and a string of high-rise buildings, and parking space lofts.

Warren McGregor, was a 53-year-old clean-shaven, mullet hairstyle-wearing, heavy metal-loving, white guy, who inherited his property development and real estate empire from his father at his passing. He and the guy he'd come to know by the name of Damien Savage (Drip), were in a bitter bidding feud down at City Hall and at the auction location to secure the permits and contracts to have a stake in the upcoming renovation of the mall, two high rise buildings, and a string of parking space lots in the center city area,

The contracts were to stretch over a seven to nine-year time period and held the potential to bring in millions of dollars to all involved. There was room for only one last developing team, and Drip and Warren were in a head-to-head heat for it. With one out of the way, the other wins by default.

"The best way to beat the competition is to have no competition, Body! That fucking white boy gotta go!" Drip spat in conveying his orders to his personal hitter. His words oozed venom.

The next meeting would be in January 2009. This day was two days before Christmas.

Body needed to groom Cold Heart for the purpose of tagging along with him for the special occasion. He had to be sure the young cat was prepared, as Drip believed in him, and had high hopes for the boy to be a great fit on the team, then eventually, close to him as a security man.

Body had twelve hours to teach and train Cold Heart on how to move, as the hit had to go smoothly, or there would be severe consequences to pay, as a lot of high profile people played a part in orchestrating the plot.

The time was six in the a.m. when Body called. Cold Heart was already up as he often got out the bed between four and six. As a hustler, he believed in the phrase, *"The early bird gets the first worms."*

He recognized the phone number. There wasn't an expectation that Body would call at that hour.

"Yeah, what up bro," Cold Heart answered.

"Get up little bro. Get dressed. I'm on my way to you now. We got work," Body stated. "Text me your address."

"I'm up already, bro. I stay ready. And I'm sending the address now."

"Check. Be there shortly. We got a heavy one," Body made him aware.

"I've been waiting for this moment, it seems like all my life."

"Okay *'Phil Collins.'* Now is the time. We got a workout that requires a sweatsuit. A black one or dark blue," Body made him conscience of.

"For sho' bro. I'm ready."

The call concluded.

Body made it to Cold Heart's house and picked him up. They dapped hands and greeted each other. Body then drove to his low-key spot he lived when not with his girlfriend or preoccupied with Drip. It was a house on Bridge Street. There was a garage to it for privacy. Body pulled the Chevy

Impala inside and let the door back down. They then got out and went inside.

Body gave his new protege a verbal rundown on things, then went over hand signs, coded words, and formality in protocol on how they would move, on order and on command. The attacking and execution training then followed. They were six hours in before it was time to call it a break and rest up. Once dark fall set in, it would be time to do the real work.

Drip had the upper hand on Warren in two ways. For one, the 26-year-old young female brunette beauty by the name Kerri Porter, who worked at City Hall, provided Drip with the addresses to each property holdings Warren owned. She was a girlfriend of Drip. He often tipped her well when he visited for business, and took her out on dates. She was delighted. This was long before the conflict with Warren. Also, Drip had first-hand information about Warren visiting a massage spa he owned in Bensalem, Pennsylvania, and had South Korean women operating the place for him. He went there after leaving the office. This was an every-other-day routine for pleasure Warren undertook, prior to going home to his wife and two daughters in Warminister, Pennsylvania, a direct route up Street Road.

Body was ordered to storm in once they cut the telephone lines (Warren prohibited cellphones inside the establishment to protect the high profile clients and customers he had visiting the spa to be naughty), hit Warren and any other males who might be inside, exit, and get back to Philly long before the cops got there.

On the days Warren stopped by, there would only be three workers on site to take care of the clients; one at the front desk, and two in the back being hands-on, mouth opened, and legs wide. An easy task to run down on Warren. He was now in the throes of death, he and the driver-bodyguard of his, the sole person Warren kept by his side the majority of the time when out and about. That was the reason why two were needed, to take them both out at the same time.

The hour was at hand. Warren and the bodyguard Dorrean exited their office suite he leased downtown Philly. The off-duty police lieutenant whom Drip had on payroll and also the brother of Body, a dude by the name Pervis Dillon, was parked out front in his black Ford Mustang, looking on at the two targets as they pulled into traffic in Warren's gray Cadillac Escalade once he'd entered it. Pervis allowed them four car lengths before he steered into a seemingly river of cars himself.

Pervis texted Body to let him know that the marks were headed their way. They were already in position and eager to do work. Pervis knew, without doubt, that Warren was en route to the massage spa due to the road they'd traveled. Dorrean pushed the full body S.U.V. east along I-676 and reached the point where the junction of Interstate 676 and Interstate 95 met. They took I-95 northbound, going toward the suburb city of Bensalem in Bucks County, Pennsylvania. They were followed the entire time and had no knowledge of it. The darkness of the night skies was a perfect cover for Pervis. December produced shorter days and longer nights.

Pervis carried along his police radio and high-powered scanner. He could switch the channels once in Bensalem. He would be able to quickly notify his brother if the cops were to be called by someone inside the spa or outside of it, once the hit was in progress. Body and Cold Heart had silencer attached to the tip of their pistols to prevent noise. They had long sharp pointed knives as well, in the event any gun jammed. Highly unlikely for a *Smith & Wesson,* but every precaution was taken

Warren and Dorrean made it to their destination. They exited the vehicle and entered. Body and Cold Heart allowed a three-minute time-lapse, then stormed in.

Body pointed the firearm in the face of the female situated at the front desk. They had masks on and were unable to be identified. She threw her hands high in the air. Cold Heart put zip ties on her wrists. They had her lead the way to the back where Warren and Dorrean were. Once at the door that separated the pleasure room from the hallway, Body had Cold Heart kick it in.

Boom!

The door burst open. Body shoved the female to the floor. Both Warren and Dorrean were naked and lying on their bellies flat atop the massage tables. The two females attending to them instantly threw their arms high above at the sight of the pistols. Warren and Dorean jerk their heads up to know what the hell was going on upon the door crashing in. The ruckus behind the force of the kick startled them out of their minds.

"What the hell!" Warren exclaimed.

Dorrean looked around frantically for his pants and jacket. He had his gun inside. They'd been caught down bad and naked. It was nothing they could do.

Body recognized the movement and intention of Dorrean. "A little too late for that, cowboy! You should've kept it on you to begin with," he spat.

"What the fuck is this all about?" Warren asked.

"You Warren McGregor, right?" Body asked.

"Yeah!! Now who the fuck asks?"

"The grim reaper!" Body responded, then pulled the trigger to the gun he had trained on Warren. He already knew it was the correct person.

Pop!

Warren took one to the forehead.

Pop!

Cold Heart then let off a round in the back of Dorrean's head, as he had the weapon pinned there already.

The two assassins then tied the two other females by the wrists and ankles. They had them all get into a closet that was there and closed the door. Warren and Dorrean were shot multiple times more for good measure per order of Drip.

That was to send a message on how pissed off he was behind the many times Warren challenged him at City Hall and during the bidding war. Their bodies were riddled with lead. They died a horrific death.

Body and Cold Heart then exited, walked the short distance to their car, and rode away with a job well done. Pervis wasn't too far behind, Nothing came over the radio air waves to indicate the police were contacted. Drip was now set up to succeed with all Warren was in the way of. The chances greatly increased for him to be granted those permits and contracts. Black Mafia Incorporation was now a larger legitimate enterprise with grand money-making companies and venues in the portfolio.

TWENTY-SIX

Von built a clientele base where his customers only brought an ounce or better each time he was called on for product. He operated mobile now and didn't have to post on the block or at a trap house. The customers he sold to dealt their product on a retail basis, and all Von had to do was, ride around town in his new car (the Dodge Magnum Nana put in her name) be available, and stack money like he wanted to.

Christmas passed and the new year was on the verge, only two days away. Von split the holiday three ways while passing out and receiving gifts from sunrise to sunset. The first part was with his grandmother (Christmas was her favorite and most cherished holiday), mother, and even Bernard at Mrs. Edna's house. They ate a meal and blessed each other with presents. Von went out and bought his mother and grandmother a pair of earrings, a necklace, and bangle bracelets. He'd previously bought his mother the same triple set before, but lost everything when he and Cold Heart were hijacked and robbed. He had the jewels in the glove compartment. They were purchased earlier that day. Lilly's birthday gifts. She was born on November 11th.

In the second part of Von's Christmas day appearances, he stopped by his grandpa's home, the great Hound Savage. He ate a little, but not too much. Von was never a big eater. He had a phobia of getting fat. Dude was young but very health conscious, due in part to his dad (from what he remembered), his grandma, and mother. There was a lot of family members there as well. Mostly grand kids of Hound's cousin Mickey Savage. Von bought gifts for his grandfather and the wife.

And the third part of his day was completed by a brief stop at Chloe's mother's home to see her and deliver gifts to Chloe's brother and sister. He and Chloe hugged and made merry with each other. That was to make what they were going through with their relationship not apparent. He left and made his way to Monyetta's house. The two would spend several hours at her parents' home. She introduced Von to them and her sister, Tiona. Von let her know he had a homie he would hook her up with. He wanted to connect Cold Heart with someone. For some reason, he held the thought Cold Heart had no girlfriend and wasn't getting any pussy. Partly true, but not totally. Tiona agreed and had in mind that one day after new years, the four of them would double date.

Monyetta, her sister, and their parents, were set to travel to the Virgin Islands to visit family there. Von's Christmas day was balanced pretty well.

On this particular day, he was out and about in his new car. He was unable to park for a prolonged periods of time. He loved the way the Magnum drove. Although gas prices were nearing a historic high, he kept the tank full, as the recession hadn't affected him as of yet. More than likely, it would at some point soon. Everyone was some type of way.

The time was around 8:00 p.m. A conversation he'd had with someone came to mind. The two hadn't contacted each other since the day. Much had happened between the time, and there was no longer any boundary lines in place to keep him at a distance from the person he was now itching to call. It was Rosa. He pulled his phone from the clip on his waistline, scrolled to the number, then called her. He didn't bother to text.

She observed the number and answered.

"Hello!"

"What's good! How you be?" Von said.

"I'm a'ight. Thought you'd never call."

"Yeah, well, I did. So, I'm interested in knowing what you got on the brain to tell me?"

"Is that right?"

"Facts!"

"Well, how bad do you wanna know?"

"Bad enough to already be in the parking lot of your apartment complex, I'm out front. Look out the window," Von stated.

Rosa pulled back the curtain of her living room window and Von flashed the lights to his car.

"Von! Are you crazy! Chloe could pull up and see your car over here, boy!" Rosa let out from fear of her cousin.

"So! What if she does? I'm free to see who I wanna see, and she is too," he made her aware.

"What!"

"Hey, this was something she wanted. Chloe was the one who said to me she would feel better if we had an open relationship. You gave me a heads up."

"You bullshittin' me, Von!" Rosa couldn't believe what she was hearing, "Look, come on in, all right.,"

"Okay."

They disconnected the call. Von got out and made his way to the front door of Rosa's apartment. She had the door open and stood to await him. Von reached the top of the stairs and they smiled at each other in a *damn I'm happy to see you* type of way. He entered the domain, with Rosa closing the door and locking immediately. They looked on at each other with gleaming eyes and illuminated faces. The smile between the two said it all.

"Well," Von began, and spread his arms wide, "I called. And not only that. I'm here. So what's up?"

Rosa went in for a warm tight hug. She then tipped on her toes to kiss him on the neck. He had a shadow of a beard now, and it was well lined. She wanted her lips to feel his skin.

"You want me to be honest, or you want me to tell you a lie?"

"I'mma always want you to be honest, sweetheart. In a straightforward and raw type of way.

"Okay, I ain't got no problem doing that. Now that I have the green light to do so."

"Well, what the hell are you waiting for? Get on with it then," he urged her on.

"The truth is, Von, I have always liked you. I always wanted you. I use to get so mad and envious of what you and Chloe had. And I know she is my cousin and all that. But I'm a firm believer in a man not being completely satisfied with only one chick. That it's best for a man to have a different female for everything he likes about women. You feeling me," Rosa spoke her peace while looking him directly in the eyes.

"Yeah I feel you. I figured it was something to that effect. You went about things the right way too. You didn't need to tear somebody else down to get my attention or to build yourself up. I was the one who got in touch with you," Von responded.

"Exactly. You made a conscious decision to hit me up. And now you're here. So what way do we take this?" Rosa asked bluntly.

Von smirked, then began to walk through the apartment, opening each room door to be one hundred percent sure no one else was there. Rosa smiled at his actions.

That's a smart dude there. He sure knows how to move. She thought to herself.

Von opened the door to one of the rooms of the two. He noticed something inside. Sneakers lined the wall outside the closet door. The room fit the appearance of a dude making it a personal space.

"I'm the only one here, Von. Nobody else."

"I know that now. Had to see for myself. Who stays here with you anyway?" he asked

"My brother from time to time, and my niece, his daughter."

"Oh, Okay. This his room right?" he asked more, having a look up the hallway at her and awaiting a reply.

"Yep, that be his room."

Von stepped into her brother's room. He looked down at the four pair of Jordan sneakers.

I had exactly four pair kicks like that in my car when them bitch-ass niggaz jacked me, he thought.

The sneakers were brand new. Still had the tag on them.

He reached down to pick one up and see what was the size of them. A size 11. His size.

What the fuck!

He picked up a different one. The same size. And another. The same.

Von then opened the closet door and took notice of the other sneakers inside. They weren't Jordans. They were *Cortez's, Chuck's, Converse, Skechers,* and clothes that resemble what a Hispanic or "*Puerto Rican*" cat would wear, as her brother was that as well. He checked the size of the ones in the closet. They were a Size 8. All of them.

I ain't tripping, am I! he thought again.

"Von, you a'ight back there?" Rosa called out from the kitchen. She began to fix drinks in the blender.

"Yeah. I'm good."

"Okay. You want a fruit smoothie?"

"I can go for one," he responded, then got back to perusing the room.

There was a phone charging on the nightstand next to the bed. An *iPhone 2, o*ne just like what he had. Those phones are extremely difficult to hack inside if you don't know the pass code. Not even the FEDS had the ability to get past such tremendous security features.

Now I know this ain't no fucking coincidence! Jordans like I had and an iPhone! No way! The same size of sneakers and all! What the fuck really going on! Like for real!

Von then powered on the phone. He wanted to be sure if or not it belonged to him. It took a little time, but nonetheless, it finally booted. Then and there, Von knew that that was his shit. The screen picture was of a black gamebred pitbull terrier. The heading read, *SAVAGE BLOODLINE.*

This my shit! he yelled in his own mind.

He put in the code and unlocked the phone. No doubt, it belonged to him.

Rosa appeared at the door of the room with two drinks. "You done checking to be sure I'm not setting you up?" she let out with a smile, then held out a tall glass of smoothie for him.

He powered the phone off and sat it back on the stand where he'd found it. Von was now determined to get down to the bottom of everything. The two walked to the living room.

"You say your brother stays here with you from time to time? He and his daughter?"

"Yeah. He and his baby-momma stay going through something," Rosa responded.

"That joker does help you pay bills and everything, doesn't he?"

"He does. Tito keeps his ass with some work to do."

"Tito!" Von retorted. "That's who he works for?"

"Yeah. Not in the streets though. At the shop."

"What does your brother look like?"

Rosa pulled out her phone and showed Von pictures of her brother and his daughter together, then a few solo shots of him posing with a large amount of cash. Von knew exactly who the dude was. He was one of the two at the shop each time he went there. However, on the night Von and Cold Heart got stuck up, he wasn't there. But the other usual one was.

Von downplayed what he now knew to be the truth. Rosa's brother had something to do with him being robbed.

The seeds of vengeance were planted in his mind at that point.

"I remember seeing him. I know who he is now."

"I thought you were about to say you remember seeing him talking to Chloe trying to convince her to take her ex back," Rosa blurted.

"What!"

"My brother and Chloe's ex Raul, are good friends."

"They *are!* Good friends? Or they *were* good friends?" he asked for clarity.

"They *are* good friends, although he and Chloe have been long broken up. And since we are on the subject of Miss Chloe, have a look at this, Rosa stated, then showed him pictures in her phone of Chloe hugging up and kissing Chino at the party they attended.

"She moved fast, didn't she? This had to be the reason why she wanted to have an open relationship. Who is that dude?"

"His name is Chino. He's a guy from around the neighborhood we grew up. That motherfucker has had the tender dick for Chloe since we were kids," Rosa let out with a chuckle.

"And he finally got the pussy," Von remarked with a smile.

"I imagine so," she responded. "And then she began fucking Raul more lately. He gave her a lot of money not long ago. Like ten thousand dollars," Rosa now spilled her guts on Chloe's activities.

Von simply responded by smiling and shaking his head. He was not bothered in the least.

The two sat on the love seat closely and talked more. They changed the subject from Chloe to them. He locked eyes with her and popped his flavor.

"So, you have *been* trying to fuck with me, huh?"

"*Mmm-hmm!* For the longest. If only you knew."

"I do now. And guess what?" he asked.

"What's that handsome?" Rosa responded, then strode her fingers tenderly along the side of his smooth face.

"We gonna do this, in a major way. But not to throw shade at Chloe or to get back at her in some type of way. We're gonna be smooth about things. Get into a legit business together. Travel and do things that young people do. You feel me."

He broke it down to her with a smile and a positive attitude.

"You know I do, Vonnie. I wouldn't have ever taken a shot at you, if I felt like you wouldn't be able to complete me in the ways I need a dude to," Rosa said sensuously, then tossed her long black natural hair over her left shoulder. She was seated to his left with her back straight, lips pursed, and all the way into what Von was articulating to her.

" I feel the same way about a female. And *hopefully,* you can be the version of Chloe she never lived up to be."

"Why invoke hope about something or someone you already got? I choose you. So don't forget that. And when we travel, do I get to choose where we can go?"

"You can. That'll be cool. Where you had in mind anyway?"

"It's an event I always wanted to experience, but never had the chance to. This is the right time of year for it too," Rosa explained.

"What? Go skiing?" Von asked.

"*That too!* But, I always wanted to go to New York City to bring in the New Year and watch the ball drop. Then, in the last week of January, we can visit Colorado, smoke some of that good ass weed they produce, and go skiing. How does that sound?"

"Sounds like a plan to me. Something I'm down for," he said.

"So when we headed up that way? Today is the twenty-ninth," said Rosa.

Von took a look at his watch. It was late, but not *that* late for the spontaneous and insomniac type dude he was.

"Fuck it! We can go tonight, and check into a room for a few days," he said then stood to his feet. "I've gotta make a stop by the house for—"

"No Von!" Rosa cut in. "Chloe will know you up to something if you go home to pack a travel bag!"

Anxiety briefly overtook her. She didn't want Chloe to become suspicious about anything.

"Calm down, shorty. I was talking about making a stop by my main house, with my grand mom," he expressed.

"Oh. Well . . . go ahead and do what's needed. I'll be ready when you get back," Rosa responded, then gave him an affectionate hug. They kissed as well.

Von appreciated the pleasant smell of her breath and the taste of her tongue. It was fruity with a hint of peppermint. His buds tingled.

He left out the apartment, got into his car, and headed to see Cold Heart, to report to him everything he now knew about who robbed them. No doubt, it was Alfredo, and more than likely, Raul was with him, and the other Spanish fuck whom was always at the shop with Tito and Alfredo.

But was Tito part of the lick too? Von pondered to himself. He had to know.

TWENTY-SEVEN

Two Days Later, New Year's Eve . . .

Lilly contacted Chloe. She wanted to talk with her. She also inquired of the whereabouts of Von? He hadn't been seen in days. Vonnie texted his mother and let her know he'd be away for a couple days on business he had, but hadn't mentioned Chloe would be with him. Lilly being Lilly when it came to her son, became curious in a sense, to know where the two teenagers stood as a couple.

"Hello!" Chloe answered at the sight of Lilly's number. She'd not long returned home. She and Raul went out shopping for the day. He treated.

"Hey, Chloe! How you been?" Lilly asked.

"I've been good. I was a little stressed out because this recession thing caused an effect on my job and I got laid off. But overall, I've been doing fine."

"You got laid off, huh? I'm sorry to hear that. I'll do what I can to get you on at the airport with me. If you'd like?" Lilly offered.

"You'll do that for me?"

"Of course, I will, baby. You're my kind of young lady. You're my friend. I have to help out."

"I thank you very much, Miss Lilly. I really do. You think, you'll be able to get me on?"

"I should. We need somebody in my area. The last person transferred to another airport when they moved. So it's a very good chance you'll get the job. I'mma need for you to come down there on the third of next month to fill out your application and other paperwork, okay."

"I'll definitely do that. Not a problem."

"Good. Now . . . where is that son of mine? I need to talk to him."

"He's not here right now. I was told he'd be away on business with one of his cousins. Some guy named Monk, he said," Chloe informed.

"That damn boy told me the same thing, but didn't say when he'd be returning."

"Hopefully it'll be before tonight, so we can bring in the new year together. But if not, oh well. Better luck next year."

"I've got a party I plan to attend tonight anyway. Vonnie not gonna spoil things for me. Not tonight," Lilly said

"I wouldn't mind going with you. Can you bring someone?"

"Sure. That's part of the reason why I called, to ask, would you like to go out and have some fun? I don't what your night to be ruined on account of my unreliable son."

"Yeah, Miss Lilly, I'd love to. I don't want my night to be wasted either."

"I'll come by to pick you up at eight, okay."

"I'll be sure to be ready."

The two concluded the call.

Meanwhile . . .

Up in the *"Big Apple,"* Von and Rosa were laid back cooling and getting familiar with each other mentally. The conversation got deeper after they'd gotten to the business with a damn good episode of sex when they'd first got there on the night of the 29th. The next day, they went shopping at *Saks Fifth Ave* and in uptown *"Spanish Harlem"* on Broad Street, and also on 125th Street near the *Apollo* theater. Rosa spoke Spanish fluently, and that made things far easier for them in the heavily populated Latin territory. She was able to relate to the Dominicans there very well. Rosa actually took a liking to New York and contemplated having a residence there.

Von and Cold Heart texted back and forth. He had a mission to take care of while Von was away. Before Von and Rosa departed for the *Empire State,* he'd left the back door to her place opened for Cold Heart, Ron, and Kareem to hideout inside and await Rosa's brother Alfredo, to show up, as they were intent on kidnapping dude, take him hostage, then murder that motherfucker for the shit he'd had something to do with. The robbery. They would press him to tell who else was involved before they murked him.

Rosa got out the shower and stood at the foot of the bed. Everything about her body resembled that of Chloe. The difference though, Rosa was way more health conscious than she, and had a flatter belly. Her skin was a shade or two darker as well. She had the robe fully opened to reveal her delicate lady ornaments. Her measurements were a 34 C-Cup, with her waistline being a 24, and thighs and ass measured out at 38. She was so enticing, and Von was ready to passionately slow stroke in-and-out with all he had once more, but wanted to wait until they returned to the suite later in the night. He needed to stay powered up to go to Times Square and then to the club from that location.

He had his back against the headboard of the bed, silk boxers on he'd recently bought, and without a shirt. His skin glistened from the palm oil he'd lubricated with, silk du-rag tried tight to press his hair and produce the thick deep waves, and one hell of a physique to give Rosa more than a night's worth of eye-candy to stimulate herself with, in addition to good dick and sensational swipes of the tongue between her pussy lips and directly on her booty-hole. He'd gone down on her already. Never had he done so to no other. Not Chloe. Not Monyetta.

"I've never asked you before," she worded.

"Never asked me what, sweetie," he responded.

"Never asked, do you like what you see? This sexy-ass body I'm in possession of?"

Rosa caressed her body with both hands slowly and seductively, and went to a slow groove belly dance, gyrating her hips and waistline.

Von's manhood came alive. He moved in upon her in a crawl atop the bed. Von then placed his face between her legs, directly on her perfectly clean shaven soul controller she had as a private. He lulled out his tongue and slithered it in and out of her love nest once or twice, then tickled her clit until she quivered and was nearly at the point of having an orgasm. Rosa kept one leg planted on the floor and situated the other atop the bed, looking to now be taken all the way to the promised land once more in ecstasy. Her juices flowed thick and succulent. She smelled fresh and so welcoming.

All of sudden, Von abruptly stopped. He backed away, returning to the head of the bed and looked on at her with a smile.

"We gonna finish later, a'ight." he said to her.

Rosa sucked her teeth and pouted. "Voonn!" she dragged out his name. "You play too much!"

He continued to smile and laugh at her. She then hopped onto the mattress and lay on him. They kissed and rolled in the deepness of the swath thickened comforter.

"You play too much, you know that," she said once more while smiling and giving him delayed kisses.

"I told you, I like to be spontaneous, baby," he remarked.

They continued to kiss and frolic.

Rosa then got up, wiped with a feminine disposal tissue (she prematurely had an orgasm) then proceeded to get dressed. She put on a G-string that was pink in color, a matching bra, and the same in socks. The Puerto Rican goddess then reached into her bag and brought out a beautiful jewelry box. She sat it atop the dresser top and began putting on each piece one by one.

Von was in the process of getting dressed as well as he stood closely to Rosa when he'd taken a look at the jewelry box and the material that were inside. He recognized everything as he'd personally handpicked the gold and diamond designed pieces exactly the same.

There was a rope-chain with a lilly pad charm; lilly pad designed earrings; and a bangle bracelet with lilly pads etched all around it.

That's the jewelry I bought my mom! he thought to himself.

He wanted to be sure. There was a need to ask.

"Rosa, where did you get that jewelry from?" he asked in a calm voice. He didn't want to alarm her in any type of way.

Von knew Alfredo hadn't said anything to Rosa about robbing him. If so, it would've been revealed by now.

"My brother gave it to me as an appreciation gift for babysitting for him, and letting him stay like I do," she responded.

"Must be nice to have a brother like him, huh," Von let out nonchalantly.

He took a step back and had a seat on the bed to text Cold Heart.

VON: Oh yeah, bro! Y'all whack that bitch-ass nigga! I know for sure now it was him and the ex.

COLD HEART: (thumbs up emoji)

Von continued to chat with Rosa

"That's nice jewelry you got there. Your brother got good taste," he complimented.

"Don't he now. He really took me by surprise with this. He just up and gave it to me one night. Made me feel really good," Rosa let stated with a smile.

"You don't say," Von added to her ecstatic feeling of goodness with those words. "But, I don't think he's done a better job than I plan to do in making you feel good with gifts."

"I bet he didn't either. Ain't no doubt in my mind, you're gonna treat me so well. That's why I wanted you so bad," she said upon completion of putting on all the jewels, then turning to tongue kiss him.

He felt on her booty with both hands as they done so, passionately caressing and providing love-squeezes here and there. They were intent on having a very good time together.

***

Cold Heart and the other two henchmen hid out in Rosa's apartment to await the brother to arrive. Von provided them with information that no one other than the brother and the sister had a key to the place, and Alfredo texted and let her know he'd be going to the house to shower and get dressed. There was a party he wanted to attend. And he would be there, at Rosa's place soon.

Von wouldn't be returning to Philly with Rosa until he knew the hit had been carried out. They had total control of the situation.

The moment they'd awaited was upon them, Alfredo made it home, at his sister's place, and was now inside the house, just entering the front door.

Cold Heart's instincts proved correct. He knew that most likely, the very first stop any man would make once arriving at home would be the bathroom. He was in the closet in the living room, with Ron and Kareem in the closet of Rosa's room.

Cold heart heard the toilet flush and knew Alfredo would be coming out at any moment. That was the cue to exit the closet and surprise the dude with a presence he'd never seen before.

Alfredo took one step from the bathroom when the barrel of Cold Heart's forty-five was pinned to the right side of his temple. Alfredo was paralyzed from fear. Petrified beyond his days.

"I should blow your mothafuckin' brains out here and now, fuck boy!" Cold Heart spat with a grimace about his face.

"What the hell is this all about, yo?" Alfredo asked.

Cold Heart thought up something to say to make him think deeply over what he may had done.

"Retribution motherfucka'!"

Wham!

Cold Heart slapped Alfredo across the side of the head with the heavy steel *Colt* firearm. Alfredo went down on one knee.

Wham-Wham-Wham!

He whacked him thrice more for good measure, sending dude to the floor flat on his chest. Cold Heart then placed a foot on his neck and pressed thoroughly.

"Aye-yo! Y'all come on," he announced to his comrades.

They appeared from the bedroom and immediately began to zip-tie Alfredo at the wrists and feet. They then gagged him.

Wham!

"Bitch-ass nigga! Wanna rob me and my homie!

Wham!

"Now you gonna pay!" Cold Heart barked.

They then stuffed Alfredo in a large thick laundry bag and prepared to put him in the trunk of the car they had and whisk him to an undisclosed location to await Von to return before they were to terminate him. Dude would be chained and locked to the concrete floor, and beaten mercilessly for the bad deed he'd participated in. He knew eventually he'd be killed.

TWENTY-EIGHT

Monk contacted his brother Drip, to notify him on the situation that had played out with Shay and Feezy. Drip had him come over to Norristown so they could talk personally, as too much chit-chat over the phone was never a good thing. Von and Cold Heart were sure to provide in detail everything that they knew, as Drip would make the final decision once he consulted with Monk, on the best course of action to take. Drip had an inside man on the force, and he could have him snoop into the evidence to find out what the cops knew.

Monk was there seated on the plush exquisite white couch in the living room of his brother's million plus dollar mansion. Drip had company there to entertain him. Actually, it was a bit of a celebration for Drip and the female he had by his side. Drip received the building and development contracts he'd sought, along with the permits from City Hall. The white female companion Kerri Porter, helped to make it all possible. He wanted to reward her for her work.

Drip urged Monk to speak on the issue at hand. "So what are we dealing with, bro? What is the situation?" he asked.

"Okay, so look. Fam, Von, got this female by the name Shay on the team and . . . ."

Monk gave him the rundown on it all. About the little girl who'd gotten killed. About the nigga, Feezy who was still on the loose. The cops investigation. The girls living in and out of the motel and unable to hustle properly. Everything. Truth be, Drip's bottom line was being effected behind the drama some fucking boyfriend-girlfiend shit gone wrong was causing, and he wasn't having that! Drip would order both them mothefuckers to be killed, and that would essentially be the end to the bullshit. Just that simple. However, the part about Feezy taking money and product from Shayla, meant that he'd taken from Drip. And she was right by blasting at him to protect the investment the first time. And the second shooting was the result from dude having someone cut her. So, there was no longer a doubt as to who she stood for and where her loyalty was at. And Drip found that to be a virtue in her he highly respected. Therefore, Shayla was granted a pass, but only under one condition: that Feezy needed to be quickly tracked down and put away long before he cooperated with the cops and told all he had knowledge about related to Shayla and her crew. Drip had the power to speed up Feezy's death. He was intent on putting Pervis on the job.

The last order Drip gave to Monk on the Shayla ordeal, was to have Von and Cold Heart be sure to keep them out of sight and out the way, in the event Feezy may had already spoken to the cops and they were looking for her to question. Once Feezy gets it, then, the girl could proceed as normal.

Monk departed Drip's home, leaving Drip to go out on his date with the lovely snow-bunny he had to keep him company. They were set to have a good time.

***

Von returned from New York. He, Cold Heart, and Ron surrounded Alfredo in the basement of the home they had him chained away in. They needed him to talk and reveal who else had something to do with the caper they'd pulled on them.

Von spoke what he knew.

"Look, Alfredo, I know it was you, that other motherfucka' who be at Tito's shop with you, and more than likely, Chloe's ex-boyfriend, Raul. Y'all were the ones who robbed me and my homie right there."

"You remember me, motherfucka!" Cold Heart barked.
Whop!

Cold Heart smacked the shit out of Alfredo with his pistol. The same Colt.45 he'd drawn down on him with inside Rosa's place. He'd busted his eye badly.

Alfredo bellowed and cried like a bitch.

Von continued. "I was in your sister's house, nigga! I saw my four pair of Jordans you kept. You have my iPhone on the stand. I know that that was my phone, because I put the pass code in and unlocked it, then turned it off again and put it back where I got it so you wouldn't know. And . . . And! When I had your sister in the hotel up in New York, fucking her like I want to, she pulled out the jewelry you gave to her, that was in my car. I'd bought it for my mother!"

Wham!

Von grabbed the pistol from Cold Heart and went up top of Alfredo's head with it viciously. He held it by the barrel and hit him with the handle end.

Wham!

He hit him again. In the mouth this time. Five teeth were claimed in the process.

"Now . . . If you don't talk . . . That little girl of yours . . . I'mma go get her, bring her here, and kill her slowly right here in front of you! Then, kill you! Now talk, motherfucka!" Von spat.

"Oh no! Please, Von! Please! Don't bother my little girl, Von! Please! I'm begging you!" Alfredo pleaded.

"Well talk nigga!" Von barked.

"And now, bitch-ass nigga!" Ron chimed in.

"We did it, Von! It was me, Raul, and a couple of homies from around the way. My other homie I work with at the shop texted me when y'all got there. We fucked up on something and owed Tito some money. He was gonna cut us off if we didn't pay him. Please bro! Not my daughter!" Alfredo begged further.

Von smirked at him very sinister like as he looked down on the poor guy propped up by one arm and his eye the size of an orange.

"What did Tito have to do with this?" Cold Heart asked.

"Tito did not necessarily *tell* us to rob y'all. But he didn't *stop* us either," Alfredo revealed.

"So he knew?" Von asked.

"No. Not really," Alfredo responded.

"When y'all took our weed and pills and sold it, did y'all pay him?" Von asked.

"We had to," Alfredo responded.

"And he never asked where did y'all get the money so fast?" Cold Heart wanted to know.

"Nope. He just took it and told us we're good," Alfredo explained.

"So that means, he had to know something about it," spat Cold Heart.

"And now, you gotta pay the price for them all, motherfucka!" Von declared, then pulled the trigger to the heavy metal firearm.

Boom!

Von had rammed the gun into his mouth and popped him. The back portion of the dude's head was blown off. Brain, bone particles, and blood splatter plopped to the concrete. The Black Rhino bullet wreak havoc in his skull, as it exploded and caused extreme damage.

***

The three bad boys of the hour—Von, Cold Heart, and Ron—took Alfredo's body and dumped him in a large trash bin. Once they'd stuffed what was left of him inside multiple trash bags one inside and the other and hauled off to a dumpster, they then went about their separate ways, with Cold Heart taking Von home, to the spot he shared with Chloe. The two friends had a deep conversation as they rode.

Cold Heart gave Von a look and a smile as he never had. He seemed to be impressed with him in a sense. He spoke to Von about what he had on his mind.

"How you feel, bro?"

"How I feel about what, bro?" Von responded.

"Getting your feet-feet wet? And the baby milk off your breath," Cold Heart expressed, then managed to agitated his trigger finger to indicate *"Kill-Kill-Kill . . . Murder-Murder-Murder!*

"Oh, that! It wasn't nothing, bro. It felt really natural."

"—Oh shit! A monster has been created! Me and Ron probably done fucked up with that one!" Cold Heart exclaimed and shook his head vehemently from side to side to stress the emphasis of *"God No!"*

Von smiled and chucked at Cold Heart's animation. "What's that, bro? Shit, it did. I was under the impression that my first body would have me feeling some type of fucked up way. But it didn't. It actually got me itching to catch another one," Von stated the exact truth about how he felt.

"Tito? Or Raul?" Cold Heart asked.

"That nigga, Raul! Hitting Tito wouldn't be a good idea."

"Why not? Ain't no way I believe he didn't have shit to do with it! I know he did. He's the one who set it up. You heard that nigga we just put away. He said, Tito didn't, quote-unquote, 'necessarily tell them to rob us, nor did he say not to,' at the time when they came to him to greenlight the move. And, we owed him money."

"You got a point there. He could've stopped it. But he didn't. And now that I think back over it, that nigga did hold us up a little longer than he was supposed to," Von stated a point.

"And the other motherfucka' who was there, disappeared for a while. That had to be the time when he called Alfredo and Raul. And how the fuck would they know exactly when we were supposed to be there to buy that large amount of product, if Tito didn't tell them?" Stated Cold Heart.

"—Fuck!" Von vented. "How come we didn't think of that before, bro?"

"Our minds were too clouded at the time. We weren't able to think properly then. Hindsight twenty-twenty, you know."

"And my people done paid that nigga all the money we would've owed him! Oh yeah! We gotta hit that pussy, bro! But when?" Von wanted to know the rundown on the plot now they'd just hatched.

"Technically, *we* ain't got to do shit, bro. We're up now, Von. Hitters can be hired and do the dirty work for us. By the way, the homie Ron, got two cousins out west who are loose cannons! Them niggaz don't play!"

"Khaddafi and Khalil! They have proven they qualified to. That shows Ron and Lonnie was able to plant our flag on that side of town. Behind the work that them two had put in," Von said.

"You talking about the lick on that nigga 'Hell Rell' and his people Anton, had bit the bullet on, right?" asked Cold Heart.

"No doubt. They are the ones."

"So we shouldn't have any problem getting them to touch Tito. But we may need to run it by Monk and Drip first."

"I'll handle that. Let's just go ahead and put that snake-ass Tito, down behind the bullshit he pulled. A'ight bro," Von emphatically said.

"If that's what you wanna do, bro, I'm down. Me and you, homie. Let's do it," Cold Heart co-signed.

"Let's do it, my nigga!" Von capped off the plot with enthusiasm.

***

They'd made it to Von's spot. He and Cold Heart dapped each other up before Von got out and entered the house. Chloe was home, laid back watching a movie in the bedroom. Von got undressed and into something more comfortable. He and Chloe began to talk as he did so.

"Hey Von," Chloe spoke first.

Von became slightly overcome by remorse from what he'd done not even an hour prior. Alfredo was the cousin of Chloe and brother of the new piece of pussy he was now getting, Rosa. He was able to look Chloe in eyes, and at the same time, not able to."

"What's good, Chloe," he responded as he took a seat on the bed. He gave her a peck on the lips and then began to get situated atop the bed alongside her.

"How was your day?" she asked.

"Pretty good! Yours?" he responded.

"Pretty good too. I got a new job today."

"Oh, you did? Where?"

"At the airport."

"At the airport!" he retorted. He cautiously looked at her. He knew exactly what that was all about. "What in the world you and Lilly got going, Chloe?"

Chloe smiled widely. She knew he would come to the conclusion fairly quickly. "We don't have anything going on. I'm her friend, and she helped me out when I told her I was laid off at my last job. I went to a New Year's party with her too while you were away. We had a ball. Lilly was fun to hang out with."

"Oh, she is. You must didn't say anything to her about us and our *open* relationship?"

"Actually, I did," Chloe responded.

"You did?" Von retorted. Apparently not believing what Chloe said.

"Yep. Only in my own way. But whether you know it or not, your mom is more down to earth than you may think. She's revealed many things to me of her private life that I'd promised not to speak about with no one else. Not even with you."

"*Hmm!* Is that so? But when will you start work there?" Von asked to change subjects with Lilly in it. He didn't feel right carrying on a talk with his mother's name included.

"Tomorrow morning. Me and your mom will be working in the same section too," Chloe revealed with a smile. "But other than that, what's your plan? What you got in mind to do? I wouldn't mind us starting a small business together to bring in extra income. How do you feel about that?"

Von had thought over all Rosa revealed to him, all that Chloe had going on behind his back. He wanted to know how well she was now doing, since mentioning the fact that she wanted an open relationship.

"To be honest, I got somebody on the side already I'm looking to go into business with. That's who I was with to bring in the New Year's," he revealed sarcastically.

"What!" Chloe retorted with an angry depth to her tone.

Von simply sat atop the bed with a smirk dashed about his face in a sinister type of way. He said no more.

Chloe now stared at him with daggers in her eyes. "What was that again, Von? Run that by me one more time, please!

TO BE CONTINUED

Lock Down Publications and Ca$h Presents
Assisted Publishing Packages

BASIC PACKAGE $499 Editing Cover Design Formatting	UPGRADED PACKAGE $800 Typing Editing Cover Design Formatting
ADVANCE PACKAGE $1,200 Typing Editing Cover Design Formatting Copyright registration Proofreading Upload book to Amazon	LDP SUPREME PACKAGE $1,500 Typing Editing Cover Design Formatting Copyright registration Proofreading Set up Amazon account Upload book to Amazon Advertise on LDP, Amazon and Facebook Page

***Other services available upon request.
Additional charges may apply

Lock Down Publications
P.O. Box 944
Stockbridge, GA 30281-9998
Phone: 470 303-9761

235

Submission Guideline

Submit the first three chapters of your completed manuscript to ldpsubmissions@gmail.com. In the subject line add **Your Book's Title**. The manuscript must be in a Word Doc file and sent as an attachment. Document should be in Times New Roman, double spaced, and in size 12 font. Also, provide your synopsis and full contact information. If sending multiple submissions, they must each be in a separate email.

Have a story but no way to send it electronically? You can still submit to LDP/Ca$h Presents. Send in the first three chapters, written or typed, of your completed manuscript to:

LDP: Submissions Dept
P.O. Box 944
Stockbridge, GA 30281-9998

DO NOT send original manuscript. Must be a duplicate. Provide your synopsis and a cover letter containing your full contact information.

Thanks for considering LDP and Ca$h Presents.

NEW RELEASES

SANCTIFIED AND HORNY
by XTASY

THE PLUG OF LIL MEXICO 2
by CHRIS GREEN

THE BLACK DIAMOND CARTEL
by SAYNOMORE

THE BIRTH OF A GANGSTER 3
by DELMONT PLAYER

Coming Soon from Lock Down Publications/Ca$h Presents

BLOOD OF A BOSS VI
SHADOWS OF THE GAME II
TRAP BASTARD II
By **Askari**

LOYAL TO THE GAME IV
By **T.J. & Jelissa**

TRUE SAVAGE VIII
MIDNIGHT CARTEL IV
DOPE BOY MAGIC IV
CITY OF KINGZ III
NIGHTMARE ON SILENT AVE II
THE PLUG OF LIL MEXICO II
CLASSIC CITY II
By **Chris Green**

BLAST FOR ME III
A SAVAGE DOPEBOY III
CUTTHROAT MAFIA III
DUFFLE BAG CARTEL VII
HEARTLESS GOON VI
By **Ghost**

A HUSTLER'S DECEIT III
KILL ZONE II
BAE BELONGS TO ME III
TIL DEATH II
By **Aryanna**

KING OF THE TRAP III
By **T.J. Edwards**

GORILLAZ IN THE BAY V
3X KRAZY III
STRAIGHT BEAST MODE III
By **De'Kari**

KINGPIN KILLAZ IV
STREET KINGS III
PAID IN BLOOD III
CARTEL KILLAZ IV
DOPE GODS III
By **Hood Rich**

SINS OF A HUSTLA II
By **ASAD**

YAYO V
BRED IN THE GAME 2
By **S. Allen**

THE STREETS WILL TALK II
By **Yolanda Moore**

SON OF A DOPE FIEND III
HEAVEN GOT A GHETTO III
SKI MASK MONEY III
By **Renta**

LOYALTY AIN'T PROMISED III
By **Keith Williams**

I'M NOTHING WITHOUT HIS LOVE II
SINS OF A THUG II
TO THE THUG I LOVED BEFORE II
IN A HUSTLER I TRUST II
By **Monet Dragun**

QUIET MONEY IV
EXTENDED CLIP III
THUG LIFE IV
By **Trai'Quan**

THE STREETS MADE ME IV
By **Larry D. Wright**

IF YOU CROSS ME ONCE III
ANGEL V
By **Anthony Fields**

THE STREETS WILL NEVER CLOSE IV
By **K'ajji**

HARD AND RUTHLESS III
KILLA KOUNTY IV
By **Khufu**

MONEY GAME III
By **Smoove Dolla**

MURDA WAS THE CASE III
Elijah R. Freeman

AN UNFORESEEN LOVE IV
BABY, I'M WINTERTIME COLD III
By **Meesha**

QUEEN OF THE ZOO III
By **Black Migo**

CONFESSIONS OF A JACKBOY III
By **Nicholas Lock**

JACK BOYS VS DOPE BOYS IV
A GANGSTA'S QUR'AN V
COKE GIRLZ II
COKE BOYS II
LIFE OF A SAVAGE V
CHI'RAQ GANGSTAS V
SOSA GANG III
BRONX SAVAGES II
BODYMORE KINGPINS II
By **Romell Tukes**

KING KILLA II
By **Vincent "Vitto" Holloway**

BETRAYAL OF A THUG III
By **Fre$h**

THE MURDER QUEENS III
By **Michael Gallon**

THE BIRTH OF A GANGSTER III
By **Delmont Player**

TREAL LOVE II
By **Le'Monica Jackson**

FOR THE LOVE OF BLOOD III
By **Jamel Mitchell**

RAN OFF ON DA PLUG II
By **Paper Boi Rari**

HOOD CONSIGLIERE III
By **Keese**

PRETTY GIRLS DO NASTY THINGS II
By **Nicole Goosby**

PROTÉGÉ OF A LEGEND III
LOVE IN THE TRENCHES II
By **Corey Robinson**

IT'S JUST ME AND YOU II
By **Ah'Million**

FOREVER GANGSTA III
By **Adrian Dulan**

GORILLAZ IN THE TRENCHES II
By **SayNoMore**

THE COCAINE PRINCESS VIII
By **King Rio**

CRIME BOSS II
By **Playa Ray**

LOYALTY IS EVERYTHING III
By **Molotti**

HERE TODAY GONE TOMORROW II
By **Fly Rock**

REAL G'S MOVE IN SILENCE II
By **Von Diesel**

GRIMEY WAYS IV
By **Ray Vinci**

Available Now

RESTRAINING ORDER I & II
By **CA$H & Coffee**

LOVE KNOWS NO BOUNDARIES I II & III
By **Coffee**

RAISED AS A GOON I, II, III & IV
BRED BY THE SLUMS I, II, III
BLAST FOR ME I & II
ROTTEN TO THE CORE I II III
A BRONX TALE I, II, III
DUFFLE BAG CARTEL I II III IV V VI
HEARTLESS GOON I II III IV V
A SAVAGE DOPEBOY I II
DRUG LORDS I II III
CUTTHROAT MAFIA I II
KING OF THE TRENCHES
By **Ghost**

LAY IT DOWN I & II
LAST OF A DYING BREED I II
BLOOD STAINS OF A SHOTTA I & II III
By **Jamaica**

LOYAL TO THE GAME I II III
LIFE OF SIN I, II III
By **TJ & Jelissa**

IF LOVING HIM IS WRONG...I & II
LOVE ME EVEN WHEN IT HURTS I II III
By **Jelissa**

BLOODY COMMAS I & II
SKI MASK CARTEL I, II & III
KING OF NEW YORK I II, III IV V
RISE TO POWER I II III
COKE KINGS I II III IV V
BORN HEARTLESS I II III IV
KING OF THE TRAP I II
By **T.J. Edwards**

WHEN THE STREETS CLAP BACK I & II III
THE HEART OF A SAVAGE I II III IV
MONEY MAFIA I II
LOYAL TO THE SOIL I II III
By **Jibril Williams**

A DISTINGUISHED THUG STOLE MY HEART I II & III
LOVE SHOULDN'T HURT I II III IV
RENEGADE BOYS I II III IV
PAID IN KARMA I II III
SAVAGE STORMS I II III
AN UNFORESEEN LOVE I II III
BABY, I'M WINTERTIME COLD I II
By **Meesha**

A GANGSTER'S CODE I &, II III
A GANGSTER'S SYN I II III
THE SAVAGE LIFE I II III
CHAINED TO THE STREETS I II III
BLOOD ON THE MONEY I II III
A GANGSTA'S PAIN I II III
By **J-Blunt**

PUSH IT TO THE LIMIT
By **Bre' Hayes**

BLOOD OF A BOSS I, II, III, IV, V
SHADOWS OF THE GAME
TRAP BASTARD
By **Askari**

THE STREETS BLEED MURDER I, II & III
THE HEART OF A GANGSTA I II& III
By **Jerry Jackson**

CUM FOR ME I II III IV V VI VII VIII
An **LDP Erotica Collaboration**

BRIDE OF A HUSTLA I II & II
THE FETTI GIRLS I, II& III
CORRUPTED BY A GANGSTA I, II III, IV
BLINDED BY HIS LOVE
THE PRICE YOU PAY FOR LOVE I, II ,III
DOPE GIRL MAGIC I II III
By **Destiny Skai**

WHEN A GOOD GIRL GOES BAD
By **Adrienne**

A GANGSTER'S REVENGE I II III & IV
THE BOSS MAN'S DAUGHTERS I II III IV V
A SAVAGE LOVE I & II
BAE BELONGS TO ME I II
A HUSTLER'S DECEIT I, II, III
WHAT BAD BITCHES DO I, II, III
SOUL OF A MONSTER I II III
KILL ZONE
A DOPE BOY'S QUEEN I II III
TIL DEATH
By **Aryanna**

THE COST OF LOYALTY I II III
By Kweli

A KINGPIN'S AMBITION
A KINGPIN'S AMBITION **II**
I MURDER FOR THE DOUGH
By **Ambitious**

TRUE SAVAGE I II III IV V VI VII
DOPE BOY MAGIC I, II, III
MIDNIGHT CARTEL I II III
CITY OF KINGZ I II
NIGHTMARE ON SILENT AVE
THE PLUG OF LIL MEXICO II
CLASSIC CITY
By **Chris Green**

A DOPEBOY'S PRAYER
By **Eddie "Wolf" Lee**

THE KING CARTEL I, II & III
By **Frank Gresham**

THESE NIGGAS AIN'T LOYAL I, II & III
By **Nikki Tee**

GANGSTA SHYT I II &III
By **CATO**

THE ULTIMATE BETRAYAL
By **Phoenix**

BOSS'N UP I, II & III
By **Royal Nicole**

I LOVE YOU TO DEATH
By **Destiny J**

I RIDE FOR MY HITTA
I STILL RIDE FOR MY HITTA
By **Misty Holt**

LOVE & CHASIN' PAPER
By **Qay Crockett**

TO DIE IN VAIN
SINS OF A HUSTLA
By **ASAD**

BROOKLYN HUSTLAZ
By **Boogsy Morina**

BROOKLYN ON LOCK I & II
By **Sonovia**

GANGSTA CITY
By **Teddy Duke**

A DRUG KING AND HIS DIAMOND I & II III
A DOPEMAN'S RICHES
HER MAN, MINE'S TOO I, II
CASH MONEY HO'S
THE WIFEY I USED TO BE I II
PRETTY GIRLS DO NASTY THINGS
By Nicole Goosby

LIPSTICK KILLAH I, II, III
CRIME OF PASSION I II & III
FRIEND OR FOE I II III
By **Mimi**

TRAPHOUSE KING I II & III
KINGPIN KILLAZ I II III
STREET KINGS I II
PAID IN BLOOD I II
CARTEL KILLAZ I II III
DOPE GODS I II
By **Hood Rich**

STEADY MOBBN' I, II, III
THE STREETS STAINED MY SOUL I II III
By **Marcellus Allen**

WHO SHOT YA I, II, III
SON OF A DOPE FIEND I II
HEAVEN GOT A GHETTO I II
SKI MASK MONEY I II
By **Renta**

GORILLAZ IN THE BAY I II III IV
TEARS OF A GANGSTA I II
3X KRAZY I II
STRAIGHT BEAST MODE I II
By **DE'KARI**

TRIGGADALE I II III
MURDA WAS THE CASE I II
By **Elijah R. Freeman**

THE STREETS ARE CALLING
By **Duquie Wilson**

SLAUGHTER GANG I II III
RUTHLESS HEART I II III
By **Willie Slaughter**

GOD BLESS THE TRAPPERS I, II, III
THESE SCANDALOUS STREETS I, II, III
FEAR MY GANGSTA I, II, III IV, V
THESE STREETS DON'T LOVE NOBODY I, II
BURY ME A G I, II, III, IV, V
A GANGSTA'S EMPIRE I, II, III, IV
THE DOPEMAN'S BODYGAURD I II
THE REALEST KILLAZ I II III
THE LAST OF THE OGS I II III
By **Tranay Adams**

MARRIED TO A BOSS I II III
By **Destiny Skai & Chris Green**

KINGZ OF THE GAME I II III IV V VI VII
CRIME BOSS
By **Playa Ray**

FUK SHYT
By **Blakk Diamond**

DON'T F#CK WITH MY HEART I II
By **Linnea**

ADDICTED TO THE DRAMA I II III
IN THE ARM OF HIS BOSS II
By **Jamila**

YAYO I II III IV
A SHOOTER'S AMBITION I II
BRED IN THE GAME
By **S. Allen**

LOYALTY AIN'T PROMISED I II
By **Keith Williams**

TRAP GOD I II III
RICH $AVAGE I II III
MONEY IN THE GRAVE I II III
By **Martell Troublesome Bolden**

FOREVER GANGSTA I II
GLOCKS ON SATIN SHEETS I II
By **Adrian Dulan**

TOE TAGZ I II III IV
LEVELS TO THIS SHYT I II
IT'S JUST ME AND YOU
By **Ah'Million**

KINGPIN DREAMS I II III
RAN OFF ON DA PLUG
By **Paper Boi Rari**

CONFESSIONS OF A GANGSTA I II III IV
CONFESSIONS OF A JACKBOY I II
By **Nicholas Lock**

I'M NOTHING WITHOUT HIS LOVE
SINS OF A THUG
TO THE THUG I LOVED BEFORE
A GANGSTA SAVED XMAS
IN A HUSTLER I TRUST
By **Monet Dragun**

CAUGHT UP IN THE LIFE I II III
THE STREETS NEVER LET GO I II III
By **Robert Baptiste**

NEW TO THE GAME I II III
MONEY, MURDER & MEMORIES I II III
By **Malik D. Rice**

CREAM I II III
THE STREETS WILL TALK
By **Yolanda Moore**

LIFE OF A SAVAGE I II III IV
A GANGSTA'S QUR'AN I II III IV
MURDA SEASON I II III
GANGLAND CARTEL I II III
CHI'RAQ GANGSTAS I II III IV
KILLERS ON ELM STREET I II III
JACK BOYZ N DA BRONX I II III
A DOPEBOY'S DREAM I II III
JACK BOYS VS DOPE BOYS I II III
COKE GIRLZ
COKE BOYS
SOSA GANG I II
BRONX SAVAGES
BODYMORE KINGPINS
By **Romell Tukes**

QUIET MONEY I II III
THUG LIFE I II III
EXTENDED CLIP I II
A GANGSTA'S PARADISE
By **Trai'Quan**

THE STREETS MADE ME I II III
By **Larry D. Wright**

THE ULTIMATE SACRIFICE I, II, III, IV, V, VI
KHADIFI
IF YOU CROSS ME ONCE I II
ANGEL I II III IV
IN THE BLINK OF AN EYE
By **Anthony Fields**

THE LIFE OF A HOOD STAR
By **Ca$h & Rashia Wilson**

THE STREETS WILL NEVER CLOSE I II III
By **K'ajji**

NIGHTMARES OF A HUSTLA I II III
By **King Dream**

CONCRETE KILLA I II III
VICIOUS LOYALTY I II III
By **Kingpen**

HARD AND RUTHLESS I II
MOB TOWN 251
THE BILLIONAIRE BENTLEYS I II III
REAL G'S MOVE IN SILENCE
By **Von Diesel**

GHOST MOB
By **Stilloan Robinson**

MOB TIES I II III IV V VI
SOUL OF A HUSTLER, HEART OF A KILLER I II
GORILLAZ IN THE TRENCHES
By **SayNoMore**

BODYMORE MURDERLAND I II III
THE BIRTH OF A GANGSTER I II
By **Delmont Player**

FOR THE LOVE OF A BOSS
By **C. D. Blue**

KILLA KOUNTY I II III IV
By **Khufu**

MOBBED UP I II III IV
THE BRICK MAN I II III IV V
THE COCAINE PRINCESS I II III IV V VI VII
By **King Rio**

MONEY GAME I II
By **Smoove Dolla**

A GANGSTA'S KARMA I II III
By **FLAME**

KING OF THE TRENCHES I II III
By **GHOST & TRANAY ADAMS**

QUEEN OF THE ZOO I II
By **Black Migo**

GRIMEY WAYS I II III
By **Ray Vinci**

XMAS WITH AN ATL SHOOTER
By **Ca$h & Destiny Skai**

KING KILLA
By **Vincent "Vitto" Holloway**

BETRAYAL OF A THUG I II
By **Fre$h**

THE MURDER QUEENS I II
By **Michael Gallon**

TREAL LOVE
By **Le'Monica Jackson**

FOR THE LOVE OF BLOOD I II
By **Jamel Mitchell**

HOOD CONSIGLIERE I II
By **Keese**

PROTÉGÉ OF A LEGEND I II
LOVE IN THE TRENCHES
By **Corey Robinson**

BORN IN THE GRAVE I II III
By **Self Made Tay**

MOAN IN MY MOUTH
By **XTASY**

TORN BETWEEN A GANGSTER AND A
GENTLEMAN
By **J-BLUNT & Miss Kim**

LOYALTY IS EVERYTHING I II
By **Molotti**

HERE TODAY GONE TOMORROW
By **Fly Rock**

PILLOW PRINCESS
By **S. Hawkins**

BOOKS BY LDP'S CEO, CA$H

TRUST IN NO MAN
TRUST IN NO MAN 2
TRUST IN NO MAN 3
BONDED BY BLOOD
SHORTY GOT A THUG
THUGS CRY
THUGS CRY 2
THUGS CRY 3
TRUST NO BITCH
TRUST NO BITCH 2
TRUST NO BITCH 3
TIL MY CASKET DROPS
RESTRAINING ORDER
RESTRAINING ORDER 2
IN LOVE WITH A CONVICT
LIFE OF A HOOD STAR
XMAS WITH AN ATL SHOOTER